Praise for

Twilight of the Dead

"Adkins remains absolutely faithful to the zombie genre while offering an exciting new twist of horror and human perserverance."
—Christine Filipak, *Dark Realms Magazine*

"*Twilight of the Dead* crackles with a sense of realism that makes it read like something that could actually happen. Break out the wakizashis niggas! The zombies are coming!"
—Andre Duza, author of *Dead Bitch Army* and *Jesus Freaks*

"*Twilight of the Dead* is an interesting new take on the zombie genre while remaining traditional enough to please long-time zombie fans. Travis Adkins is a talent to watch in the world of horror. Don't miss this book!"
—Eric S. Brown, author of *Cobble* and *The Queen*

"With original twists and good old-fashioned suspense, *Twilight of the Dead* is a must-have for any zombie fan, or indeed any fan of the horror genre. Highly recommended."
—Meghan Jurado, author of *Dead World*, featured in *The Undead*

"I didn't want to lay it down! ...The details that go into this book from the fighting techniques to the surrounding areas were spectacular... The author takes this book to places others only imagined."
—James Maynard, The Zombie Junkyard

TWILIGHT
of the
DEAD

written and
created by
Travis Adkins

with an
Introduction by David Moody

and cover art
by Noel Hill

Permuted Press
The formula has been changed...
Shifted... Altered... *Twisted.*
www.permutedpress.com

INTRODUCTION

What would you do?

Don't tell me you haven't thought about it. I know you have. It's human nature. We live in unpredictable times and there are now more ways than ever that it might happen. It hasn't happened so far today, but there's always tomorrow...

What am I talking about? The end of the world.

I bet you have a routine. Most people live their lives by them. Maybe you get up early, have breakfast, get ready for work, say goodbye to the family then head to the office or to school or wherever it is you spend your days. You probably have another routine when you get back. You'll see certain people, go certain places, do certain things at certain times... you get the idea.

Have you ever stopped to think about how fragile it all is?

Everything could change in the blinking of an eye. In five minutes from now your life could be turned on its head. In the time it takes for a missile to strike, a bomb to explode, an earthquake to hit, an infection to develop or a car to crash every aspect of your life could be changed forever. And there's absolutely nothing you can do about it.

So I'll ask you again: *what would you do?*

Let's be more specific. Let's consider a particular apocalyptic event. Let's look at a nightmare that will shake society to its very core and leave no-one untouched. Let's imagine that today, all around the world, the bodies of the dead are rising. No-one knows why it's happening and no-one can stop it. What we do know is that the situation is deteriorating by the hour. The bodies are attacking the living and infecting them and the contagion is spreading with terrifying speed. The dead are increasing in number exponentially. Where there were two just a couple of minutes ago, there are now probably four, and those four will soon become at least eight (probably more) and those eight sixteen and... and you know it won't be long before the living are outnumbered by the dead.

So, one last time, what would you do?

You might do nothing. You might not be able to deal with any of what's happening around you. You might end it all with a gun to your temple, a rope from a rafter, a cut to the wrist or an overdose of pills. But let's assume for now that you're going to try to survive. It's not going to be easy. For a start you'll have the immediate problem of having to deal with vast crowds of the dead. You'll have your work cut out keeping out of sight and you'll probably end up a virtual prisoner, locked away in some dark, dank shelter somewhere. Maybe you'll be fortunate and you'll find yourself a decent place to hide. No matter how strong and secure as your base may be though, you're still going to struggle to find enough water, food and medical supplies and sanitation will be poor and the electricity and gas sources will be down and... and let's face it, in many ways it would be easier just to give up and roll over.

But if you had a chance, even the slightest chance, you'd take it, wouldn't you?

In *Twilight of the Dead*, Travis Adkins presents us with a world which has been literally torn apart by the reanimation of the dead. Most of the population have been destroyed and are now walking the streets as rapidly decaying 'skin-eaters' – vicious cadavers with an insatiable appetite for the flesh of the living. And yet, in the midst of this nightmare, a small group of weary individuals have somehow managed to survive. In the five years since the beginning of the apocalypse they have sheltered in Eastpointe, a walled community. Their lives have changed and they have adapted to their circumstances but they still cling desperately to the past. Theirs is a small corner of the world which is frozen in time.

These people have done better than most. They've succeeded where the rest of the world has failed and from the ashes and crumbled remains of the past they've managed to somehow build new lives for themselves. But while the residents of Eastpointe work and play and remember who and what they used to be, the undead hordes wait for them on the other side of the concrete wall, baying for their blood.

On the face of it Adkins' survivors' world appears deceptively normal. But it's a world full of conflict and uncertainty. A world where a lonely teenage girl can be watching a feel-good movie or reading a pulp romance novel one minute, before picking up a gun and a blade and slaughtering the undead the next. This is a world which is balanced precariously on the edge. Everything is calm and controlled but then you turn the page and... and I'm not going to spoil it for you. Read this book and you'll find yourself on a bullet-train ride through hell. You won't know what horror is around the corner until you've already reached it and you're squaring up to it eye-to-eye. Adkins takes us from deceptive normality to outrageous, stomach-churning horror in seconds.

Twilight of the Dead deserves your full attention. Not just because it's a damn good, full-on blood and guts and brains and bullets zombie Armageddon, but because it's that and so much more. This is a book that's going to scare the pants off you *and* make you think, because this is a book about you and me and just about everyone else you know. This is a book about regular, everyday people who just happen to find themselves trapped in hell. It's about your neighbour. It's about your family and the people you see each day at work and school. Take a second to look around you now at the faces of the people you see. Would they survive? Could they fight for their lives against millions of diseased corpses? Could *you*...? This is a book that's going to make you ask, "What would I do?"

Read it, enjoy it, then ask yourself again...

"What would I do?"

—David Moody
Halesowen, England
2nd July 2006

for Phantom and Spike,
the coolest cats to ever own such a proud human

the END of the WORLD

is a PROCESS

not an

EVENT

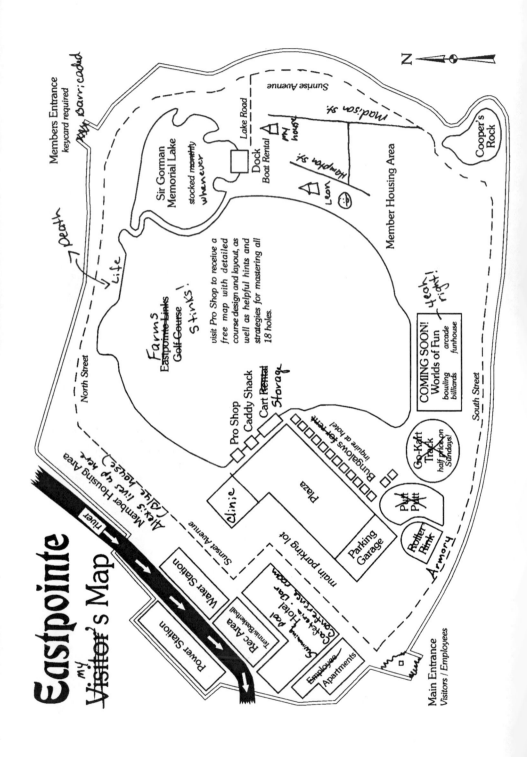

PROLOGUE

The Corridor

Perception determines reality.

Growing up, she may not have believed this proverb or even understood it, but as she peered down the dark corridor yet again, no other adage rang more true. *This* is what she was seeing and so that made it very real. In actuality she was pulling her bedsheets closer in clinched fists and mimicking every sensation and emotion of the *fake* life.

But what was fake and what was real?

It didn't matter. She was in the long, dark hallway again and she had to deal with it. Concrete walls were erected on both sides, keeping her in, the cold and callous bricks rough on her fingertips. Miles —*it seemed* —of nothingness stretched out in front of her and behind her and she was lost somewhere in the middle, the blackness overwhelming and the sensation of hopelessness already seeping in.

And then began the pounding, thumping, thunderous sound that originated somewhere far ahead of her, reverberating through the hallway and in her eardrums, disrupting any thoughts she could be having and shaking the very floor she stood on.

This much was always the same: the concrete corridor, the dark, the noise. And up to a certain point, the events that followed were also the same.

Probing with outstretched arms she made her way forward, one foot after the other. Though she had learned through the years to be silent in every movement she made, somehow she wasn't able to suppress the sound of her loud and exaggerated footfalls no matter how softly she stepped.

Frustration.

Her steps always remained out of sync with the pounding noise ahead of her and the result sounded a lot like some kind of music fit only for neanderthals, like the beating of tribal war drums urging her forward.

Fear.

A light began to appear at the end of the corridor, rectangular in shape with a hollow belly. When she got close enough to realize the light was the outline of a door and that beyond that door the sun was shining through the cracks, she stopped. Someone —*or several someones* —were on the other side, banging on the door, wanting to get in.

Uncertainty.

She called out, "Who's there?"

Her voice carried itself through the corridor without reverberation or echo.

And then there was silence. The thundering ceased and all she could hear was her own stuttering breaths —cold intakes of oxygen drawn softly from her concrete sarcophagus.

Then it came —a reply to her question —an even more ferocious beating against the door, so hard and violent that the light began to distort and wobble, likely pushing the durability of the frame to its absolute limits.

Then began the part of her dream that made even less sense than the rest of it. With no more thought or hesitation, she walked to the door. Her eyes, open wide, saw nothing but the light. Her ears, listening intently, heard nothing but the pounding, beckoning sound that pulled her near. Even her footfalls —which had been so noisy before —were now lost amidst the din.

The door itself was a heavy-duty metal bastard. Three locks adorned the space above the handle and each one begged to be unlatched.

She turned the one on top first. With a modest *click* it let her know it was undone and useless. The banging slowed a bit and the silent intervals became steady and somewhat rhythmic. She turned the next lock. It too made a modest click. The banging intensified once more, remaining rhythmic, cheering her efforts. So with a satisfied exhale she turned the final lock.

The banging was constant now; no silent intervals.

boomboomboomboomboom

She reached down and placed her hand on the doorknob, feeling it to be much warmer and inviting than the coldness of the corridor and its concrete walls. The sun was out there, she knew. There was light out there to extinguish this dismal darkness. There was warmth —and, perhaps —*hope.*

She turned the handle and let the door swing open.

Sunlight shot into her eyes like daggers, brightening her face and blinding her momentarily. It was a good sensation, even if only temporary.

But then came the hands —thousands of cold dead hands attached to cold dead arms attached to cold decaying bodies, clothing ripped and shredded and polished with a layer of blood, dirt, and muck. Eyelids rotted off, fully exposed eyeballs looked at her with a glassy, soulless stare. Thousands of faces with blue skin and formaldehyde-filled veins, tendons and muscles pulling away to show cold, white bones.

A thousand dead bodies wanting to partake of *hers.*

And this is where the dream sometimes varied.

In some instances —*most* instances —the dead hands would latch onto her and pull her out of the dark corridor and into the sunny area occupied by this mob of hungry corpses —and there they would rip at her shirt and claw at her jeans and, while she screamed in terror, they would open their mouths and feast on her flesh, taking off chunks of her skin with each grisly bite, some of the greedier ones pulling her arms off at the sockets with a violent tug and taking them elsewhere to chew on separately. Her intestines came next, pulled from her open belly like sausages and dragged into the crowd like a bloody rope. And after several seconds of intense agony, with her eyes open wide she finally transpired, staring up at the very mob that had taken the sun from her, casting their shadows down across what remained of her body.

Yes, that is how the dream ended in most instances, and —despite its gruesomeness —it was actually the ending she preferred.

But what she got this time was the finale she dreaded most; the one where all the dead arms lowered to their dead sides and instead of pulling her out they invited her *in*.

—To join their ranks.

She brought her own arm up to her face to study it under the sunlight. It was blue and cold. Frantically, she pressed her palms to her cheeks and felt that they, too, were cold. She looked down at herself to see her clothes ripped to shreds, maggoty decaying skin showing through. Finally she stopped everything and stood completely still, hoping and praying to feel something in her chest. Her heart should have been beating at a frantic, adrenaline-pumping pace, but instead it was utterly dormant. She felt nothing.

She was one of them.

And so she stepped out of the corridor to join her new comrades, basking in the glory of just another day, all cognizant thought swept from her mind. Only one motive was driving her now:

Hunger.

WKTT
FM
104.7

Transcript from
The Morning Show with
Face-For-Radio Rick (Richard Snyder)
and Easy-Going Earl Boy (Earl Boyland)

WKTT-FM 104.7 - 05/07 - Adam Yvel, typist

RICK: Good morning. They're telling the FCC to warn us to avoid using the Z-word. But what else do we have to talk about? It's everywhere now. They may have been able to contain it at one time. Quarantine it somewhere. And maybe they tried.

EARL: Well I'll tell you this and it isn't a threat, its...

RICK: Thank God. We got a call. Good morning caller. Thanks for sparing us another Easy-Going tirade.

EARL: [expletive] you Face-For-Radio Rick.

RICK: Where are you calling from?

CALLER: Hello?

RICK: Yes caller we hear you. Where are you calling from?

CALLER: Hey. Good morning Rick. Good morning Earl. Long time listener first time caller.

EARL: We always welcome our virgin callers. Don't worry. We'll be gentle.

RICK: Yes Easy-Going Earl we never get tired of hearing your catch phrase.

CALLER: Thanks guys. You're downtown right?

RICK: Smack dab thereabouts.

CALLER: Hate to be where you are. Hear its chaos.

EARL: Getting there.

RICK: How are things in your area?

CALLER: Well I'm looking out the window right now and I see dead people. Pardon the cliché.

EARL: From east coast to west coast. They're all over the place. Like a [expletive] Michael Jackson video. Except we're not dancing and neither are they.

RICK: Seriously, who remembers the eighties?

CALLER: They say it takes massive head trauma to bring one down.

RICK: Whoa. Stop right there. We cannot condone killing anyone.

EARL: We're not condoning anything.

RICK: Nor can we give instructions on how to do it.

CALLER: But those freaks are killing people. Have you seen what they do?

RICK: Don't say it. You'll just gross us out.

EARL: This is such [expletive].

CALLER: [expletive] right, its [expletive].

RICK: I just wish someone would tell us what exactly is causing this problem.

CALLER: They're eating people. That's the problem.

EARL: What a way to go.

RICK: We're not supposed to talk about that remember?

EARL: We're not even supposed to say the Z-word.

CALLER: Can I?

RICK: Yes. Technically you're allowed. But we're not.

CALLER: Zombie. Ghoul. Flesh-eating dead person. And here's one for you: Somnambulist. Did I say that right?

EARL: I believe you did sir.

RICK: Well done.

CALLER: So what are we supposed to do? Just step around them on our way to work? Say don't eat my family while I'm out trying to earn a living?

EARL: We supposed to just drive by and wave?

RICK: I guess so. Until they stop treating them like they're still alive. This isn't a problem that's just going to go away.

CHAPTER
ONE

Awake

It was the doorbell —and not the nightmare —that woke her.

She had slept long past it, though not without considerable effort. Her comforter was in a ball against the wall and her sheet was wrapped around her in such a way that seemed nigh impossible at first glance.

Raising her head, she inspected the clock on the nightstand.

Nine forty-five.

Time to wake up anyway.

The doorbell then rang again, the noisy *ding-dong* sound of it one of the few remnants of the world before.

She rose up and began unraveling her bedsheet, unwinding it from around her body and pushing it aside. She swung her legs over and put her feet down. She extended her arms and arched her back, feeling it crack in several places, then reached down to the floor to retrieve her jeans. She found them in the same rumpled state she had left them the night before. She straightened them, slithered both her legs inside, then stood to pull them up to her waist. After a zip and a fasten she was stumbling tiredly from the bedroom and into the living room.

Sunlight was bursting through the gaps in the curtains, its golden rays capturing millions of undesirable dust molecules floating in the air. They stirred and undulated from her path as she broke through them, disrupting the calm that had settled over the house since the night before and welcoming in the new day in their own grandiose, miniscule style.

All the artificial lights in the house were switched off —save for the nightlight in the hallway —just as she had left them.

The carpet was soft on her feet and maybe even a little bit damp. There was a well-worn path from the bedroom to the couch and a very noticeable lesser-worn path from the bedroom to the front door. She followed this path and by the time she reached her destination her stumbling feet had found their coordination and her morning grogginess had dissipated enough that her brain would be useful.

She could catch glimpses of movement through the modernistic diagonal windows in the door, but not enough to determine whom exactly was out there. So she gathered her best morning voice and asked, "Who is it?"

And the muffled, masculine reply answered, "Leon."

She yawned ferociously, swiped her hair and tucked it behind an ear, then went about the process of opening the door. First she pulled away the metal bar and set it aside, then she released deadbolts one, two, and three, then finally she turned the handle and pulled open the heavy wooden monster.

Sunlight hit her straight on in its typical unforgiving manner, mercilessly wounding her morning eyes. She had not grown accustomed to this despite the many times it had already happened, nor had she even considered this annoyance when she decided on a house facing east.

Yet sure enough, when her pupils shrank enough to filter away all this new light, standing there on her porch, she saw, was Leon Wolfe. Wearing jeans, a plain blue shirt, and sporting his styled hair, he appeared to have been awake for at least two hours already and had something to show for it. In his hands he held a styrofoam container, which he was extending to her in offerance, all the while grinning his obnoxious grin.

She glanced at the container through the screen door, then back at him. "And this is...?"

"Breakfast."

"Breakfast?"

"I took a chance," he explained in his typical, arrogant, know-it-all demeanor, his head cocked slightly to one side. "I didn't see you in the cafeteria. Haven't seen you anywhere, actually. Not for a week."

She thought about it for a moment, then opened the screen door and snatched the styrofoam container from his hands. After opening it for a quick inspection she saw that he wasn't lying —that it wasn't another trick —and that there was actually breakfast inside. Grilled bread (better than toast), scrambled eggs, a slice of ham, a sealed cup of what looked to be orange juice, and one of those pesky little plastic forks. She closed the container and looked at him oddly.

"Why are you bringing me this?" she asked.

"Because I know how you are," he replied. "You don't stock your refrigerator and you don't leave your house until you're two minutes away from starving to death."

She groaned.

She knew that accepting this would give him a small amount of satisfaction —and that was something she'd rather avoid —but then again, having breakfast delivered would spare her a trip out of the house. This way she could just stay inside most of the day, at least until dinnertime.

She stepped away without a word, leaving him standing there holding open the screen door. She then found a spot on the couch between two piles of unfolded laundry and placed the styrofoam container on the coffee table in front of her. A bit hesitant, she peeled open the orange juice and took a sip. It tasted like orange juice and not *something else* —which was a good start. She licked her lips. For concentrate, it wasn't bad at all.

"Is this an invitation to come in?"

She glanced back over to the door, took a deep breath and shrugged her shoulders, then mumbled, "You're still here? Whatever then."

He stepped inside and let the screen door swing closed. Though he didn't know it, he was the first person she had allowed to come inside.

"Juice taste all right?" he asked.

She shrugged.

"A Florida chick like you has probably tasted better, but, oh well."

She nodded sourly.

"Well, good morning, Leon," he said with sarcastic dryness. "Nice of you to think of me and bring me breakfast. I thought the world had forgotten I lived here."

She didn't bother looking at him. She was almost tempted to roll her eyes, but even that would require too much effort. "Good morning, Leon," she repeated. "Nice of you to think of me and bring me breakfast. I thought the world had forgotten I lived here." She paused for a moment, then added, "And I like it that way."

He smiled. She would have preferred him to have gotten angry and stormed out, thereby leaving her the hell alone.

"Can I sit?" he asked, motioning to the cushion next to her.

She put down her orange juice and shrugged her shoulders.

There was a pile of unfolded laundry where he wanted to sit, but true to Leon fashion, instead of pushing it aside he made an event out of it.

"Ah, what do we have here?" he teased, his hand probing closer. "*Female underthings*?" At this point he appeared ready to take something and —more than likely —tease her. "Hey, I recognize *this* one..."

She turned quickly and snapped, "*Stay out of my stuff,*" as she knocked his hand away. She then used her forearm to swoop all the clothes off the cushion and create an even messier heap on the floor. After mumbling, "Show some respect and stop being a goddamn brat," she turned forward again, hoping maybe he would leave her alone to eat. Her stomach *was* growling, after all.

Leon remained standing, scratching his head.

Books, some open and some closed, some disregarded without care, were scattered across the floor. Videotapes minus their dustjackets were stacked in three piles next to the television against the far wall and compact discs without their jewel cases were stacked haphazardly in a cylindrical pile on the stereo. A layer of dust had begun to settle over most everything. Now added to all this was the clothing she had just strewn about to help stir some of it up.

"Your housekeeping's worse than mine," he commented.

"My maid's on vacation," she countered. "Is there some reason for you being here?"

"I brought you breakfast."

"Yes, I told you thank you."

He slowly eased himself down on the cushion next to her where the clothes used to be. He didn't get close to her, but he didn't sit far away either.

She tried her best to ignore him as she cut up the breakfast ham, being careful not to cut into the styrofoam in the process. She took a bite. The ham wasn't too bad, but it was kind of salty, which was to be expected.

After a moment Leon clicked his tongue, attempting to garner her full attention, and said, "We need to talk, Courtney."

It was inevitable. She exhaled deeply and dropped the plastic fork into the scrambled eggs. She turned her head then, not enough to look at him completely, but just enough to see him in the corner of her eyes. She asked, "Are you just going to keep babbling on? What's the use of bringing me breakfast if you're not going to let me eat it while its warm?"

"I just want to talk," he replied. "The way you are, it won't take long."

She let her gaze fall to the carpet.

He began, "I've been doing some thinking."

She couldn't resist: "Congratulations. I know that must've been hard."

"Whoa, whoa, whoa!" he exclaimed, putting his hands in the air. "This is going completely wrong. I didn't come here to argue with you."

"You're being irritating."

"I'm not trying to be irritating. I'm trying to be... I don't know. I thought I could be playful with you now. Maybe I'm trying to make you smile."

"It's not working."

"I can tell."

Then there came a noise from outside —someone shouting, "*Toss me the shuttlecock!*" Then someone answering, "*Shuttlecock?*" and another person replying, "*The shuttlecock!*"

Peering across the room and through the screen door, she eyed some of her neighbors starting a game of badminton across the street. Cindy was over there and it looked like Mike and Delmas were there too. They'd need a fourth player and she knew that that was where

Leon would rather be, instead of in her messy house having the 'one week after' chat. The people across the street were *his* friends —not hers —and they never got tired of shouting 'shuttlecock!'

Idiots —like *him*.

However, Leon didn't seem distracted by the new noise. He hadn't even turned his head. He restated, "We need to talk."

"Why?" she asked.

"Because."

"Then just say what you're going to say."

"I don't *know* what to say. I was hoping you could do half the talking. *You know* —like two people do when they're having a conversation."

With a deep, frustrated sigh, she tilted her head back and looked at the ceiling. She saw a couple of dusty cobwebs up there and quickly put her head down again. The house really was a mess.

"Fine," she snapped. "Then I'll just say it and we can get this over with: It was a *mistake*."

"That's what I thought you'd say."

"Then why'd you bother?"

He grinned his annoying grin. "Because that's the typical scapegoat answer."

She gritted her teeth and groaned, simply *not* in the mood for a morning-after talk —a *week-after* talk —with Leon Wolfe. She said, "You slept with a girl. That's not a new experience for you, is it? Not *you*, the local gigolo, the local slut. Do you go back and talk with *all* your conquests? Try to string them along in case you want to go back for seconds someday?"

He chuckled softly, then stood and walked to the door. Instead of leaving like she would have wanted, however, he leaned against the nearby wall and put his hands in his jeans pockets. "I thought your attitude toward me might've changed," he said. "I couldn't figure out why you showed up at my door because I knew you hated me — And you *still* hate me."

"Yes," she replied.

"But I don't hate *you*." He paused a moment, then mumbled, "Gigolo... *I wish*." He chuckled again.

She leaned back on the couch and threw her feet onto the coffee table, being careful not to spill the styrofoam container. Even though it was a gift from Leon Wolfe —of all people —it meant she wouldn't have to go over to the cafeteria at least until later today.

He said, "Tell me why you don't like me and then I'll get out of your hair."

"Well, gee," she began, turning to glare at him. "I can't seem to forget that one time when you served me a glass of vinegar and told me it was ice water—"

"Wait," he interjected. "That was almost five years ago. I was a *kid.* Jesus, we were only like —what —*seventeen*?"

"You were an asshole then and you're an asshole now."

"I *did* get in trouble for that, you know. Made to stay on food service duty for *month*. You know how much it sucks to be a lunch lady for an entire *month*?"

"Well, I was sick for almost that long."

"Because of a little vinegar? I kind of doubt that."

She turned away to stare at the opposite wall. There might be emotions growing behind her eyes and that was the absolute last thing she wanted him to see.

"It was a joke," he explained. "A *prank.* Granted, *yes*, a bad one. But I didn't single you out. I was hoping to get one of those cranky Odd Fellows running this place. It was just plain random that it was *you* who got that glass of vinegar." He paused for a moment, staring off at nothing, then softly added, "So why else do you hate me? Is there any other reason?"

She didn't say anything.

After waiting for an answer and not receiving one, he looked around the room again, gathering his thoughts, then said, "You came to *me*, remember? Completely out of the blue. So did you get what you wanted? Did you get it out of your system?"

"What do you care?" she mumbled.

"Because I see the way you *live*," he replied, motioning with his outstretched arms to the wholeness of the room's interior. "Jesus Christ, Courtney, this is *depressing*."

She turned to look at him then, despite the pressure building in her eyes, and said as fiercely as she could, "*Leave*."

"Tell me why you hate me first."

She looked away again, a sensation running through her veins causing the muscles in her arms to tighten and her fingers to begin closing into fists.

A moment passed.

"Are you going to tell me?" he asked again.

Then she mumbled, "*I could have fit in here if you hadn't ruined it.*"

"What?"

A spark lit in her gut. She stood and stomped over to him and when she got close enough she pressed her forefinger hard into his chest. She gritted, "*You jerk.* You don't *get* it. What you did *did* single me out. You and all your other jerk friends —the way you laughed at me and teased me from then on. Things were hard enough *without* all that."

Looking shocked —and a bit scared by her sudden aggression — he stuttered, "Nobody made fun of you."

"The hell you say," she retorted. "Do you realize how hard it was to make friends? Impossible. *That's* how hard."

"But you didn't even *try.* You just went around with your sassy attitude pretending you didn't need *anybody.* You can act as high and mighty as you want, doll, but I see through you."

And with that, she hit him. Not a girly, feminine slap on the cheek, but a full-fledged, closed-fisted slug on the chin; the perfect spot — she knew —if you wanted to knock someone the hell out. Besides, it just felt right. It seemed that his chin and her knuckles were just destined to be together.

Reeling, clutching his jaw with one hand and holding the wall with the other, struggling not to see the inevitable stars, he mumbled, "*Ouch.* Jesus, you hit hard for a skinny girl."

She knew that now was the opportune time. This was when she could tell him that the morning after their little encounter she had immediately sent the clothes she had worn to his house to the laundromat, then took a two-hour shower simply to get rid of the last scent of him. She could tell him how it irked her to no end that his Maine accent occasionally caused him to pronounce R's as *ah's.* She could tell him how his narcissistic, *nothing's-wrong-in-the-world* attitude had no business being around her. Furthermore, she wanted to mention just how thoroughly the very sight —the very *thought* of him —disgusted her.

Instead of saying these things, however, she pulled back her fist.

Talking simply required too much energy.

Seeing another punch in his future, he grabbed her wrist and forced it down to her side. "Wait. Just wait." He paused a moment and used his free hand to adjust his jaw once more. "Okay, maybe I deserved that."

She cocked her head to the side as if to say, '*Well... DUH.*'

"I don't know anything about you," he said. "I just know everyone has some kind of story about how they got to Eastpointe, and stories about people they know that *didn't* get to Eastpointe. I just—"

"Leave," she again gritted.

"Wait, I'm going to try to explain this to you," he said. He slowly let go of her wrist, certainly wondering if he would regret it, then softly continued, "I'll be the first to admit that I wasn't blessed with an overabundance of brains, so I'm a little slow catching on to things. But I'm starting to figure you out."

"Oh really?"

"*Yeah* —You were in love with him."

She took a step back. "What? Who?"

"Gordon Levi."

She didn't reply just yet, but instead stared at him angrily.

"Tell me I'm wrong."

"That's entirely none of your business."

"Aha!" he said, his eyes widening with enthusiasm. "You just inadvertently answered my question."

She took a deep breath and let it out slowly, letting her eyes drift away. After a moment she asked, "So, what kind of name are you going to call me first?"

"I'm not going to call you a name," he replied. "Why would I do that?"

"Then what are you going to point out that I don't already know? That he was twice my age? Or just something as simple as him being black? Or that I was just seventeen and I didn't know what I was doing?"

"I'm not saying anything."

"Then why are you bothering me with this?"

"I'm just trying to figure you out." He lifted his hand close to her face and seemed ready to make some kind of tender motion she knew she wouldn't be comfortable with —especially from *him*.

She shied away.

He lowered his arm. "If you loved him, then I'm sorry he didn't make it."

"Just go, Leon."

Instead of obliging her, he stayed right where he was and explained, "Before everything went nuts, I was in high school, like you. I played baseball and I guess, well, that pretty much sums up and defines my life til that point. I didn't really get over that whole locker room mentality, alright? So, what I did to you, that *vinegar thing*, it was to impress other people, the new people I met here. It was wrong of me and it was immature and it was stupid. I admit it and I'm sorry. But I've grown up since then. We all have."

"Will you leave now?"

"Just one more thing." He smiled then, that cocky smile, but whether he was forcing it or not she couldn't tell. "This might just be a psychological issue, but I have a thing for bad girls."

"Well," she groaned, "I don't have a thing for pretty guys."

He laughed. "You think I'm *pretty*?"

She quickly caught her slip of the tongue and compensated for it by pointing to the door and stating, "*Out*."

Then came a mistake, when she caught his gaze and allowed herself to hold it. Their blue eyes meeting and staying met made her very uncomfortable.

"You're a gorgeous chick," he said. "Always have been. And when you're not yelling at me or hitting me, I think I actually *like* you."

This statement caught her much by surprise and it might even have flattered her had his New England voice not ruined it.

She stated, "Did I mention I hate your accent?"

Another smile. "Oh, come on. I've had five years to blend my style with everyone else's. The accent's going away, so it's not all that bad."

She sneered. "Yes it is. Leave."

His smile faded a bit then. He pushed open the screen door and held it there while he paused in thought. With his back still turned, and in a tone that sounded both sarcastic and apologetic, he softly stated, "I didn't realize I was the sole cause of you being unhappy. I'm sorry."

Then he left, heading down the concrete walkway and across the street, probably to join in the game of badminton.

Courtney closed the main door, putting the outside out of sight again.

And that was that.

She returned to the couch, but instead of digging back into her breakfast she put her hands through her hair and rested her palms against her temple.

She got even angrier. She didn't get to tell him about her repetitious nightmares and how she still had them even with someone in bed beside her, so her one night of weakness hadn't helped matters at all.

He probably wouldn't have understood anyway.

ROCK FORGE
Army Research Laboratory

Addendum - to be filed separately
Compiled by Dr. Dalip Patel (civilian status)

Title: Reanimation of the dead becomes global phenomenon.

Exegesis: This office has not been charged with determining cause of phenomenon. Cause is as yet undetermined by any scientific agency. No known way of engineering virus capable of such results.

Exegesis: Reanimated dead instinctively seek consumption of living human beings. There is no datum on record to confirm whether reanimated dead seek consumption of lower living life forms e.g. cats, dogs, mice.

Problem: Deteriorating effect on soldier morale was completely unforeseeable.
Specifics: 90.25% of soldiers surviving combat with reanimated dead are showing immediate symptoms of post-traumatic stress.
Solution: No solution reached thus far. Military has been too short on manpower to allow any troop down time. E.g. recuperation period

Problem: infected civilians and soldiers show signs of depression.
Specifics: death and reanimation 24 hours following infection is inevitable. This information is widespread.
Notes: This datum should have been guarded under military law.
Solution: Euthanasia. e.g. any infected person, civilian and soldier alike, requesting merciful death should likewise be granted a lethal dose of barbiturates. IMPORTANT - Upon stoppage of heart, head should then be removed (decapitation) and both head and body burned to ash (incineration.)

continued...

```
 Problem: many soldiers do not believe reanimated dead are actually
          dead, and therefore hesitate to destroy them, resulting
          in heavy casualties in our armed services.
Specifics: some soldiers believe reanimated dead to be still-living
          victims of mind-altering virus.
 Solution: Commanding officers MUST order soldiers under their
          command to shoot-to-kill. e.g. destroy the brain.


 Problem: a small percentage of soldiers believe reanimated dead
          are capable of feats of superhuman and/or metaphysical
          nature. e.g. super strength, levitation, magic
Specifics: No datum on record to prove reanimated dead have any
          unique ability/strength not previously possessed by the
          person they used to be.
  Notes 1: Living human muscles deteriorate under exertion, (e.g.
          weight-lifting), then regenerate (heal) bigger and
          stronger.
  Notes 2: Muscles of the reanimated dead deteriorate under exertion,
          but do *not* regenerate (heal). In theory, older reanimated
          dead should be weaker than newly reanimated dead.
  Notes 3: No reanimated dead have been witnessed to move (walk)
          faster than an estimated four miles per hour, and this
          speed was witnessed only in newer reanimated dead.
 Solution: There may be no way to relieve soldiers of superstitious
          belief, even with scientific data proving otherwise.
```

CHAPTER TWO

Five Years Ago, When it Began

There was mayhem ensuing outside, instigated mostly by the National Guardsmen and not by the walking corpses. At seventeen, Courtney understood this much. Her father was watching the chaos through the living room window and ranting about it in a hushed tone. Sitting on the couch across the room, maybe she was supposed to hear him and maybe she wasn't, but she *did*, so this was one of her last memories of him.

His words were: "Look at them. Idiots on power trips. Just out of high school, three months of boot camp, and now they're walking around with a gun strapped to their back." Then, in singsong, he added, "*This is my rifle, this is my gun, this is for fighting, this is for fun.*"

Finally she spoke up. "What are you talking about, dad?"

He glanced at her long enough to show her a fake, *everything's-all-right* smile, then gazed out the window again. "Those guys," he said. "They're supposed to be protecting us. But did you see what they did to Mister McGreevy down the street? Took him out of his house; bullied him around. They're just kids, barely out of high school, no more than a year older than you, Court. They're too stupid to go to college, to get a scholarship or whatever, so they join the

Service. Get bullied around in bootcamp. They learn responsibility, but not intelligence." Another gunshot spliced through the air. Her father winced, but otherwise didn't pause. "They talk about how wearing the uniform gets them girls. So the fact remains that they're still *stupid*, but now they're on a power trip because they've got a gun. They're still *kids*, though, so they're scared. Just as scared as the rest of us. Add all that up and you've got a bunch of scared little *kids* who have *guns*, who are given positions of *authority*, but no intelligence to use it properly, and are therefore on one *gigantic* power trip. Promotions occur from within, so there's always going to be an idiot in charge. Disaster, I say. Disaster."

He had scared her now quite thoroughly, but she didn't tell him. The National Guard —the frickin' *Army* —was outside in the streets shooting off their guns and that was scary enough. Now she was hearing that they might not be the heroes her father was expecting. Even worse, his pessimistic attitude was beginning to make perfect sense and it frightened her to the very core.

"Did you get your mom a glass of water?" he asked.

"Yeah," she replied.

"Take her some aspirin?"

"Yeah."

"Check the bandage?"

"Yeah."

"How's it look?"

She hesitated a moment before replying, "*Gross.*"

A look of worry showed on his face for the briefest of moments, then subsided. He mumbled, "Goddamn medics. It's just a *bite*. Why the hell can't they make it better?"

Courtney cried then, putting her palms over her eyes and resting her elbows on her knees. She made sure she wept softly. She didn't want to be the center of attention.

Her father was a strong man —a smart man. He lifted weights regularly in the basement. He had a government-funded job in an office designing respirators. Like everyone else on earth, he had had a life and a history and so he was unique —and just as could be said about most people, he was so unique no amount of words could describe him. Like many daughters, Courtney saw *her* father as one of the strongest men in the world. But he was scared and he had made it evident. He let it slip. Maybe it was by mistake or maybe he just didn't care anymore. She was used to seeing him handle problems one way or another, either by muscle or by brains, but here he was helpless. She knew he understood that as well as *she* did.

When the dead guy had broken through the back door, her dad took it to the ground and pummeled it with alternating left and right fists. He had been watching the news enough over the past week to know what was happening across the country, but he never figured it would spill onto the north Florida coast. Nobody broke into the Colvin home —*nobody* —dead or otherwise —and security systems be damned, her father was *pissed*.

But then the dead guy got back up and bit into her mom's shoulder. It wasn't much —it wasn't much at all. Just a scratch. Nobody was supposed to get sick from a *scratch*.

Her dad went after the intruder again, attacking it this time with the entire kitchen table, lifting the table up and slamming it back down again and again on the dead man's spine. The dead man still moved after that though, albeit pathetically, as it seemed paralyzed from the neck down. They stood there and watched it, the three of them —Courtney, her father, her mother, until Courtney realized:

"Dad, that's Mister Coolidge!"

Her father's eyes opened wide at that point, when he too realized he had just fought with Mike Coolidge, the guy who had the house that neighbored theirs in the back. He was a mess now and had several small bite wounds of his own across his arms. Her father put on a pair of dishwashing gloves and dragged the wriggling body onto the back porch and tied it to the grill with a roll of duct tape. He was then going to go to Mister Coolidge's house to check on his children and make sure they were safe.

He didn't get the chance.

That was when the National Guard rolled in and royally fucked up everything.

They were somewhat helpful at first —making sure everyone was okay, treating the bite on her mom's shoulder, sealing off the streets with tanks, patrols, and barbed wire. It should have made for an impenetrable barricade. They were even treating the situation rather lightly, in her opinion, by posing with the walking dead and taking photographs with full-on smiles.

But then bad things started happening. They started losing contact with other battalions stationed throughout the north Florida coast. Then a couple of their captains got eaten near the barricade. However, it wasn't until CNN aired the graphic attack on the White House, complete with images of a line of marines getting overrun and secret service agents getting picked off and chewed on, did things go utterly downhill.

The National Guardsmen outside Courtney's home started fighting amongst themselves as they argued over who was in charge or who was *going to be* in charge. Any of the soldiers who were pacifistic and willing to take orders just wanted someone —anyone —to be given an impromptu promotion so the confrontations would end, but the more aggressive ones continued shouting back and forth until it escalated into violence. A couple of them shot each other, which —among other factors —caused a couple of the pacifistic soldiers to shoot *themselves*. Even elderly Mr. McGreevy was assaulted when he tried to bring order to one of the gun-toting youths. Apparently no civilian was going to be permitted a voice in this debacle.

This all led to Courtney's mom resting in bed, sicker than she'd ever seen her, pale and vomiting, and her father staring out the living room window cursing the soldiers who were supposed to be their saviors.

It went on this way for a couple of hours. It was then that her father started seeing the Guardsmen going door to door and taking people from their homes —forcefully at times —and loading them into deuce-and-a-halfs. Courtney always believed her father knew what was going on before she did, which was probably why he told her to go upstairs and put some clothes into a backpack. When she came back down with backpack in tow, he was already unzipping it to stuff in a couple of oranges, bottles of water, and some hastily-made sandwiches. He hugged her, told her he and her mother loved her, and kissed her on the forehead. He seemed uneasily calm.

She really didn't have enough time to have a good cry or even time to think up any words to tell her father. The Guardsmen were already at the door.

The first soldier aimed his gun at her father while the second stated, "*Uninfected women and children only.*"

With that, the soldier took Courtney by the arm and ushered her out the front door. She heard the second soldier ask if there was anyone else matching the criteria and heard her father tell him no, followed by, "Take care of my girl." She didn't hear anything after that. The soldiers didn't answer her father or even acknowledge he had said anything.

Tightly gripping the straps of her backpack with the fear it would be confiscated, she was put in the back of the deuce-and-a-half, which had only been partly modified to resemble an armored personnel carrier. There were other women and children in there with her — all people she knew, all equally frightened, and most of them she would see die before the day ended.

The big diesel monster took off down the street with a thunderous roar and would later join with a convoy of humvees, tanks, halftracks, and more deuce-and-a-halfs.

It all seemed to happen so quickly.

And that was how it began, five years ago.

WE COULD HAVE DEALT WITH THIS
PROBLEM WHEN CASES WERE FEW AND
FAR BETWEEN IF IT WASN'T FOR YOU
HUMAN RIGHTS MOTHERFUCKERS!!!!
I HOPE YOU ALL GET EATEN
ASS FIRST!

The Convoy

Courtney believed that no one, including the soldiers, knew exactly where they were going to begin with. Maybe they thought they were safe as long as they kept moving, but all she knew was that it was deafening in the back of the deuce-and-a-half. Kids were crying, moms were crying. Most everyone was screaming for answers and receiving none at all.

Courtney stayed mostly quiet. It was at this point she began to wonder when and if she would see her parents again. The "if" part — actually realizing this 'zombie' problem could really be really, really *bad* —end of the world type of bad, and actually realizing there may never be a "when" —was most of the reason for her silence. And then there was another lingering thought; a thought that had her hating herself *and* questioning her own situation: In the rush, her father had used wheat bread to make the sandwiches. She hated wheat bread. She knew he knew she hated wheat bread. So, she postulated, he wasn't in any real danger, not if she was mad at him for using wheat bread —she still needed to explain to him one more time how wheat bread made her gag.

She kept the bottles of water her father had stuffed into her backpack, but gave away the rest. The oranges and sandwiches shut up some of the kids at least for a little while and gave their moms — and Courtney —a bit of a break. It made her feel like there was at least a little something she could accomplish while being held hostage by the military. It made the situation seem less bad.

Two women sitting across from her —whom she recognized as her lesbian neighbors four houses down —were spreading a rumor that they were all being taken to the LaCosta Community Building. Apparently the National Guard had seized it for use as a rescue station. Sheriff's stations and hospitals were getting too crowded and dangerous, so citizens in the area were being urged to make their way to the community building. It was under armed guard, the women said, and there were doctors there that could administer aid to anyone who had been bitten by a zombie. They saw it on CNN, they further stated, shortly before the White House attack. Rescue stations were popping up all over the country.

What got Courtney, however, was the casual way people were

throwing the word 'zombie' around. It was real. It was happening. *Zombies.*

—What the *hell*?

Someone else, a girl Courtney recognized from her fifth period Botany class, made a point that if the Marines —and the entire United States for that matter —couldn't protect the White House, the most blatant, symbolic icon of their country, then how could they possibly protect a few people tucked away in some community building along the north Florida coast?

This statement quickly shut up the two women who had been talking about the rescue station, completely obliterating their upbeat attitude. This also turned out to be a mistake, because her gay neighbors' positive outlook had been the only thing preventing everyone in the deuce-and-a-half from resorting to tearful panic.

Had Courtney been able to relive this time of her life, she would like to have been the one to restore order —the one to explain how everyone was going to be all right —explain to them that if the enemy is already *dead*, then how tough could they possibly be? Looking back, Courtney wanted to be the one to *help*, because when this all really happened she was no different than the rest: Trembling and feeling completely pathetic and helpless.

The convoy wasn't stopping. If they were really going to take them to one of the self-described "rescue stations," then they would have already arrived there.

After ripping the velcro and lifting up the camouflaged canvas on the side of the deuce-and-a-half, she could catch a glimpse of the outside. She was able to recognize, just barely, that they had crossed over to Georgia. Furthermore, as twilight fell across the coast, they were crossing more and more areas that had been stripped of electrical power. She knew that most streetlights were equipped with a sensor that told them when it was dark enough to turn on, but none of them were lighting up. Houses and apartment buildings were also darkened. Apparently the friendly folks running the power stations decided it was time to up and leave —or, more likely —they were *forced* to leave.

Courtney knew that if the National Guard could just come to her door and drag her away from her father, then it was highly likely they were dragging everyone else out of their homes as well.

It was her first taste of martial law.

She figured that the Army thought it wiser to remove people from their homes so they could be safer, but in reality, well-boarded windows and doors were ten times safer than the 'rescue' the uniformed men claimed they could provide. It didn't matter where a mob of zombies decided to ambush someone, but being stuck with a company of soldiers meant being forced to sit back and watch while scared little kids in uniform waved their guns around.

Courtney had hoped that her father was wrong; that his pessimistic view of soldiers had been just that —*pessimism.* Unfortunately, in the days following her father's speech she witnessed more testosterone-driven power trips than acts of heroism from her would-be saviors. She wanted to be back home. She was willing to bet that her father was turning their house into a virtual fortress at that very moment —taking apart the tables and removing all the interior doors from their hinges and nailing them over the windows. It seemed like something he would do —something *strong,* something *smart.*

Then, causing more panic, one of the women with Courtney thought it was wise to mention that anyone bitten by a zombie was bound to die and become one of them. It was the *bite,* she said, and not death by any other cause. If you were bitten, you became one of them. There was no cure, she said. You would die, you would come back, you would bite others, and the cycle would repeat unto infinity.

For weeks and even months later Courtney would try to convince herself this wasn't true. If it *was,* then it meant her parents were really dead. Her mom had been bitten and Courtney knew her father wouldn't leave her all alone. They still seemed to love each other, at least as far as Courtney could tell, and they would be together until the end. Her mother would have died and came back and attacked her father.

And the cycle would repeat unto infinity.

This all really didn't sink in for Courtney just yet. She had no sooner begun to remember how sick her mother was when the deuce-and-a-half she was riding in started to slow down. All that could be heard was the sound of the vehicles in the convoy burning their diesel.

She lifted the canvas and peeked outside once more. The sun

was barely looming over the horizon. She could see the interstate directly below but didn't recognize which one; She had never been this far into Georgia. Then, a few seconds after the truck came to a complete stop, she stuck her head out even further to try to find out what exactly was happening. Others in the deuce-and-a-half were doing the same, and up ahead in the next truck in the convoy she could see other heads popping out through the canvas. It seemed no one —whether at the front of the convoy or at the back —knew anything and they weren't given any information by their uniformed chaperones.

Looking beyond, all the way to the front, Courtney was then able to see what had stopped the massive line of trucks, halftracks, and humvees: a gaping chasm where a bridge should have been. It was enough to stop any army —provided, of course, that that army was *alive*.

The convoy remained halted there for what seemed to be at least several minutes, but nobody was doing anything. She kept hoping she would see a bridgelayer drive by.

But then, off to the right, something else got her attention. There were several people —six or seven, at first —coming over the hill, stumbling over the guardrail and crossing the interstate, headed for the convoy. A few moments passed and by the time Courtney realized what was happening, that these were not survivors seeking refuge, the soldier driving the truck shouted, "*DEAD ONES!*"

First came the sound of screaming from within the deuce-and-a-half, then came the sound of automatic machine gun fire. She saw hundreds more —just like the others —come stumbling over the guardrail. Bullets were hitting them, she saw, but they kept coming. Even though they were only silhouettes to her, she could see some of them being ripped to shreds by the mounted gun on the halftrack up ahead. At least thirty seconds of nonstop shooting passed, but the line kept advancing and soon they were only several yards from the convoy. Whenever one of the shadowed figures finally fell another was there to take its place, and there were still hundreds more of them coming over the guardrail —literally thousands in all. Before Courtney brought her head back inside the truck, one of the figures in the vanguard stepped into the headlights of the truck behind her and she saw its face.

It was a man, but the nose was missing and an eyeball was out of its socket and dangling against its cheek like a paddleball. It was limping from a bullet that had destroyed its left kneecap. But it kept coming, it's mouth open, teeth shining and saliva drooling all over its chin.

It looked *hungry*.

Then the hysteria truly began.

The women and children with her were all screaming, some already splitting the velcro and pouring out of the truck through the ripped canvas. Courtney, all alone with no friends or relatives, found herself knocked down and nearly trampled underfoot. Then, when she was able to look up again, she saw that those with her were not *jumping* from the truck —they were being *pulled*.

There was screaming and the sound of gnashing teeth.

Surges of automatic gunfire were few and far between now, being replaced with the quieter *pop-pop-pop* sound of handguns. Though she knew very little about the military and even less about war, she did know that handguns were called *sidearms* and they were used as a last resort when all the bigger weapons had failed.

She brought herself to her feet, instinctively gripping the straps of her backpack as she cowered shoulder-to-shoulder with the six or so women and girls that were still in the truck. They stayed towards the center, away from the sides. Dead arms were ripping through the canvas and grasping at the air inside.

Something she remembers more than anything else was that there were no children left inside the truck with her. There had been at least twenty of them earlier, but now they were all *outside*, and young, pre-pubescent screams were the last reminder that they had even existed.

Looking back on it, Courtney wasn't sure how she herself survived this part. She and all the others had allowed the children to be taken. They hadn't even tried to protect them. They were too busy protecting *themselves*. By rights they should have met their own end alongside them. But there was no justice. She knew that anyone who was alive five years later was alive because others had died, more than likely distracting the undead just long enough for the rest to escape. In the months that would pass, however, things would change and she would learn enough to help others while she helped herself.

But *then*, during the slaughter of the convoy, she knew her actions were utterly *shameful*.

There were hundreds of dead arms probing through the canvas of the deuce-and-a-half and one of the cold hands finally caught a prize —the woman next to Courtney. It grasped at her skirt and pulled her just enough for other hands to latch on. They yanked her through the canvas, kicking and screaming, and then she was seen no more.

No one had tried to help her.

Courtney wasn't sure if she *could* have been helped, but she wished she had at least tried. She had seen the woman's face, gripped in terror, begging with incoherent screams for the others not to be cowards —to *help* her.

But no one so much as extended a hand.

Then there was a jolt —a sudden impact that reeled Courtney and the others, sending them off balance. The entire truck —two and a half tons of it plus passenger weight —had been sent careening down the interstate. They felt several bumps, probably caused by hundreds of bodies being rolled over and crushed beneath the tires. When she and the others brought themselves to their feet again, this belief was further reinforced by the fact that there were no more dead arms reaching through the canvas. A single blindingly-bright light was now shining at them through the back.

Together but alone they opened the tail flap. The truck behind them, another deuce-and-a-half, had rammed theirs and now the two deuce-and-a-halfs had become one big hunk of metal junk. As Courtney peered over the headlight that illuminated the entire transport area, she saw the driver of the other truck, a military man, be pulled out through his open door and into the arms of several hungry walking corpses.

She doesn't remember now what happened to the others that were with her, but she knows they didn't make it. She only remembers climbing onto the steaming engine of the truck behind her and then up and over the windshield and then onto the flimsy canvas on the roof.

Maintaining her balance on her hands and knees, she saw the scene in its entirety: Thousands upon thousands of dead people, some split into smaller groups as they feasted on someone who had been alive, the others still in mobs as they tried to get a meal of their own —all brightened by the headlights and searchlights of the scattered trucks in the convoy.

It was *luck* —and nothing more —that the truck carrying her had been sent out of the encircled area with a push from the truck behind it and into the guardrail on the side of the interstate.

It was dark on the other side of the shoulder, but she didn't see anything moving. She could see what might be a small creek down the hill, followed by a lot of trees, but nothing was moving —nothing that would *get* her.

She jumped. This leap of faith was far from graceful. Somehow she had turned sideways but —again, out of luck and nothing more —her backpack full of clothes had softened the fall. However, there was an immediate pain in her ankle as it came down on a sharp rock jutting out of the ground.

She lay there for a second and in that time wondered if this was where a mob of hungry hands would circle around her and tear her apart like she deserved —if this was going to be the end of her.

She heard moaning to her right. Investigating with a simple turn of her head, she saw a soldier lying about ten feet away clutching his knee. His camouflage uniform was covered in blood and the pain in his face was evident.

She heard moaning to her left. Turning her head the other way she saw another girl there, roughly her own age, crying into her palms. She didn't seem physically hurt in any way, but she didn't get up and move. She just cried.

And then there was a set of camouflaged arms that hooked Courtney beneath her armpits and lifted her to her feet. The attached voice said, "Let's get out of here."

Though she knew her ankle might be broken, she still couldn't summon sound from her voicebox. She just stood there, looking into the soldier's face, trembling.

The soldier picked her up into his arms. He carried her down the hill at a full running stride, crossed the creek, and then went up and over the opposite hill, away from the slaughter.

He ran for what seemed like the longest time.

Fax Transmission

TO: Colonel Franklin Darlton [sic?]

FROM: Rodney L. Lloyd, Sheriff

**# OF PAGES
W/ COVER:**   1

COMMENTS:

Colonel Darlton [sic?]: my office, in cooperation with the Briars County Detachment of the Kentucky State Police and the 201st National Guard Unit, is currently maintaining a rescue operation out of the Briarston YMCA. The space in this building is ample and we are receiving a constant flow of refugees (for lack of a better word). We have twelve doctors on hand to aid the wounded.

As you can imagine, no one here has any experience in dealing with a catastrophe of this magnitude, and the policemen and soldiers here are not finding any effective means of fighting the unending waves of corpses that are throwing themselves at our door. We can barely shrug them off long enough to make an opening to safely bring in more civilians.

We heard a rumor about your **BLACK BERET PROJECT** and would be extremely grateful if you could dispatch a Black Beret to this location to train my officers and the soldiers in an effective means of combat. There is a flat rooftop on this building that can be used as a makeshift heliport, or as a drop point for a fast-rope descent.

Please advise.

RLL

Why She Survived

They ended up at Camp Rigero, a National Guard Reserve Center just off the coast near Carson City. The parking lot in front of the base was littered with corpses —the kind that didn't seem to get up again, all with extremely apparent head wounds —and the fence beyond was patrolled by dozens of uniformed soldiers carrying very big guns.

The soldier who had rescued her, remembered simply as "Ryan", was dragging her by the arm at a very brisk pace, forcing her to find her own footing, pain in her ankle notwithstanding. There were several stray zombies here and there in the parking lot, but snipers behind the fence quickly picked them off. She and Ryan ran to the base and screamed to be let in as if it were the last American embassy in a hostile nation.

The soldiers opened the gates.

It was here she lived for eight weeks. The base had its own power generators, so they were never without light, and sometimes the pasty stuff that oozed out of the packages in her daily allotment of rations was actually pretty good. On top of that, fresh water was plentiful; several rows of water tanks occupied the area between the barracks and the northern rifle range. However, as secure as she should have felt, most of the time spent at Camp Rigero was uneasy, and not for the most obvious reasons. Of the eighty-seven others surviving there with her, eighty-one of them were male.

No one asked for her input. Most never even asked for her name. She figured it was for the same reason she survived the slaughter of the convoy.

When she had leapt off the deuce-and-a-half and hit the ground, there were two others close by that needed just as much help as she did: a soldier and another girl. Yet Ryan chose to help *her*. She knew why and —looking back —the reason sickened her.

The other soldier, the one bleeding and in a terrible amount of pain, was for all intents and purposes a *brother* to Ryan. Courtney always thought that soldiers were told to never leave anyone behind, but that nameless soldier was left as fodder for the zombies.

Ryan could have chosen to rescue the other girl instead of Courtney. She didn't even appear to be injured. But that girl was also a lot more ample than Courtney. Courtney —with purple highlights through her hair and tight jeans around her legs, showing her slim physique —was the one and only person Ryan decided to help. He hadn't even seemed to look twice at the others.

Courtney realized that if she were blonde instead of brunette, she would have made for the absolute *perfect* damsel in distress. She could remember how *manly* Ryan acted the night before they arrived at Camp Rigero, believing himself to be a heroic savior and Courtney to be an utter weakling in *need* of a heroic savior.

And maybe that's how it really was then.

—Then. But not now. Not five years later.

She saw less and less of him in the following weeks until he became just another face in the hallway. However, each time she saw him, he glared at her in an unflattering way much like the other soldiers did —like she was there under *their* protection and she should be doing something to return the favor —and by that they didn't mean menial chores. Furthermore, as days passed, they began to look at her as if they wanted to exact their payment sometime soon. They were just waiting for the right time, it seemed, when man's law could be made more flexible for the times they were living in —maybe just as soon as it was confirmed that all the higher-ups were truly gone.

—Idiots on power trips, just as her father warned.

Over the course of the first week, fewer and fewer uninfected civilians were arriving at Camp Rigero. Even worse, the *infected* ones were being turned away at the gate. All of the soldiers knew by then that to get bitten meant twenty-four hours of painful sickness, followed by death and reanimation.

She was beginning to wonder if she wanted to continue living like this or if she even wanted to continue living at *all*.

But then everything changed.

She heard the sound of the helicopter —the noisy, deafening sound —and, like everyone else, she ran to see what was happening. Excluding the soldiers ordered to remain at their posts, they all hurried to the heliport where a mammoth Army Chinook was hovering patiently overhead with its bay door wide open. She could see a dozen or so figures sitting inside.

A rope was flung out, dangling from high in the air, and not long afterward someone was rappelling down fast and graceful. Several large padded packages were then dropped and landed hard on the heliport. The figure —by now obviously a male someone —unhooked the line and the helicopter spun away, leaving him there without so much as an explanation.

Soldiers were looking to their captains for some kind of explanation, but the captains could only shrug their shoulders in response.

The man was wearing a pseudo-military uniform that up until that point had not been seen by the general military. Most noticeable was the black beret on his head. Below that was a full polarized visor that reflected the sunlight with a copper glow and completely obstructed his face. It seemed to be secured comfortably snug by a spandex hood below the beret. His actual uniform, however, was a tight black and turquoise bodysuit with a high collar. He wore black gloves that fit close against his forearms and extended nearly to his elbows. Lastly were his boots, which appeared to have thick metal embedded in the heels. In this full garb, none of his skin was at all visible.

There was a rifle strapped to his back and a handgun in a holster on his right hip. On his left hip was a sheathed sword.

He was tall and imposing and quite the spectacle.

Then came the unveiling —the removal of his copper-colored visor.

He was black and a great deal older than most of the soldiers — probably in his late thirties or early forties. However, as they would all soon discover, he was highly articulate and had a strong, domineering voice to go along with it. Also, it seemed he was prepared for the inevitable skepticism.

"My name is M. Gordon Levi," he stated. "No *'sir'*. No *'M'*. Just Gordon. I'm a Black Beret. I'm here to help."

Then followed a barrage of questions by the soldiers.

The Black Beret began answering these questions, piquing the curiosity of everyone, but when he made it known that he was without rank —a total civilian yet under military authorization —the soldiers began to lose interest.

"I'm a member of the Black Berets," he explained again in a very practiced way. "A unit trained and specialized in surviving the new world crisis. Yes, I *am* a civilian, as are most Black Berets. As you might've guessed, actual military —in *any* branch —is an endangered species. What few of us there are have been sent to places like this to train you and increase the number of Black Berets. Like I said: I'm here to help."

In the minutes to follow he would repeat his mission statement over and over exactly the same. Courtney wondered how anyone with such a bold voice would have any problem at all getting others to fall in line, but the soldiers didn't make it easy for him.

Gordon Levi, unfazed, was ready to provide a demonstration.

Later that day, entirely at his request, he ventured alone through the gates of the base and into the uncontrolled outer parking lot. Courtney watched on, her fingers trembling as she wrapped them around the links of the chain fence. There were three zombies on the other side, one male and two female, and she knew anyone with a gun and three bullets should have had no problem putting them down. However, Gordon left his guns behind. He wore only the outfit from before and carried only the sword.

The zombies were fast. No area of their skin appeared decayed and they were able to walk at full strides. They were approaching in a huddle, weaving through a line of cars that had been parked there and forgotten.

Gordon met the zombies halfway.

He unsheathed his sword and in one motion decapitated the first. Its head rolled off its shoulders immediately and hit the pavement with a very satisfying *thunk*. Gordon stepped gracefully away and spun twice, taking off another zombie's arm on the first spin and its scalp on the second. The third and final zombie, equally unfazed, extended its arms and lunged at its meal. Gordon extended the blade and —using a simple jab and the zombie's own forward momentum —put the metal at least five inches through its eye socket, most certainly splitting the brain in half inside its protective shell.

Finished, Gordon knelt down and used the zombie's shirt to wipe the blood and gore from the blade of the sword. He then calmly sheathed it.

Courtney didn't remember *everything* that happened, nor did she care to, but she did remember everything Gordon said —and the soldiers' rebuttals —with utmost clarity.

Upon returning through the gate, Gordon addressed the crowd: "Are we finished playing *playground* here? Have you seen enough, or do you want to keep playing reindeer games? Because I *refuse* to continue butting heads with you."

One of the captains spoke up and his sarcasm was already evident. "You want to teach us to be ninjas or something?"

Murmurs and chuckles rumbled through the crowd.

"Yay, a *smartass*," Gordon countered, passive-aggressively maintaining his composure. "That's *exactly* what we need." He took a few moments to eye the soldiers one at a time, effectively silencing them, then continued, "A sword is the least of it. A Black Beret is almost as effective without a weapon at *all*, but give him the right rifle and the right handgun and a Black Beret with only a week of training can deal more damage than any of you trigger-happy bozos."

The soldiers got understandably angry at this point and several of them appeared ready to verbalize their displeasure. One of the captains held up his arm to keep them silent at least for a little while longer.

Gordon continued, "Ammunition's running out, boys and girls. There's too many of you who have heavy trigger fingers. There's even more of you who expend entire magazines because you like to see blood and guts flying everywhere. Well, *bravo*. All you've accomplished is proven that you get your rocks off by shooting up something *formerly* human. But guess what? There's going to be millions more." He paused a moment to let this sobering fact sink in. "So what happens when you're out of ammo? I'll tell you: You'll have to *fight*. And I mean really *fight* —there'll be no more of this hanky-panky gunplay. You'll be fighting with your *hands* and with a *sword*." He jabbed his knuckles together and motioned to the sheathe on his hip. "These weapons never need reloading and you'll never run out of ammunition."

"We won't be ninjas, Captain," one of the soldiers in the front chimed. "We'll be Shaolin monks!"

Gordon quickly approached that soldier, put his palm on his chest, and pushed him to the ground. He could obviously lay a whipping to living people just as well as he could to dead people. However, instead of doing more, like holding the soldier down and bloodying his face, Gordon simply stepped back. He removed his cover, revealing a shiny bald head, and held the black beret high in the air for all to see.

"This means something!" he shouted. "Wearing this beret means never having to doubt yourself! It means not being afraid anymore! Anyone who trains under me will receive one. I've got plenty of berets and uniforms in those fancy little boxes over there and plenty more en-route. I've even got manuals for the reader types." He motioned to the packages that had been dropped out of the Chinook, then continued, even more seriously: "You'll be a *weapon*. You won't need endless amounts of ammunition —you won't need any more fully automatic *hogs*. You'll have a rifle, a sidearm, and a sword. That's all you'll need." Then he capped it all off with, "We'll win this war."

It was quiet for a while after that. The midday sun was getting hot and the soldiers were getting even hotter.

"That's the plan?" one of the captains asked. "This is the best that all the strategic minds could come up with?"

Without hesitation Gordon replied, "Yes."

The captain stepped forward, looking doubtingly at his men, then turned to face Gordon once more. "There's nothing else?" he asked. "They're not going to round everyone up and get us the hell out of here? They're just going to drop off a...," (Here he paused to make quotation marks in the air with his fingers), "...*Black Beret?*"

"Black Berets are being dispatched throughout the country," said Gordon. "You needed help, so you *got* it."

The captain approached him and stood very close, then in a very soothing tone told him, "I'm sorry, Mister Levi. But you're not a soldier. You're a civilian. You haven't earned your stripes. I don't care how *cool* you are, the men here aren't ready to listen to you. Besides, *sir*, in case you can't tell, our enemy is already *dead*. They're going to rot away and everything will be back to normal. So why fight them? We're safe here and we're handling things just fine. And since all the best strategic minds in our great country have left us *stuck* here, we plan to enjoy the calm."

Gordon walked away from him and didn't bother arguing. He focused on the crowd once more and addressed them instead: "Anyone interested should raise their hands now and make yourselves known. I'm not going to waste any more time trying to convince you."

There was silence —maybe even crickets chirping.

However, from her position in the far back, this was the point when Courtney timidly raised her hand. Every head turned to her and she lowered *hers*, not wanting to feel their eyes watching her.

Gordon didn't hesitate to point to her and say, "There's one. Any more?"

There wasn't. Even after waiting —perhaps even *hoping* —no one else raised their hand.

Then Gordon motioned like he was parting the oceans and the crowd of soldiers shuffled out of his way. He walked through them and straight to Courtney.

"What's your name, honey?"

She stuttered a moment before she finally got out: "Courtney Colvin."

He eyed her in a very suave way and said, "Well, Courtney Colvin, you made the right choice."

They walked away together.

She could hear several racist remarks being spoken, which she thought was funny since no one had said anything until they discovered it was a *white* girl that decided to follow Gordon. But to her it didn't matter what those soldiers thought. None of them had much of a personality to speak of anyway, so a racist remark was probably the best they could come up with. Whether her decision was right or wrong, one way or another she would never have to rely on them again.

ROCK FORGE
Army Research Laboratory

RESEARCH RESULTS PART ONE (ABRIDGED FOR REVIEW)
Submitted by M. Gordon Levi, Director of Unarmed Combat
with cooperation from members of "Project Black Beret"
under authorization by Col. Franklin Darlington

<u>Effectiveness of unarmed combat vs. reanimated dead (target).</u>

WHEREAS the majority of all existing martial arts require an opponent to be conscious of and aware of pain:

e.g. Karate/Tae Kwon Do: Kicks and hand strikes = Mostly ineffective. Attacks do not do sufficient damage to the target's brain to cause termination and a target will not back down under duress.

e.g. Judo/Aikido: Throws by joint manipulation and/or leverage = Mostly ineffective. Target will attack again after being thrown. (Note: It has also been found that targets with later forms of decay will simply lose the body part being manipulated and the throw will fail.)

e.g. Wrestling/Jiu Jitsu: Submission holds, armlocks, chokes = Mostly ineffective. Target is not conscious of pain and will not respond to a joint lock or any form of submission maneuver. Also, though target occasionally draws oxygen, it is not required for the target to function, and therefore the target will not respond to choke holds, whether by air or by blood. The only practical use of Jiu-Jitsu in this instance is the Guard position, which will be discussed in full later on.

e.g. Krav Maga/[Soldier Style]: Unarmed versus weapon = Not applicable. It has been discovered that targets will use [tools] to some extent to accomplish a goal, but as of this time none have been observed using a [tool] as a weapon.

WE FIND that the world as a whole was not prepared.

continued...

BE IT THEREFORE RESOLVED that the BLACK BERET will adopt a hybrid unarmed fighting style, aptly titled "BLACK BERET STYLE", consisting only of the most effective maneuvers and techniques in existing Martial Arts.

INCLUDING, but not limited to: (1) Rather than using speed with the intent of causing pain, Karate and Tae Kwon Do kicks will be modified to PUSH AWAY A TARGET. (2) Throwing techniques from Judo and Aikido will be softened to prevent breakage of target's joints and therefore failure of the maneuver. (3) Wrestling and Jiu Jitsu styles will not be incorporated, as they require prolonged contact with a target. Only the Guard position will be favored. (4) Krav Maga and various other [Soldier Styles] of combat have little to offer, but this will be discussed in full at a later time. (5) Newly-devised techniques will become available after guarantee of effectiveness.

BE IT THEREFORE RESOLVED that anyone, regardless of race, gender, religion, branch of military, civilian status, or any other qualifying factor, will be eligible for training as a BLACK BERET.

WE THEREFORE RECOMMEND that this information be adopted into the AD HOC BLACK BERET TRAINING MANUAL.

MaL

The Fall of Camp Rigero

She learned to fight.

She was taught maneuvers from various martial arts: Karate to attack, Judo for throws, and Jiu-Jitsu for defense. She learned throws and variations of throws, kicks and variations of kicks. The first rule of throwing a zombie, she learned, was that it was necessary to grab the creature in an area of its body that wouldn't easily snap and ruin her leverage. Also, it was best to keep in mind a domino effect: if possible, throw a zombie into another zombie.

When kicking, she learned, it was best to *push* rather than attempt to injure. They needed to be kicked squarely on the ribcage, otherwise it was possible her foot would penetrate the zombie's chest and get stuck inside. Rarely was it possible to kick high enough and hard enough to even *damage* a skull, let alone cause enough penetrable brain damage to put down a zombie for good. After all, it wasn't like zombies could be knocked unconscious like normal people. The theory, she was told, was that all a zombie required in order to function was the very core of its brain.

Next she learned the wakizashi. As Gordon explained it, long swords —*katanas*—were too heavy to swing with a single arm alone despite how action movies portrayed using them, and knives were simply too short to keep enough distance between herself and the target. The wakizashi, on the other hand —a shortened version of the katana —could be swung with one arm alone if necessary while the other was used to defend, especially when confronted with two or more targets.

He told her how he and the other specialists forming the Black Berets were given real zombies to practice and perfect all these techniques on at a place called Rock Forge. He told her how the zombies had been completely wrapped in airtight black plastic that still allowed them to remain mobile, yet prevented them from infecting anything or *anyone*. He then told her how the zombies all too often resembled "gimps out of bad porno movies."

It gave Courtney a laugh, which felt good. It was something she hadn't done for weeks.

He explained that *here*, however, cotton training dummies would have to suffice. He didn't want her in real danger unless it was absolutely necessary. Besides, he doubted any of the soldiers would be willing to help him capture a zombie and wrap it up. They would have to make do with their makeshift dojo —hollowed out from a large storage room that used to be an indoor shooting range. But after pushing some boxes aside and moving some heavy metal cabinets and laying down some carpet, the place served its purpose well.

This training was all she had to set her mind to —and, while training, it allowed her to block out more painful thoughts. It was also the perfect distraction from the lustful eyes of the soldiers.

Next she learned precision shooting with a .22 Hornet rifle, modified with an add-on for the Black Beret —a night vision-capable telescopic scope. This rifle was for longer distances. For shorter distances she was given a Socom .45 caliber handgun with an attached silencer, laser sight, and built-in flashlight. Gordon called it "The complete sidearm." It was lightweight and highly accurate. The silencer was so no more zombies than necessary heard any shot fired. A Black Beret never wanted to attract attention. The purpose of the laser sight was self-evident —just highlight a target with the red dot and *boom*. Even young girls like her, who had never even *held* a gun before, could feel confident that they would hit their target. It seemed that Gordon and the rest of the founders had thought of everything. The key to shooting, she learned, was patience and easy, steady breaths. If a zombie didn't fall after the first headshot, then a second one would surely put it down. She would just need to stay calm and *do it*.

When she learned the basics of the weapons of the Black Beret, Gordon began showing her more and more advanced techniques, including how to move and how to listen and how to function in a team. They were exhausting every lesson provided in the hastily-printed Black Beret manuals Gordon and his team had put together. Since she had been the only one willing to learn and therefore his only student, she progressed quickly. He explained that he was one of the founders of the Black Berets —one of the originals —which meant she was learning straight from the source. However, she just liked to think she was talented.

Every other day he would take her to the landing strip on the eastern side of the base and teach her how to drive. Her father had taught her a little, but now she was learning the ins and outs of the humvee and their very loose, standard transmissions. Unlike her father, however, Gordon would let her go as fast as she wanted — until, of course, he had to warn her to slow down since they were almost out of runway.

However, three weeks after the training began she started to notice Gordon's deteriorating morale. She didn't think it was because he had lost contact with another Black Beret —a friend —stationed at the LaCosta Community Building, but rather because he only had one student to concentrate his efforts. He probably imagined getting a somewhat warmer reception upon his arrival at Camp Rigero and that the soldiers would eventually see things his way. She could tell he felt he had a lot to offer everyone and was feeling rather depleted at not being able to do a damn thing about it.

It was a week later that he came into the dojo and made it official. Whether she really deserved it or whether he was just bored of it all, she couldn't tell.

"You're a Black Beret," he said. "Congrats."

He gave her the uniform, gloves, boots, visor, and —*most importantly* —the beret. He then showed her how they should be worn and helped her zip up the back of the suit.

After she was fully geared up, sans visor and beret, she asked what the deal was. The uniform clung to her skin and the black and turquoise color didn't seem at all like something any branch of the military would willingly create. It was too flashy.

He laughed and explained, "It's actually a *wetsuit*. The material's called *trylar*. Nothing short of a really sharp knife can cut it. If you ever get bit wearing that, it'll feel like a vice clamping down on your skin and it'll most definitely *hurt*, but the teeth won't penetrate the suit. As for the tightness, well, as you might have noticed, those baggy uniforms everyone else is wearing only gives those dead guys something to grab hold of. And *no*, the military didn't make them, they *seized* them from the manufacturer. Hence the lame design."

She looked in the mirror when he said this, turning fully around, and replied, "I think its kind of cool."

And he mumbled: "Figures."

Things changed a lot then, when she no longer wore sweatpants and a tank top to training with Gordon, and instead wore the uniform.

He started looking at her differently.

She looked older. More experienced. Stronger.

What happened then was something she somehow expected to happen a lot sooner at Camp Rigero. It was never *rape*, though he was easily a foot taller and twenty years her senior and could easily have taken what he wanted. After all, the *rest* of the world didn't really seem to care about her opinion or her age, nor did they even trifle with petty things like chivalry. At least Gordon had been different from them. While she was nervous and didn't want it to happen, it didn't mean she was not willing —there was too much to lose by not letting it happen.

So she let it happen.

He seemed to have been getting bored with teaching her and she felt it would only be a matter of time before he gave up, leaving her with no one. So, as long as he taught her how to fight the way he did —how to survive —then she would let him have his moments after each session. At first it was like a kick in the gut to her self-esteem, (especially in the somber moments afterwards when he'd be too ashamed of himself to speak to her,) but she knew that at least she wouldn't have to rely on those testosterone-driven soldiers anymore and at the same time she wouldn't be *alone*.

It was around then that she realized just how in truly bad shape the world was —and not by the same logic everyone else had used to arrive at the same conclusion. No, she realized this when even the kindest and most honorable man became just that —a *man* —who had put aside his noble behavior and his reservations about sleeping with a much younger girl despite knowing the girl needed him and therefore would not refuse him.

But, after receiving the uniform, she wasn't just a girl anymore. She had become everything he originally promised in his motivating speech in front of all the soldiers.

After a couple of weeks being with him didn't feel wrong anymore. She was starting to enjoy it. He was strong, but gentle, and reminded her of her father —and not in some sick, twisted, perverted way. It was the only relationship of any kind she had ever had. No matter what he did —no matter what she *let* him do (because she could have told him no even when it hurt) —she couldn't bring herself to be angry with him.

She didn't know exactly how she felt about him and she never got the time to explore it fully.

Gordon Levi —and everyone else at Camp Rigero —would soon be dead, and her last mental picture of the place would be of an army of the undead conquering an army of the living.

The base was overrun one cloudy September day only eight weeks after she had arrived. It looked like it might rain, which would have been the first rain in over three weeks. None of the soldiers or their captains had bothered considering what such a dry spell would do to the river nearby —the very same river that served as a natural barrier on the unfenced side of the compound.

She had been in her barracks when the ruckus started, getting ready for that day's training session that was to begin within an hour. Sirens started blaring and a few seconds later machine guns were firing incessantly.

M16's. She recognized their sound easily enough by then.

The noise outside was reminiscent of the chaos when her convoy had been attacked. This time, however, her body was tight and her mind was focused and she knew how to use them. She knew she would never again feel satisfied by simply running away in a fearful panic. This time she was *ready.*

She left her barracks in full Black Beret gear and had every intention of joining the fight, but outside waiting for her was Gordon, who stopped her immediately. He wasn't wearing a uniform, just pants and a button-up shirt. Blood was running down his forearm from a large hole near his elbow. Before her brain could decipher what this meant, he was using his healthy arm to guide her away.

"Get out of here," he said. "They're in. They came across the river. Hundreds. All over the heliport."

Soldiers were everywhere now, she saw, all in the process of loading their machine guns as they ran in the direction of the battle. None of them seemed to notice her or Gordon.

She didn't move. She just stood there, looking up at him, then at his bleeding forearm. He knew what she was going to ask, so he went ahead and told her.

"They took a chunk right out of me," he said, chuckling sourly. "And I was *just* getting ready to put my uniform on for our training.

Of all the luck." He tried to force a smile, but didn't quite pull it off. "Pack whatever stuff you can and get your ass over to the garage. Take a humvee. You won't need a key to start it."

"And leave you here?" she asked.

"That's the one thing I never got to teach you," he replied. "Sometimes it's okay to run. This isn't a fight you can win. This place is done for."

So she left.

There was more to it than that, of course, but these were some of the memories she felt were best left unremembered. The pleading with him to come with her, his apologies for being stupid and getting bitten, his reminder that he wasn't going to live anyway, the snub-nosed pistol he pulled from his pocket, followed by his last words, *"Don't worry, you won't catch me walking around,"* —these were all things she didn't care to be reminded of ever again.

ROCK FORGE
Army Research Laboratory

FOR THE EYES OF Col. Franklin Darlington ONLY
From: Dr. Henry "Hank" Freeland (civilian status)

I am completely not qualified to be making this report. I am not an expert in this. I can name at least ten people off the top of my head that are far more qualified than I. Dr. Patel should be doing this. Not me.

My findings, as erroneous as I hope they are, is that <u>decay in reanimated dead is coming to a stop</u>. Dead cells are somehow stabilizing. Harsh weather conditions and other external factors may begin to break them down, but on the flipside, the right weather conditions could have them functioning for a lot longer than we first expected.

Maybe you should have done more than simply dispatch a few Black Berets. Sorry man, but I don't have the patience to use bullshit etiquette anymore. This is some serious shit. Maybe nukes are our last and only option now, but who can authorize that? Is there anyone even manning the silos anymore?

If you want, have another researcher double check my results. I hope I was wrong.

You can call me a wimp or whatever, but I'm out of here. I'm taking my kids and I'm going far away. By the time you read this I'll have left the installation.

My best to you,

Dr. Henry "Hank" Freeland

P.S. Don't let your brain get sucked out through your eyeballs. Let em come out your nostrils instead.

All Gone

She faced a long and lonely road ahead. She tried to concentrate only on the pavement rolling under the tires in front of her. Thoughts of returning to her real house on the north Florida coast crossed her mind on more than one occasion, but she knew what would be waiting for her there. She didn't even consider finding another rescue station like Camp Rigero since she was certain soldiers were the same pretty much everywhere. So, since all bad things that had happened so far had happened to the south, and —knowing no other way to go —she headed north.

She killed her first zombie that very day.

Just like all the vehicles in the garage at Camp Rigero, the gas-powered humvee she took had several cans of fuel mounted along the sides. She waited until she was on a long, flat, open stretch of road before she stopped and got out. She fed gasoline into the tank one can after another until it started spitting back at her. When she opened the door to climb back inside, she heard something rustling in the weeds on the side of the road.

She stood and watched it for a while, the pitiful thing, as it struggled towards her on the bloody stumps where its knees and elbows used to be. It was covered in dirt and left a trail of coagulated blood in its wake. Whether it had been male or female, she couldn't tell.

She watched it a little longer.

It took nearly an entire minute just to cross the first lane.

Though she would never admit why, she allowed it to crawl all the way up to her. It could open and close its mouth well enough, but it couldn't angle its head in a way to bite her leg that didn't send its deformed body off balance. Even if it could have bitten her, the wetsuit she was wearing wouldn't have given it anything to sink its teeth into. Its teeth could only slide up and down on the slick trylar.

She quietly pulled the silenced Socom from the holster, whispered, *"I guess it won't be you,"* then put a bullet in the creature's brain. There was a *zip* sound when the gun fired and a *thud* sound when the creature's body all at once fell to the pavement.

It was the first of many zombies that she would put down for good —but for hours after her first one, she wondered if she would start to feel guilt over killing something that was already dead.

But she felt nothing —Nothing at all.

Maybe she wasn't even capable of feeling anything just then.

She kept driving. She stuck to interstates that stayed well away from big cities. Also, since the ocean was the only thing that ever seemed to stay the same, she stuck close to the coastline. In some places fire was raging uncontrollably. In other places the roads were so jammed with abandoned vehicles that she had to drive into the median to get around them. Everywhere she went, however, all was dark and all was dead.

Stopping for personal needs wasn't too difficult; she simply found an isolated spot and got out of the humvee long enough to do whatever she had to do. But finding a place to wash up was a bit more difficult, as clean, out-of-the-way creeks were hard to come by. The powdered soap and small packets of men's shampoo provided in each ration didn't help much either. She eventually sacrificed cleanliness for a safer state of mind, since constantly looking over her shoulder while she bathed wasn't doing her nerves any favors.

She always stopped to sleep in places she thought were safer than others. These included more desolate stretches of road where houses were few and far between, which meant the former residents of those houses wouldn't be wandering anywhere close by. Still, she would make certain every door in the humvee was locked up tight before she curled up in the back and nodded off. Sometimes an occasional dead person would find its way to her and come pounding on the side of the vehicle, and at first she would always roll down a window and shoot the creature in the head. Later though, when she realized the windows in the humvee were truly shatterproof, she would just cover her ears and sleep through the siege. When she woke she would simply start the engine and drive away, sometimes running over the creature that had been trying to get her.

Making a straight line up the coast, into South Carolina she went, then North Carolina, through Virginia and Maryland into Delaware, barely missing Pennsylvania, through New Jersey and New York, into Connecticut, and finally entering Rhode Island. She didn't know how far she would end up going —maybe even into Canada provided she could find a working gasoline pump somewhere —or maybe even so far that she could wave at Santa, Frosty, and Rudolph.

Eventually she lost track of how many days had passed since leaving Camp Rigero.

Halfway through Rhode Island, however, signs of real life were becoming apparent. It started with very colorful graffiti scribbled on a bright white billboard:

LOOK HERE → *More survivors ahead. Keep going.*

She slammed the brake and stopped the humvee and there she sat for the longest time, staring up at the message.

She knew her will was deteriorating and eventually she would stop caring — maybe even intentionally neglect to lock up the humvee some day before nodding off. Besides that, she was *starving*. There had only been one box of sixteen rations stored in the back of the humvee and those were gone. She hadn't eaten in at least three days. On top of all that, the fuel strapped to the sides was almost gone as well. She didn't know anything about pumps and the like. She didn't know if she could even *find* a working gas pump, let alone be able to operate it and fight off any undead opposition at the same time.

She knew that if she wanted to stay alive, she couldn't stay alone.

Then again, how old was the graffiti? Was the person who wrote the message still alive? If so, exactly how many other survivors *were* there? Was it just another rescue station like Camp Rigero, full of the same obnoxious soldiers who would eventually turn to barbarism and rape? Could she just stay long enough to eat, sleep, and refuel? Would they even allow her to leave if she didn't like it there?

There were just too many questions and no easy answers. It was too much for a girl of seventeen to try to think about.

The worst that could happen, she reasoned, was that she would die. Furthermore, she knew she was definitely done for if she stayed alone. If there were any other survivors up ahead, she could check them out from afar and if she met them and if they tried to do anything bad to her, she would shoot as many as she could before shooting herself.

So, either way, the worst that could happen was that she would die. That was the best answer she could come up with.

So she put the humvee back in gear and kept going.

Roughly every five miles or so someone had written another message in one bright color or another and each one seemed to answer an unspoken question. Whoever it was that wrote them somehow had in mind the kind of person who would be reading them.

The first one read: *We have walls here.*

The second: *STILL ALIVE and looking good.*

The third message was so long that some of the letters at the end were scrunched together and running off the side of the billboard: *IF YOU ARE NOT NICE, GO AWAY YOU WON'T BE TOLERATED*

(Below that someone added: *THAT MEANS NO DIRTBAGS ALLOWED.*)

And finally, the last one read: *Turn at Matunuck Exit. Follow Road.*

A Child of Pop Culture

She was different when the apocalypse happened, not so much in appearance, but in demeanor. Change was bound to happen one way or another as she got older, but the end of the world tended to bring changes in the extremes.

Appearance-wise she remained pretty much the same. After arriving at Eastpointe she had the stylist at the plaza cut her hair just above her shoulders so, when tucked behind the spandex hood on the visor, it would fit easier. She also declined more purple highlights, but her hair was still beautiful on its own; soft brown which rested flat and flowed straight from her scalp in a single wave.

Having relocated from the north Florida coast to Rhode Island, her tan was long gone and replaced with a pale porcelain hue, though admittedly this could also have been caused by seldom venturing outside her home and experiencing even the slightest warmth of direct sunlight. Or, perhaps, her body —so accustomed to constant summertime —had not adjusted to the long, harsh Rhode Island winters. She had never even *seen* real snow before then.

Other than that, her appearance had not changed much in five years. She remained short and petite and very cute.

She had always been a child of pop culture —MTV, showy clothes, and dreams of marrying James Spader. She had been popular throughout school and usually always had a say on what her friends could like and dislike. Even she would admit she was nothing more than a teen brat. She could remember a guy named Bobby Ware who stole the teacher's edition of their Geometry book and gave it to her. She promptly used the book to cheat her way through Geometry throughout the semester, never even bothering to thank the guy because she knew he just wanted attention from her.

And that's pretty much how her life worked. She could get anything she wanted, she was never teased or ridiculed, and she never had to thank anyone for anything. Underneath it all, however, she knew she wasn't a very interesting person.

Therein lay the problem: What were the chances any *interesting* people had survived? Before acquiring the necessary skills, it was by luck and looks alone that *she* had managed to make it to Eastpointe. It certainly wasn't because of her personality.

She had been the two hundred and seventh survivor to drive through the gate. Once she settled down she would have tried meeting other people there in the hopes they were a cool sort, but her enthusiasm had been dashed by that prick Leon Wolfe. Light brown hair past his ears and obnoxiously good-looking, he was the same type of jerk she probably would have dated —and have her heart broken by —had the world not changed and her youth not been wasted.

She was just starting to accept that by living within the walls of Eastpointe she would have to do just that —*live* —despite all the horrors she had already been through. It seemed everyone else there was living, moving on, that sort of thing. So why couldn't she?

It started in the cafeteria.

Eastpointe didn't have much going on then. A couple hundred more survivors would roll through in the weeks after her, but until they found people with the necessary talents they had to forsake things like running water and electricity. However, they still had a cafeteria in the hotel and they were still able to serve what food hadn't gone rotten.

Working the lunch line that day was Leon Wolfe, a kid from Maine who was also one of a handful of people trained as a Black Beret along the way. Like Gordon Levi, Leon's trainer also met his demise before finding the solace of Eastpointe's high walls. Courtney always felt there should have been some sort of unspoken comradery between the seven Black Berets who made it to Eastpointe and maybe an even larger understanding between kids who were popular, but Leon Wolfe —the arrogant jerk that he was —mixed a glass of vinegar in with all the glasses of water and it was Courtney who got it.

She had been very, very thirsty and didn't question or suspect anything. She didn't even have time to smell the noxious aroma; she just tilted back the glass and took two full chugs.

It hit her hard.

She went to her knees, spitting and vomiting while Leon and several others were laughing their heads off. She had been strong on her own when she drove the humvee all the way from Georgia and at the same time managed to avoid getting eaten. She knew how to fight. She felt strong now. However, after a week at Eastpointe she was growing accustomed to the relative safety of the place and its relaxed atmosphere. There had only been a couple of actual soldiers there, but they weren't in charge and they weren't like the other soldiers she had met. No one there was on a power trip. There were no lustful eyes constantly watching her. For all intents and purposes, everyone there was normal. Unfortunately, she didn't know that some of them were also going to be dickheads.

Seeing them laughing at her was too unexpected —too much to deal with. In her anger, she just sat there in the middle of the cafeteria and bawled her eyes out, creating quite a scene. She wondered if there were new rules here that she didn't understand. She wondered why these people had done this to her. She wondered what she did to deserve this.

Then she remembered the kids —the little boys and girls with her in the back of the deuce-and-a-half —and how they met their ends. Even at Eastpointe, the very young or very old were very much a minority, as were out-of-shape types. She remembered why she survived initially —not because she was strong, but because she was *pretty*. She remembered all the others who deserved to be alive but weren't.

She remembered Bobby Ware and the stolen teacher's edition Geometry book. She remembered her mom and dad. She remembered *Gordon*.

And she missed them all.

With more people arriving at Eastpointe and with the various skills they brought with them, they were able to get the power plant working and the water running. They were strengthening the walls and renovating the houses.

But she had nothing to offer. She had no talents.

She chose a small newly constructed home to live in by herself. When it came time to celebrate her eighteenth birthday, she was allowed to go to the abandoned Eastpointe Plaza and take anything she wanted. It had all the amenities of the malls in Florida and she found this shopping spree surprisingly comforting.

She was able to find most of the things she owned before the apocalypse. She got a television —though she accepted there would never be any new shows to watch, a VCR and videotapes of her favorite movies —mostly Disney flicks, (she loved the gargoyles in Hunchback of Notre Dame), a stereo and her favorite CDs, her favorite sappy romance novels, and all the clothes she liked right down to the rainbow-colored socks with individual toes. She even got posters of her favorite bands —whose members were all probably wandering around as dead people with guitars still strapped to their backs —to decorate the walls in her new home.

And so she existed.

Tucked away in her house with all the conveniences she wanted, she lived in her newly created world. With no interesting people left, she felt it was best to read her books and watch her movies and listen to her music.

From within her own walls, the only reminder that all was not truly well in the world was the iron bars welded into the window frames. Every window in her house had them. Bigger windows like the two in the living room were given a vertical, prison-style treatment. Smaller windows like the ones in the bedroom were given a quick yet reliable crisscrossing metal grating. All were welded in place to suit a very simple purpose, which certainly wasn't for aesthetic viewing pleasure. They would be her last defense if the undead ever breached Eastpointe's walls.

In a world *ruled* by the dead, the living were again forced to live.

Courtney, however, simply existed.

Nestled in the triangle of Potter Cove, Snug Harbor, and the same great Atlantic Ocean Courtney saw in Florida, Eastpointe was a private community of small vacation homes for rich folks and fishermen. Just like one of the graffiti messages on the interstate proclaimed, there was a wall around all of it and it stretched as far as her eyes could see. A pre-apocalypse sign posted in front of the guard shack at the main gate read: *Welcome to Eastpointe - Golf - Swimming - Recreation for the family.*

There had been a rear entrance at one time, but was now bricked up and barricaded. The wall was high and solid concrete. It probably served the purpose of keeping the eyes of poor people —or, to be politically correct, *'non-members'* —from peering inside.

Eastpointe, even from the beginning, had everything a small town needed to be self-sufficient. As more and more people came, more and more of those luxuries became available. Getting the community's small hydroelectric power plant up and running came first. Then came the pumps at the water treatment facility and getting clean, running water constantly flowing. The only thing they had to do without was telephones —which, as they all discovered —none of them actually needed.

Taking from a stockpile of chemicals large enough to last for a decade, they were able to get the indoor swimming pool at the hotel up and running. Swimming had always been something Courtney enjoyed, so it was about this time that she wanted to leave her house to go there.

She had been avoiding everyone for so long that she knew they would be questioning her sanity, so she created a facade of maintaining that she was still a child of pop culture. Any time she left her house she made sure to look her best. She showered and waxed and shaved, plucked her eyebrows, and applied makeup and mascara. She wore cool clothes and a sexy two-piece bathing suit to go swimming in. She kept to herself.

The facade worked.

She was certain everyone saw her as she wanted to be seen: a snobby chick who —despite the circumstances —still looked down on everyone around her.

However, the community's in-house supplies, which were taken mostly from the Eastpointe Shopping Plaza, would not last forever. Pre-packaged food, light bulbs, toiletries, and other items of significant importance were dwindling.

Though still maintaining her *right-as-rain* attitude, she at last found a way to contribute. In doing so, everyone at Eastpointe — including that self-righteous bastard Leon Wolfe —soon found it evident that she was indeed trained by Gordon Levi.

Courtney, along with the six other Black Berets —*including Leon, much to her chagrin* —a couple of soldiers and some other gutsy people, ventured outside the walls of Eastpointe and began an operation to loot and pillage the neighboring towns. It wasn't like anyone in those towns were going to complain. After all, they were all dead, and for all Courtney knew, anyone who was alive in the world was alive inside the walls of Eastpointe.

Courtney found it surprising that the group never really had trouble locating what they needed. While a lot of the places they went to had already been ransacked and things like appliances and guns removed, the looters left behind everything that was significant for *long-term* survival.

The Black Berets brought back supplies by the truckload, including the most important ones, the items a town would need to stay entirely self-sufficient forever: *farm animals.*

Left untouched due to the strict human-only diet of the undead, cows and pigs and sheep and chickens and even a couple of horses were herded all the way back to Eastpointe. Over the span of several months, the acres upon acres of golf course was turned into a thriving farm community and irrigation ditches were dug from the river by the power plant. Large gardens were planted and harvested, always being certain enough vegetables were gathered to last everyone through the entire winter season. The livestock gave birth to new livestock and there was always an endless supply of meat as long as the Eastpointe citizens didn't get too greedy.

With over five hundred people in Eastpointe and the resulting melting pot of backgrounds, the inevitable power vacuum started to develop. Soldiers preferred a military style of authority, politicians wanted the common electoral system, and a Scientologist just wanted to 'clear' everybody. From what Courtney understood with her limited knowledge of the happenings outside her home, the matter was settled by an older man named Ervin Wright, who had been a member of the International Order of Odd Fellows. He introduced the Odd Fellow system of government and everyone eventually agreed it to be best suited to the purposes of Eastpointe.

With this system, every individual issue concerning the welfare of Eastpointe was assigned to an elected committee. Respectively, a committee was elected to address concerns of the power plant, water treatment and irrigation, land management, security, and so on. Every issue, regardless of its importance in hierarchy, was given a committee. Members of committees were elected to varying lengths of terms so some would expire before others, yet the rest of the members in rotation would still be knowledgeable of current affairs. To assure all of the committees were functioning properly, a Superintendent was elected for a six-month term. This Super-intendent would also see to creating more committees as other concerns arose and when his term expired he would not be eligible to run for Superintendent again until he served terms in three different committees. This guaranteed no one person would ever amass too much political power within Eastpointe.

Voting was held once a month in the conference hall at the hotel and all votes were taken with a simple showing of hands. Courtney only attended the ones she was requested to, and usually when she was it meant one of the committees needed something that was outside the safe walls of Eastpointe. They knew what she was capable of. With her training and her attitude they never saw nor treated her as *just a girl.*

She liked the respect.

And, when requested, Courtney and the rest would oblige them.

The undead were everywhere outside the walls of Eastpointe and it seemed more and more were migrating to Rhode Island to be where the food was. It was always tough —and it was always scary —every time her group had to venture into some dead town to retrieve something.

There were losses sometimes.

Sometimes a member of their group would get bitten by a zombie and —more often than not —that person would request sleeping pills to end their pain. After they had passed, someone else had to put a bullet in their head to prevent them from rising again.

Courtney never did it. She always left the room when talk of euthanasia began.

Everyone figured the zombies would rot away within a year, but as more time passed, everyone noticed that they appeared pretty much the same. During winter, the snow would cover them up and bury them, and then in the summer they would be seen wandering outside the walls again. Very rarely did they see one who had decayed enough to render itself immobile.

The years passed and the committees stopped finding reasons to send her outside. By then the town had become fully self-sufficient and the Plaza restocked with enough supplies to last almost indefinitely. There had not been another survivor to enter the gates of Eastpointe in quite some time, even though they had spray-painted directions to the community on nearly every billboard in a fifty-mile radius.

And all the while, Courtney existed. She maintained her facade. Sometimes she cried, sometimes she slept, but she always did so alone. She had dreams about Gordon at first —that he showed up at her front door, decaying and hungry. After his memory faded however, she began having the dreams about the corridor and what waited for her at the end of it.

She thought that maybe the nightmares would go away if she weren't alone, which was when she sought out Leon Wolfe.

She heard rumors from listening to other girls at the swimming pool that he had slept with nearly every available female at Eastpointe. While she didn't know if it was true or not, she did know he was easy enough on the eyes and her hatred for him would make it easy to forget him afterwards. And —if it was true he was the town slut —she would have no trouble seducing him.

She would regret her actions later, of course, but at the time she was so starved for some kind of release that she looked beyond her anger at him and focused instead on what he could do for her.

Yet she didn't get the release she was hoping for. Even in someone else's bed, with someone else sleeping beside her, the corridor still haunted her. Now she was embarrassed again, knowing he thought she simply couldn't resist him and simply *had* to come over for a joy ride.

She thought the worst would be behind her, especially more than five years after the first corpse decided to rise again. Furthermore, she thought that her story would have ended upon arriving at Eastpointe, and —like in her sappy romance novels and favorite Disney flicks, '*lived happily ever after*' would be displayed in fancy letters.

But at Eastpointe, her story had not ended.

It had only begun.

Courtney Colvin - 4th Period English - Mrs. Harris, Instructor

My dramatic reading assignment will be The Seven Ages of Man by good old Billy Shakespeare. Please let me go last and at least give me a "C". 😊 Thank you. (Did I mention you're the coolest teacher ever?)

The ~~Seven~~ Eight Ages of Man by William Shakespeare

All the world's a stage,
And all the men and women merely players:
They have their exits and their entrances;
And one man in his time plays many parts,
His acts being seven ages. At first the infant,
Mewling and puking in the nurse's arms.
And then the whining schoolboy, with his satchel,
And shining morning face, creeping like snail
Unwillingly to school. And then the lover,
Sighing like furnace, with a woeful ballad
Made to his mistress' eyebrow. Then a soldier,
Full of strange oaths, and bearded like the pard,
Jealous in honor, sudden and quick in quarrel,
Seeking the bubble reputation
Even in the cannon's mouth. And then the justice,
In fair round belly with good capon lined,
With eyes severe and beard of formal cut,
Full of wise saws and modern instances;
And so he plays his part. The sixth age shifts
Into the lean and slippered pantaloon,
With spectacles on nose and pouch on side,
His youthful hose well saved, a world too wide
For his shrunk shank; and his big manly voice,
Turning again toward childish treble, pipes
And whistles in his sound. Last scene of all,
That ends this strange eventful history,
Is second childishness, and mere oblivion,
Sans teeth, sans eyes, sans taste, sans everything.

The eighth age is sitting up again
From widst the void she come and
Feasting on the flesh of the other ages

Sorry Courtney, Shakespeare
was WRONG //

CHAPTER THREE

Eastpointe, Present Day

Her 'week-after' chat with Leon left her feeling awkward most of the day. She eventually finished the breakfast he had brought, but still felt hungry. She tried re-reading one of her Harlequin romance novels, even skimming ahead to the parts that she liked, but it was all just too fake. She wasn't sure if the world *ever* worked like it did in one of those books, let alone now that all the survivors of the apocalypse were living in the same town together. She knew some people were pairing up simply because they didn't have too much of a choice. Romance had nothing to do with it.

Ergo, her decision to consummate with Leon Wolfe.

She popped *Beauty and the Beast* into the VCR and tried sitting through it, but the cheery songs just weren't sinking in. She then sifted through her collection of James Spader movies, but most of them were the risqué type and she really didn't want to be put in that kind of mood. After all, her favorite man in Hollywood probably wasn't even alive anymore. She didn't want to be reminded of that.

She decided to make do playing some music on the stereo while picking up the pigsty she was living in. She had never had anyone over before Leon and she didn't much like the thought of him knowing she lived in a messy house. He would probably go around telling people she wasn't as content as she claimed to be —that she just liked putting on a show. Well, now she would have a clean house to prove that she was just fine and dandy. It was like fitting the last piece of a puzzle into place.

It took her most of the day and she still didn't get entirely finished.

But by five o'clock her stomach was growling again, which meant it was time to make her daily trip to the hotel cafeteria. She took a shower, then put on her bathing suit and slipped her clothes on over it in case she felt like taking a dive in the pool afterwards. After all, nothing at home seemed to hold her interest that day.

She then ventured outside. Her neighbors had finished their game of badminton, much to her relief, and she hadn't heard '*shuttlecock*' being shouted since that morning.

—They were so immature.

Her golf cart was sitting there, shiny and new-looking just as she left it. She plopped down on the seat, pushed the ignition button, and put her foot on the accelerator. The quiet *vroom* sound of the engine was nice and steady as she headed down the road.

The air in Rhode Island was never as warm as it was in Florida, even in the middle of the summer. She still had not gotten entirely used to it. She still half expected to feel a skin-scorching breeze every time she opened her front door, but it never came. She had thoughts that maybe someday, in another five years or so, she could return to the coast.

But for now, Eastpointe would have to do.

She exited the streets of the main housing area off Sunrise Avenue and passed by the farms, trying to stay far enough away that the smell of manure would not burn into her nostrils. The road furthest from the farms was the main stretch near the high concrete walls, so this was the one she was forced to take.

The wall itself —probably ten feet high —cast a long shadow across most of South Street. However, it was still not able to mute the sound of the occasional breathless moan originating on the other side. Sometimes she could even hear something trying to claw away at the concrete stones in an attempt to get through.

She was used to it. So was everyone else.

She passed the armory on her right, (which at one time had been a roller rink), then proceeded past the big garage where all of the larger gas-powered vehicles were stored.

The road ended at the main gate. There were a couple men with rifles positioned here, along with a little rottweiler resting lazily between them and serving no purpose whatsoever. The men were sitting back in lawn chairs and exchanging half-assed ideas for starting a football league of some sort. Courtney didn't know their names.

There were two sets of gates that had to open in order for someone to get in or out. The middle area where the abandoned guard shack rested acted as sort of a decontamination zone.

Beyond that at the outermost gate, a lone zombie was standing with its icky fingers wrapped around the wire links, gazing longingly at the two men and the dog that were ignoring it. It wore a dark business suit with the sleeves ripped off at the elbows. Its skin was almost a pale blue color, all blood having long coagulated and pooled in its lower extremities. It remained silent, though it was most definitely still hungry.

On the wall next to the gate someone had posted a sign that read:

BEWARE THE JABBERWOCK
THE JAWS THAT BITE
THE CLAWS THAT CATCH

To which she mused, *Beware the Jubjub bird and shun the frumious Bandersnatch. Yeah, I get it.*

Next to that sign was another:

Be careful out there.
If you come back dead,
then no cake for you.

That sign was there every time she passed through. She figured someone should have taken it down a long time ago. Nobody went out the gate anymore —not since the Committees had sent her and the rest of the Strike Team on the last retrieval mission over two years ago.

Courtney turned away from the gate and took the road heading toward the hotel parking lot. The men sitting in the lawn chairs stopped talking long enough to wave at her, so she smiled and waved back.

It wasn't too hard.

She crossed the parking lot and maneuvered her cart between the yellow lines next to six or seven other carts, where she stopped and cut the engine. She hopped out and stepped into the large shadow of the Eastpointe Hotel.

It was a big building, but not humongously big. It had a shiny stonewashed color about it. There were five floors not including the basement and sub-basement, (which she had never had a reason to visit), with the lavish rooms reserved for committee members to live in during their terms and the penthouse given to the acting Superintendent.

She wasn't even sure who exactly the acting Superintendent was. She missed out on the last four elections.

She opened one of the glass doors and stepped inside.

There was a lot of noise coming from the cafeteria to her left, which was to be expected at that time of day, and after smelling roast beef in the air she knew there would be long line at the buffet.

Her eyes drifted away, passing the doors leading to the swimming pool and the conference room and eventually focusing on the door opposite the cafeteria. She'd never been through that door before.

Despite her growling stomach, food didn't seem all that appealing just then. There was too much on her mind to be solved with a simple helping of roast beef. Somehow she knew that before she even left her house.

That day she had a hankering to venture through the *other* door. So she did.

Suds & Salutations

The bartender was someone Courtney had seen on one or two occasions at the swimming pool. She was a pretty girl that was roughly Courtney's age and also shared the same height, figure, and happy-go-lucky attitude —but whether hers was faked or not, Courtney didn't know. She had long, shiny blonde hair with the last few inches dyed red and black. Though longer, it was styled straight and flat like Courtney's. She dressed similarly as well.

Another child of pop culture.

She was probably someone Courtney could have been a friend with had events happened differently —and she didn't mean just at Eastpointe. The bartender reminded Courtney of the kind of person she used to have as part of her social circle —the pretty yet not overly interesting type. If the world as a whole had not changed, maybe this was someone she would be finishing college with. That sounded about right to her. At her current age, she *would have* just been finishing up college, provided she had only signed on for four years. She would never know now.

It was weird for her to think about things like that.

The bartender was busy washing glasses in the sink, but looked up as Courtney entered the room.

"Hi there," she said in a laid-back Pennsylvanian voice. "*Courtney*, right?"

A bit surprised, Courtney asked, "You know my name?"

"I'm a bartender," she replied with a smile. "I know everybody."

Courtney looked around. The place was dark, with booths only dimly lit with soft, candle-like lights overhead. The stools around the bar itself were polished and shiny and the large mirror in the back was smudge and fingerprint free. Cocktail glasses hung from wire racks and long, perfectly situated rows of bottles stretched out along the wall. Despite its upper-class atmosphere, there was country music playing quietly on the jukebox. Courtney and the bartender were the only ones there.

She pulled out a stool and climbed on.

So this is a bar, she thought. *Whoop-tee-do.*

From behind the counter, the other girl strolled over and stood in front of her. She leaned close and very politely whispered, "You know you need work credits in order to drink here, right?"

Courtney sighed, then reached into her front pocket and pulled out a handful of silver tokens. She placed them neatly in a stack on the bar and asked, "Is this enough?"

The bartender's eyes grew wide for a moment. The tokens still had their glossy finish, which meant they probably hadn't been circulated throughout Eastpointe. She replied, "That's plenty. Don't you ever spend any?"

"Just in the cafeteria and swimming pool," Courtney replied. Then, wondering if the girl might think her a prostitute or something for having all those credits, she quickly added, "I earned them *legitimately*."

"Yeah, I know," the girl said. "You were one of those going out the gate a couple years ago."

Courtney nodded. She was a bit surprised a bartender would know something like that. Then again, she knew everyone at Eastpointe had a tendency of keeping an ear to the ground.

"You don't *have* to work, do you? You've got like a free pass now."

Courtney nodded once more.

The girl cutely rolled her eyes and said, "Must be nice." She extended her hand and introduced herself. "Alexis Turner."

Courtney shook it and replied, "Courtney Colvin."

"I know. So, what can I give you?"

Courtney looked away to investigate the rows of bottles behind the bar. She had to squint to read their labels. She saw Amaretto, Schnapps, Chambord, and a bunch of other names she didn't recognize. She looked back to the bartender and asked, "What about —like... *beer*?"

Alexis raised her upper lip and replied, "All the beer went bad a long time ago. Unless you want to try the home-brewed kind. But it's kind of nasty."

Courtney shrugged. "I don't know what I want."

Alexis turned her head to examine the bottles for herself, then turned back and said, "You'd probably like a Manhattan."

Courtney didn't know what it was, but assumed it involved mixing alcohol from different bottles. It sounded fine with her.

Alexis grabbed several bottles off the shelf and set about making the drink. She started with sweet vermouth and whiskey, then added a dash of bitters and topped it off with a cherry. It was kind of pretty.

Courtney spun around on the stool, checking out the room's layout again. After a moment she turned to face the bar once more. She asked, "Doesn't anyone else come in here?"

"Of course," replied Alexis. "But not for another hour or so. Most of them have jobs."

"Oh."

Alexis slid a wide-rimmed glass of red liquid to her. Courtney checked it out, then stirred it a bit with a straw before taking a sip. It wasn't bad.

So this is alcohol.

Alexis pulled up a stool on the other side of the bar and sat down.

Courtney wondered if she had been one those laughing at her in the cafeteria during the vinegar incident. She couldn't remember. She further wondered if Alexis was still laughing and just trying her hardest not to show it.

—But it didn't matter. She was just a bartender and as long as Courtney had credits to spend, nobody would be teasing her.

The Manhattans kept coming. After a while Courtney started to notice how the drink was losing its flavor and it took bigger and bigger gulps just to taste it. By then she was slouching forward, resting her elbow on the bar and her head on her palm and using her free hand to lazily lift the glass to her mouth and back down again.

It was sort of relaxing.

Time passed —slowly at first —but every once in a while she would glance at the clock on the wall and notice the second hand had moved quite a bit. Other people were filtering in from wherever they had came from and sitting down on the stools or in the booths. A couple of them eyed her curiously, probably wondering what force of nature had brought her out of hiding, but none of them sat close to her.

She liked it that way.

Alexis continued to chat with her between drinks, but Courtney didn't really mind. It seemed like she might actually be able to get along with her newfound peer, though she wasn't ready to socialize with more than one person a day.

However, no sooner had she considered this when someone sat

down on the stool right beside her.

"Hi Courtney."

She turned her head to match the voice to the face, then turned forward again. She mumbled, "*And so my day is now complete.*"

"Hi Leon," said Alexis.

"Hi Lexy," he replied.

They exchanged a mutual grin. Courtney immediately realized that they had been intimate at some point or maybe still were. It made her sick to remember that she had willingly made herself just another notch on his bedpost.

"What can I give you?" asked Alexis.

Leon leaned forward and very slyly replied, "How about *A Goodnight Kiss*?"

Alexis laughed. "I keep telling you we don't have champagne."

"You *do* keep telling me that, don't you?" he replied. "Fine. How about just *Sex on the Beach*?"

At this point Courtney mumbled, "*Gee you're so suave.*"

They didn't hear her.

"I don't have another bottle of Grenadine yet," Alexis told him. "They're looking through the boxes in the basement again. They'll find one eventually."

Leon leaned back, eyed all the bottles one more time, then stated, "Jim Beam. Water. Rocks." He then fished a token out of his shirt pocket and slid it across the bar.

Alexis took it and started mixing his drink.

Leon —as far as Courtney knew —was also one of the few who were given a free pass in Eastpointe. He had risked his life with her and at one point was even mobbed by a group of zombies. Only the trylar suit he was wearing had stopped all the teeth from actually penetrating his skin. Otherwise he wouldn't be here now, annoying her simply by his presence.

He turned to her and said, "I come here in the evenings sometimes."

She shrugged her shoulders and replied, "So?"

"*So,* I didn't want you to think I came in here just to see your pretty face."

She sighed, then turned to face him, showing a sneer. "Why can't you just talk *normally*? Your voice is so annoying."

"Oh —the witty barbs continue. If you keep being this insightful we'll have nothing left to talk about."

She rolled her eyes and took another drink of her Manhattan.

Alexis slid a glass of black stuff to Leon. He took a sip.

"You two get along so well," Alexis teased. "I'm beginning to think there's something going on."

"It's supposed to be one of those love-hate relationships," Leon said, playfully watching Courtney out of the corners of his eyes. "But right now the needle's stuck in the hate area."

"Just shut up," Courtney snapped. She finished her drink and slid another token to Alexis. "More red stuff please."

Alexis took the token, but didn't drop it in the bucket on the other side of the bar. Instead she rolled it across her knuckles in a practiced way as she watched Courtney.

Courtney watched her too, wondering why she was getting stared at.

After a moment Alexis returned the token to her and leaned over the bar to whisper, "I know the Manhattans are good, but you should just drink water for a while."

"*What?*" Courtney snapped. "Why?"

"Your eyes are getting cloudy. Your face is pale. You've been slurring your speech for the last half hour. Shall I go on?"

Courtney, in no mood for this, slid the remainder of her stack of tokens over to Alexis and said, "You can have all of them. Just treat me nice. Another Manhattan please."

Alexis turned her gaze to Leon for a moment, then back to Courtney.

"Are you drunk, Courtney?" Leon softly questioned.

"*No,*" she replied, her voice becoming louder. She glared at Alexis. "A few minutes ago you were being really nice to me and now you won't even give me another drink? What the *fuck* is your problem?"

Other heads in the bar —ten or eleven of them —started turning toward the ruckus.

"Courtney, I'm not being mean to you," Alexis told her, keeping a soft tone. "But if I give you another drink you're going to be sick."

Courtney swiped all the tokens off the bar and sent them flying. They clattered to the carpet below. She climbed off the stool. "I don't need this," she declared. "Why'd I bother? Hell with you guys. I'm going swimming."

She promptly fell to her butt.

She then sat there, looking at the floor, wondering what had caused her to be so close to it and why her hair was hanging so messily across her face. After a moment she mumbled, *"This sucks."*

She could hear someone laughing across the room. She quickly turned her head and saw a woman in one of the booths watching her and giggling.

"Keep it up," Courtney growled. "And I'll come over there and smack the grin right off your face."

"Okay, that's enough," said Leon. He got off his stool and knelt down beside her. "I'll take you home."

She looked up at him and whispered, "You know I could kick her ass, right?"

"I believe you could, doll," he replied. "So there's nothing to prove."

He put his hands in her armpits and pulled her to her feet. She wobbled there for a moment, trying to find her coordination. It was worse than morning dizziness.

When the hell did this happen?

Alexis pointed to the glass of Jim Beam and asked, "Are you coming back, Leon?"

"Yeah," he told her. "Can you put it in the fridge for me?"

She nodded.

With that, Leon put his hand under Courtney's arm and guided her across the room. She glared back at the people watching her. She kind of wanted to slug them all on the chin.

They exited the bar and crossed the parking lot. The sun was completely behind the hotel now. She wasn't sure exactly how long she had been in the bar, but she knew twilight was at about nine o'clock. That would make for about three and a half hours.

She further concluded that three and a half hours and twice as many Manhattans was not a good mix. She should have learned how to drink before just jumping right into it. Being led outside like a mental patient was kind of embarrassing.

Then she noticed Leon was leading her in the wrong direction.

Courtney pulled her arm away and said, "That's *my* cart over there."

Leon grabbed her arm again just before she looked ready to topple over once more. He said, "Okay. We'll take *your* cart." He paused for a second, then muttered, "*They're all the same. What does it matter?*"

She found she couldn't do much on her own. Leon situated her in the passenger seat and dug the long forgotten seat belt from underneath. He strapped her in, probably thinking she could fall out or something. She wondered why. It wasn't like golf carts were particularly fast or anything and there weren't exactly any wild turns.

He hopped in the driver's seat, started the ignition, then went forward out of the yellow lines. He exited the parking lot and took the road headed for the main gate.

He was a slow driver.

Courtney didn't like it.

As they passed the gate, she could see that the business-suited zombie was still on the other side of the fence in the same position he was before. He still had his icky fingers around the links in the fence, still keeping quiet, still being ignored by the two guards and the rottweiler. However, this time Courtney went by the zombie opened his mouth and snarled at her, spilling chunky saliva all over its shoes.

She, in turn, flipped him off.

Leon laughed. "I bet he's *really* pissed now. He's probably gonna sneak up on you and bite off your ass."

She turned her head and angrily told him, "*Don't even joke about that.*"

"Sorry."

They took the road Courtney usually traveled —the one furthest from the farms, much to her relief. She didn't think she could handle the smell of cow manure just then. She'd rather smell the aroma of dead people emanating from the other side of the wall. She wasn't feeling good at all, especially riding in the passenger seat without any control of how the cart would move.

They entered the main housing area.

As they passed, Leon took the time to wave at friends who were out in their yards. A couple were playing badminton again. Some were just idly wasting the evening away on their well-manicured lawns under large, multi-colored umbrellas, casually indifferent to the neighborhood kittens wrestling at their feet. However, all of them smiled and waved at Leon.

Finally he stopped the golf cart in the small patch of gravel in Courtney's front lawn and shut off the ignition. Courtney didn't do anything just yet. She just sat there, staring at the iron bars in the windows of her home. They seemed new to her somehow.

Leon reached over and went to unfasten her seat belt, with the buckle just so happening to be in the area below Courtney's belly. When his hands got too close, she pushed them away.

"*Nuh-uh*," she slurred. "You don't get to go there again."

He shied away and climbed off the cart. He muttered, "*Please. Get over yourself.*"

She fumbled with the buckle until it unfastened, then slid her butt off the seat and put her feet on the ground. Her front door seemed a long way away. She studied the ground between her and the porch, noticing a lot more hills than what used to be there before.

Being drunk sucked. Courtney wondered how *anyone* could enjoy this.

"I've gotta walk back to the hotel," Leon told her. "So if you need help getting inside, you'd best tell me before I get halfway down the road."

She looked at him, then studied the miles of yard between her and the front door again, then returned her focus. She said, "Yeah, a little help might be nice."

He nodded, then walked around the cart and put his hand under her arm. He guided her across the lawn, helped her negotiate the two porch steps, then opened the screen door.

He couldn't get the front door open.

"Push in and turn left," Courtney whispered.

He did and the heavy wooden door swung open. He guided Courtney inside.

"Which direction do you want to go?" he asked. "Couch or bed?"

"I think...," Courtney began, concentrating, "*Bed.*"

He escorted her down the hallway.

"You cleaned the place up," he commented. "Looks nice."

"Thanks."

"Was it on my account?"

"Get real."

He took her into the bedroom and let her plop down on the edge of the bed. She looked up at him for a moment. He had an odd expression on his face —maybe a look of guilt, maybe a look of pity. She couldn't tell. All she knew was that the skin on Maine guys glowed ever whiter in darkness. For Leon, this meant his blue eyes were given a halo.

It sucked that he was cute.

She was tempted to do something then, like kiss him or something, but she didn't know why. She didn't even like him. If only he were more mature —like Gordon —maybe things wouldn't be so complicated.

"I'm gonna go now," he said. "Take care of yourself."

She nodded, then put her head down and started unlacing her shoestrings. Before he left the room, she whispered, "You're not that much taller than me and you're certainly no James Spader."

She hadn't meant for him to hear, but he did.

He countered, "And you're no Michelle Pfeiffer. So what's your point?"

She shrugged.

She heard the front door being pulled closed and the screen door swing shut. She kicked off her shoes and fell back on the mattress. She watched the ceiling twist for a while before closing her eyes.

Another Day

The corridor nightmare came again for the fourth night in a row, complete with the ending she hated most. And —for the second day in a row —it was the doorbell that woke her.

Wow. I must be getting popular.

She rose up, feeling a numb throbbing in her skull. Her stomach was a bit queasy and there was a weird tangy aftertaste in her throat. She recalled the bar, the Manhattans, the stumbling, and Leon Wolfe bringing her home. She was immediately embarrassed.

The digital clock on the nightstand told her it was ten thirty.

She just knew that this day would be worse than normal. She was tempted to not even answer the door, but figured it could be something important —Not *too* important though or the air raid sirens would be blaring. At least she knew it wasn't an emergency.

So, after looking down to realize she had fallen asleep fully dressed and therefore didn't need to put jeans on, she got off the bed and went to the front door.

It wasn't even shut properly. Sure, it was *closed*, but none of the deadbolts were latched and the metal bar that was usually propped underneath the knob was still leaning against the wall where she had left it yesterday morning. To think, if something had somehow gotten past the main walls in town, they could have just walked right in her house.

But then she remembered that even Leon Wolfe had trouble turning the handle. It was kind of funny.

She opened the door —again, forgetting she would be blasted with a morning dose of sunshine —and saw, standing on her porch, the bartender from last night. Her straight blonde hair was shining even brighter under the sunlight. The very ends, still dyed red and black, contrasted so heavily they almost seemed like they would fall off.

Courtney was forced to think for a moment before saying, "*Alexis.*"

A smile showed on her face as she replied, "You remembered."

"I wasn't drunk," Courtney told her, trying her best to sound convincing. "So of *course* I remember."

"You were totally tipsy and you were getting mean. That's why I cut you off."

Courtney rolled her eyes and looked away. She mumbled, "*What do you want?*"

Alexis motioned to the porch and asked, "Come outside for a minute?"

Courtney sighed. The bartender didn't seem mad at her or anything, so the purpose of this visit must be for something else entirely. She was kind of curious —and besides, she was feeling kind of bad about yesterday. She knew she needed to salvage the last of her pride.

She opened the screen door and stepped onto the porch. Alexis motioned for her to sit down, so they both took a rest on the edge and propped their feet on the first step. Alexis reached off the side of the porch and retrieved a can of Sprite and a baggie with two little white pills rolling around inside. She handed the items to Courtney.

"What's this?" she asked.

"Sprite and aspirin," Alexis replied. "For your hangover. You know, that thing you're having *now*."

Courtney held the can of Sprite in her hand and inspected it. It was very cold. She asked, "Didn't this stuff expire like a long time ago?"

Alexis smiled. "Those are like Twinkies. They last forever."

Courtney thought about it for a moment, then popped the top of the can and put the pills on her tongue and swallowed them down with a couple hesitant slurps. It turned out that the stuff was still good after all. She hadn't had Sprite in over five years.

She asked, "You probably hoard this stuff, don't you?"

"And sell it to customers for an extra token," Alexis admitted, grinning mischievously. "Completely off the books. Gotta look out for numero-uno."

Courtney felt herself smile too. She sat the can down beside her and whispered, "Sorry for the trouble last night."

"Don't worry about it."

"That's not why you're here?"

"Well, sort of." Alexis then turned a little bit so she could face her more directly and continued, "Last night in the bar you just looked like you were tired of being alone."

Courtney shot her a glance and whispered, "Are you *hitting* on me?"

Alexis' face turned red for a second, but she quickly smiled it away. "*No.* God, girl, you need to get out more."

Courtney grew even more skeptical. "Then did Leon put you up to this?"

"No," she replied. "Look, there's only a couple girls here I get along with and neither of them are that interesting. I just wanted to get to know you. That's all."

Courtney sighed. She knew if Alexis was looking for someone interesting, then she was looking in the wrong place. She wasn't sure if any interesting people were even alive anymore. She sure hadn't met any.

Alexis looked away for a moment to wave at the memo-lady walking down the road, who was probably delivering flyers about the upcoming Fourth of July celebration. Courtney didn't know the memo-lady's name, but she did know the Fourth of July Committee thought up new rules and restrictions every year. They took that stuff into way too much detail. The lady dropped a bright orange sheet of paper in Courtney's never-checked mailbox, then continued on down the road giving letters to people who actually cared.

Alexis said, "See? You don't even try."

"What do you mean?"

"You didn't even wave."

"I wave sometimes," Courtney stammered. "Like at the people guarding the gate."

"Well, *yeah*, but do you know their names?"

Courtney shook her head side to side.

Alexis very matter-of-factly stated, "That's my point."

"I know the names of most of the people that live on this street though."

"Well, that's because you've had almost five years to overhear what other people were calling them."

Courtney sighed and took another drink of Sprite. Her stomach was beginning to settle and her headache was less throbby. The stuff was working fast. God bless bartenders.

"Before you got to Eastpointe something bad happened to you, didn't it?" Alexis asked.

Courtney, taken aback by the abruptness of the question, replied with a question of her own: "Why? Did something bad happen to *you*?"

"Something bad happened to *everybody*," Alexis said with a frown. "I'm just wondering what makes you the way you are."

"I don't want to talk about it."

"Why not?" Alexis pressed. "You seem interesting. You were one of those zombie fighters. You must have some cool stories to tell."

"*Cool?!*" Courtney snapped. "The guy who trained me got bitten and for all I know he might not have had time to shoot himself like he planned. I loved him and maybe right now he's walking around out there somewhere. Aside from that, I have no idea what happened to my mom and dad and I'm a thousand miles from home. I risked my life for you people by going out those gates even after you treated me like dirt." She paused for a moment, sort of surprised she had blurted what she did. So she added, "And I don't think it's any of your business."

Alexis looked away and softly stated, "I had to kill my own brother you know. Elliot. He died and got back up. I had to hit him with a bat a bunch of times." She then grunted and made a motion like she was going to stand up. "You're not the only one who's a long way from home. Something bad has happened to all of us. I just wanted to get to know you because it's hard to make friends. If you want me gone, just say so."

Put on the spot, Courtney realized that left alone she would just go back in her house and maybe sleep, maybe read a book, or maybe watch a movie. But none of it sounded like fun. With the end of the world came the end of all things new, so it was only a matter of time before she grew depressingly tired of doing the same things over and over again. She just wished it wouldn't have happened all at once. A few days ago she was perfectly content —or, at least —had convinced herself she was perfectly content.

She swallowed her pride and said, "No, I don't want you to go. You can stay if you want."

Alexis relaxed once more.

Courtney told her, "I like that you came by. I'm just not good at talking."

"Then just start whenever you feel comfortable," Alexis replied. "I don't mind hanging out."

Courtney squinted up at the sky. It was blue and beautiful. Little clouds were rolling by in their typical, indifferent puffy style. Then she looked down and studied her arm. Her skin was so much whiter than it had been in Florida. The sun was so much hotter there. She missed jumping off the cliffs and swimming in the ocean. Rhode Island kind of sucked in comparison. *True* —the same Atlantic Ocean was only a couple miles away from Eastpointe and it probably had its share of cliffs to jump off of and salty, foamy waves to swim through, but to actually go and *do it* was basically a death sentence.

"Okay," Courtney began. "I know what to say."

"Go for it," Alexis replied.

Courtney took a deep breath and stated, "I don't understand the rules here."

"Rules?"

"*Rules*. I mean, everyone else has had almost five years to adjust and learn how things work. But I've stayed by myself since I first got here. I didn't get to pick up on things one at a time like everyone else did. I didn't get to *move on*. Do you know what I mean?"

Alexis shuffled her feet. She thought for a moment, then said, "Sort of like once you're out of circulation for too long, it's hard to get picked up and read again?"

"If you want to compare me to a magazine, then... *yeah*."

Alexis nodded. "I think I understand."

Courtney continued, "What do we have to hope for now? Nobody else seems to *get* that. The world's *over*." She motioned to the can of Sprite. "This stuff's gone. It'll never get made again. Same goes for Oreos. Cheerios. Spaghettios. *All* the O's are gone."

Alexis giggled.

"And nobody seems to care," Courtney added. "It's like I'm waking up and realizing everyone knows something I don't —like they know the secret to being happy but they're not telling me."

Alexis tried to show her a comforting smile, but it wasn't very convincing.

"What's going to happen now?" Courtney asked, putting her palms in the air. "We survived the end. But somehow there's still going to be a future. I mean, are guys like Leon Wolfe the best we have to hope for? Are these little houses all we're going to get? We don't even have a *chance* to improve because we have to stay in these walls. And everybody knows the rules to being happy with that except for me."

"Let's put it this way," Alexis began. She motioned with her fingers in the air as if she were scribbling cursive letters and told her, "*Welcome to Yesterday. Population: You.*"

"*That* is what I've been trying to explain."

"Okay, so let me tell you what you want to hear." She turned fully this time to face Courtney directly. "You can't go on thinking along the lines that you're going to grow up and get a job and maybe get married someday. I mean, for you and me, these were supposed to be our college years —Our time to get all the fun out of our systems while making that wondrous transition into adulthood. Am I right?"

"I guess," Courtney replied.

"Well, now there's nothing to transition *into*. There's no grownup world anymore. We're not going to be doctors or lawyers or veterinarians or whatever, getting into our cars every morning and going to work. The old world is gone."

"I kind of noticed that."

"Well, the world's not going to go back to normal —at least not in our lifetime. And you're worried that guys like Leon Wolfe are the best we can hope for?"

"Something like that."

"Right now there's no such thing as boyfriends, fiancés, or husbands. Nobody worries about titles anymore." Alexis paused and sheepishly lowered her head. She continued, her tone even softer, "My family didn't exactly have it easy when the world was normal. We didn't have much money. You think I could afford the kind of clothes I'm wearing now? You think a guy like Leon Wolfe would have even given me the time of day back then? But I don't worry about it. I try to be happy. If I don't, it gets me thinking about bad things. I mean, we survived the end of the world—"

Suddenly, with almost impeccable timing, a wail pierced through the air and echoed through the street. It seemed that somewhere beyond the high walls of Eastpointe a zombie was getting cranky. It wasn't anything unusual —there were at least three loud roars every day. Most of them came from zombies who had been trying to scale the wall outside for weeks on end and not getting any favorable results.

Alexis continued, with a point already made, "This place can be depressing if all you're hearing is *that*." She motioned with her thumb in the direction of the wailing. "If you don't do something to make yourself happy, you're gonna go nuts. For people our age, it can be like spring break if you let loose those inhibitions. You just need to *try*."

"*That* is supposed to be what I wanted to hear?" asked Courtney. "Take my shirt off and run down the street like it's Mardi Gras?"

"That's not what I meant," said Alexis, rolling her eyes. "What I mean to say is that this town is the world as we know it. You're not going to meet anyone that isn't already stuck inside these walls. But people *accept that* because at least there's *people*. We have electric power and running water. We have a *town*. And some of us —if you would just take the time to socialize —aren't all that bad. You know all this already, but *that* is what you wanted to hear."

Courtney put her head down. She waited to see if Alexis' speech would sink in and give her comfort, but it didn't. Not really. Maybe there just was no simple answer. Maybe that was the point. Maybe at least now she knew that everyone else didn't know the answer either.

—They were just pretending they did.

"I see you at the pool sometimes," Alexis said. "You always go alone. Like I told you, there's not many people here and these are the only people to choose from. You have to find friends where you can. I like you. If you want a friend, then you know where to find me."

"I'm not sure I want to go back in the bar," Courtney told her, smiling uneasily. "I don't know if I even want to *look* at another drink for the rest of my life."

Alexis laughed. "You'd be in even worse shape if I hadn't cut you off. You never even had to hug the porcelain. Consider yourself lucky."

"Then... *thank you*, I guess."

"I live by the power station," said Alexis. "The only blue house on the street. Most nights I just watch movies."

"I watch a lot of movies too," Courtney replied.

"Well, then you're welcome to—"

Then came another interruption. Not the random wailing of a

zombie this time, but the wailing of a siren originating somewhere near the hotel.

It startled Courtney and Alexis and brought them both to their feet.

Since they hadn't heard any kind of siren for so long, they immediately assumed the worst: that the walls had been breached. However, after taking a moment to realize that the siren they were hearing wasn't the really *bad* one —*the one everybody feared* —and that the one they were hearing was a high-pitched repeating whistle, it shocked them even more.

"That's the siren that goes off while the main gate is open," Courtney said. "But nobody's gone outside for almost two years. Not even scouts."

They looked at each other, shocked at what they were both thinking.

Alexis uttered, "That means they're letting somebody *in*. A new arrival."

"Somebody was still alive out there?" Courtney added, speaking for both of them, "—After all this time?"

Like most everyone else in Eastpointe, they had to drive to the gate to see the new arrival with their own eyes.

CHAPTER FOUR

New Face in Town

Even though the gate guards were out of practice from nearly two years of doing nothing but sitting on their asses, the procedure to admit the new arrival went quite smoothly. Courtney didn't notice any difference between the way she was brought in and the way this other survivor was brought in. Actually, when she thought about it, every arrival she had seen while living in Eastpointe was exactly the same.

Meticulous.

First came the siren. It reminded people that, *"Hey, the gate's open at the moment, but don't worry."* The siren was then followed by however many gunshots were necessary to remove any undead opposition nearby. In this case there was only one.

The business-suited zombie finally got the headshot it was asking for, which appeased Courtney. After all, she had given it the middle finger yesterday and was kind of worried it might hold a grudge. At least she didn't have to worry about that one anymore.

Then came the part where the outer gate would screech along its rails as it opened up. Whoever was outside would then drive their vehicle into the 'decontamination area' between the inner and outer gates. The outer gate would close, the sirens would cease their noise, and instructions would be shouted down to the new arrivals.

There was just one this time —some man driving a jeep with bloody bits of hair and scalp dangling from the bull bars in front. Courtney knew how those bits of body parts got there. When she had been out on her own before arriving at Eastpointe, the bull bars on her humvee looked exactly the same.

It was caused by plowing over zombies at high speeds.

Then came the part when the man in the jeep was ordered to step out of the vehicle. The inner gate screeched open and the guards came inside the decontamination zone. They searched the vehicle and the man, asking him to raise his shirt and lift his sleeves so they could check for any evidence of infection.

Courtney could remember her own fear and uncertainty when this scrutiny was being performed on *her*. Despite the .45 Socom holstered on one hip and the wakizashi sheathed on the other, she was scared while the guards searched her and her humvee. She knew she was taking quite a risk by putting her faith in people she didn't even know and quite possibly insane for purposely letting her guard down. The new arrival, however, didn't appear too startled and wasn't noticeably trembling. He stood back and didn't say a word as they searched his jeep.

Normally, after this part, the new arrival was welcomed in, briefed on the situation by the New Arrival Committee, introduced to the Superintendent, given a house —as there were plenty that were still unoccupied —and allowed once-only free shopping at the Eastpointe Plaza in order to gain back some of the possessions they were most certainly forced to leave behind and to help ease the tension of arriving in a town full of strangers. Then, after they were settled in, they were interviewed and given a job they were most suited for. While the Committees kept hoping another doctor would waltz through the gate —as there were only three in all of Eastpointe —most new arrivals ended up being a mechanic, farm hand, or electrician.

However, before he could even be let out of the decontamination zone, one of the guards saw something on the man's inner forearm that gave him quite a start. Courtney and Alexis and the others watching then saw it too.

A bite wound.

The guard asked the man, "When did that happen?"

And by this question, Courtney knew what the guard really meant was: *How long before I have to shoot you?*

Instead of panicking, the new arrival calmly stated in a very elegant and persuasive French-Canadian accent: "I can explain this. I just need to speak with whoever's in charge."

A little more conversation followed, but the voices became so hushed that neither Courtney nor the others were able to hear. It ended with the new arrival being seated on the back of a golf cart and escorted to the hotel.

But he had been bitten.

What the hell was going on?

Ockham's Razor

The Procurement Committee —long defunct but now apparently reinstated for some emergency reason —came and got her later that evening. At the time, Alexis was sifting through her collection of movies trying to find any she wanted to watch again or any she hadn't seen already. Courtney was lying on the couch, listening to music through headphones and trying to get used to having someone else hanging around. It wasn't too bad though. It was reminiscent of *before*, when she would have friends over at her house in Florida. The Procurement Committee, however, interrupted just before she could get entirely comfortable with it again.

They came knocking and very politely said, "Miss Colvin, we'd like you to come to the conference room if you don't mind."

She asked, "Why? What's going on?"

"It will all be explained once you get there," they told her. "Come along now."

So she did.

Alexis followed her to the hotel in her own cart since her bartending shift was almost ready to begin, but Courtney ventured alone into the conference room and sat down in one of the chairs around the circular table.

Leon was there too. So were Vaughn Winters and Delmas Ridenour. Soon Mike Newcome showed up, followed by Christopher Gooden.

The remnants of the Strike Team.

They all appeared to be just as uninformed as Courtney.

Though it had been two years since a meeting of this type was held, everything appeared the same as it used to. The brown executive-style walls of the conference room remained outdated and ugly. The marker-stained whiteboard was still nearby in all its imposing glory and the Flag of the United States of America and the state flag of Rhode Island were still hanging from their respective poles on either side. The big oval table and the comfy leather swivel chairs that surrounded it were also just as Courtney remembered them.

The four members of the Procurement Committee were sitting in less-comfy chairs lined along the wall and a typist was sitting in the far corner of the room, ready to transcribe the events of the meeting for posterity's sake. Ervin Wright, the man who originally introduced the Odd Fellow system of government to Eastpointe, was sitting in the chair reserved for the Superintendent. Courtney figured he must have gotten re-elected at the last showing of hands.

At least now she knew for certain who was in charge.

Though the Superintendent and Procurement Committee members had changed since these meetings were taking place with greater frequency, all appeared as it should.

However, this time around, someone new was with them in the room.

The man who had arrived that morning was sitting in the chair next to the Superintendent. He was wearing clean clothes now, so he must have been allowed to visit the plaza sometime that day. He was short and kind of stocky, as if his muscles were simply out of shape, and his hair was already thinning even though he only looked to be in his early thirties. Like most others in the post-apocalypse world, he was very pale. Since everyone had heard him speaking in a French-Canadian accent at the gate they assumed he came from somewhere near Montreal.

They were half right.

After the doors to the conference room were closed to give them privacy, the Superintendent stood and introduced the stranger.

"This man is Dr. Aaron Dane," he said, motioning with a relaxed gesture. "When the zombie problem first began to get out of control, he was put aboard *The Atlantic Princess*, a cruiseliner that usually ports up north. In that time, the ship was commandeered and modified to be a floating research lab." He turned to the new arrival. "Am I telling this correctly?"

The man nodded and said, "That's the short version."

"He's been on that ship for over four years," Ervin continued, "But he's found his way to us and he's got some information you all might be keen on hearing." He motioned back to the man. "Dr. Dane, the floor is yours."

The man stood and glanced at everyone around the room, pausing noticeably longer when his eyes reached Courtney. She lowered her gaze to the very boring surface of the table and stared at it to let him know she wasn't interested. His eyes eventually left her and once he felt he had everyone's attention he began rolling up the left sleeve of his shirt.

Just as most of them had already seen when he first arrived at Eastpointe's gate, there was a gaping bite wound on the thick, meaty area near his elbow. Teeth marks were evident, but up close, under the fluorescent lights, somehow the wound looked *old*.

He displayed his exposed forearm for a moment, then stated, "I was bitten over a year ago."

Vaughn Winters, a member of the Strike Team who Courtney always thought was kind of creepy with that long black hair of his, posed the question everyone in the room wanted an answer to: "Then why aren't you *dead*?"

"I'm a scientist," Dr. Dane began, rolling his sleeve back down and buttoning the cuff. "That's the short explanation of what I do — or what I *did*, anyway. Like your Superintendent was explaining to you, I was put aboard The Atlantic Princess to do research. The Army had sought me out and took me forcefully out of my home and tossed me in with some other researchers. We were ordered to figure out why the dead were rising, but we were never able to determine the cause. We still don't have a clue." He paused a moment before solemnly adding, "*No one does.*"

At this point Dr. Dane smoothed the back of his trousers with his palms and sat down again. He clasped his hands together and put them on the table, leaning forward very casually. He then continued, "We were forced to work in very close quarters with the reanimated dead, drawing samples from them, gauging bite strength, things of that nature. Sooner or later something bad was bound to happen. And it *did*. I'm the last one left." He lowered his eyes. "I kept on working though —even with malfunctioning equipment and limited tools and nobody answering my distress signals and all my dead colleagues locked away in the forecastle and in staterooms and making all kinds of racket. I was just floating aimlessly. I had no idea how to pilot a *cruiseliner*."

"So how did you get here?" asked Vaughn.

"Luck," Dane replied. "The ship beached itself on Point Judith a few days back. I climbed off, found a jeep with the keys still in the ignition, and here I am. And forgive me if I seem disturbingly calm about all this, but I've had over two years all to myself to consider what I would say if I ever found other survivors."

"Like I told you," Ervin soothingly told him, "Nobody will judge you."

"Everyone here has been great," Dane said, agreeing with the Superintendent.

"*Whoa*," Vaughn interjected. "You still haven't told us how you survived a zombie bite."

"Because I found the *Cure*," Dane replied. "Being all alone aboard a ship in the Atlantic with nothing but the sound of zombies to keep you company kind of makes you want to find a distraction. So I kept researching."

"So how did you get bitten?"

Dane lowered his head and looked away slightly. He then softly stated, "Because I *let one bite me.* I was alone. I thought I found the Cure but the only way to test it was to test it for *real*. I figured if it didn't work, then at least I wouldn't be alone anymore."

This statement brought back memories for Courtney. She remembered the day she escaped Camp Rigero when nobody else had. She remembered getting out of the humvee to refuel it. She remembered the zombie crawling towards her and how she let it get so very close and even gave it a sporting chance before she put a bullet in its head.

"Wait a second," said Vaughn, carrying the brunt of everyone's skepticism, "So you were bitten and you swallowed the antidote—"

"*Injected* the antidote," Dane corrected.

"*Whatever*," Vaughn continued. "Then in theory you should be immune to zombie bites." He paused a moment to show a smirk to everyone in the room. "So you won't mind if we stick your hand out the gate and see what happens, right?"

One of the members of the Procurement Committee, who had been sitting quietly for some time, decided to tell Vaughn, "Show Dr. Dane some respect please."

Vaughn shrugged his shoulders and leaned back in his chair indifferently. He mumbled, "*I was just saying what everyone was thinking.*"

"I wouldn't exactly be thrilled with the idea of getting nibbled on," Dane told him, remaining civil. "I'd be infected again. I'm not *vaccinated*. The Cure is a creation in and of itself. It's not an antitoxin or an antidote. I should stop referring to it as such. I can't call it a vaccine either because it doesn't last indefinitely. Simply put, it destroys the infection then leaves the system."

Then Courtney's good pal Leon decided to speak up. "I'm not understanding any of this," he said. "Antitoxins, antidotes —what are you getting at?"

"There's still no name for the disease those monsters carry," Dane answered. "It's not exactly poison, but it's not exactly plague either. It's somewhere along the lines of *infection*, but no one has isolated the difference between the saliva in a zombie and the saliva in living humans. We could never even determine why reanimated dead only sought out humans and not lower life forms."

"Like politicians," someone blurted.

"No, more like cats and dogs," Dane replied, ignoring the joke entirely. "It's all so complicated. Everything we know about them is only what we've been able to discover in the last five years and I'm not even talking *collectively*. If the science community as a whole could have gotten together on this, perhaps an answer to all these questions could have been found. Problem is, we started losing contact with sister stations all over the globe shortly after this crisis *began*. If everything worked like it should have, researchers in one area could be studying one aspect of the problem while researchers in a different area studied another. But instead, after all contact was lost, what we had was every researcher starting from *scratch*."

"So how exactly did you come by a *cure* then?" Leon asked.

"Like I said: by going from *scratch*," Dane replied. "I first accepted that death is a *process*, not an *event*. Except in the case of a nuclear bomb or something of that sort, different tissues and organs die at different speeds. When a zombie bites someone, the germs spread through the body like a plague until they finally conquer the brain. *Brain death* seems to be what matters. After the brain is dead, the germs move in and reactivate it to a certain extent."

"But you said no one has isolated the difference between zombie saliva and human saliva," Vaughn pointed out. "So how do you know its *germs* causing it? How are you even positive it's an *infection*?"

"I can only theorize," Dane replied. "It works like an infection and dead people will only reanimate if they were bitten by a zombie —not if they died a natural death. So it *must* be an infection. I accepted this early on and that's why I didn't take the time to isolate the bacteria in zombie saliva. I had better things to focus my efforts on." He paused for a moment, then added, "Do you really want to sit here and argue common knowledge?"

"I'm not arguing anything," Vaughn replied. "I couldn't care less. I don't plan on ever becoming infected and I don't see the point of this meeting. What are we getting at here?"

"You should let Dr. Dane finish speaking," Ervin said.

Vaughn sighed and leaned back once more. He started twiddling his thumbs.

All was quiet for a while. Even the typist stopped his keystrokes, as he had nothing to transcribe at the moment. It almost seemed that Vaughn had been everyone's source of enthusiasm and once he gave up so did the rest.

Finally Ervin said, "Dr. Dane is talking about a *cure* here, people."

"We get that," Leon answered. "It's just that he's awfully long-winded. Why can't he just get to the point?"

"Fine then. I will," Dane said. He crossed his arms and for the briefest of moments looked grumpy instead of pacified. He stated, very slowly, "*I have the Cure to the zombie plague.*"

"*Yeah*, that's what we're hearing," Leon told him. "We just don't *believe* you."

Vaughn started chuckling under his breath. Even quiet Mike Newcome muttered, "*I've only been here five minutes and I'm already bored.*"

"Tell them the specifics," Ervin said, trying to stay upbeat. "Tell them what you told *me.*"

"That's what I've been trying to do," Dane replied. "I've been trying to explain that up until the point the infection reaches the brain, a person can still be saved. We can't help the ones who are already dead. There's no coming back from that. But we *can* stop the poison from reaching the brain and an infected person will recover."

"It doesn't make sense," argued Leon. "If you don't know the exact bacteria that zombies carry, how can you have a cure for it?"

"I didn't need to know the exact bacteria," answered Dane. "It's irrelevant. There wouldn't be a name for it anyway, so I would have to name it. Do you want me throwing an invented name around?

What purpose would that serve?"

Leon grunted and shrugged his shoulders. No one else said anything.

"Like I told you," Dane continued, despite the calm, "Death is a *process*. Even though mitosis ceases after brain death, some tissues and organs will still live for up to twenty-four hours. Once the virus conquers the brain, it reactivates it. Any tissues and organs that are still alive upon brain death will continue to decay, but when they reach a certain point, they *stabilize*. And *no*, we don't know *why* they stabilize. They just *do*. That's why some zombies have been around since the beginning. Parts of them that were dead *before* brain death will continue to decay until they rot off. Parts that *weren't* dead, on the other hand, will continue to function. It's how they can still walk around."

"Why are you telling us this?" Leon asked.

"Because I want you to understand that until the infection takes over the core of the brain, a person can be injected with the Cure. It will eliminate the infection and the sickness will go away and the body will begin to heal itself —provided that there hasn't been a significant amount of blood loss or irreversible damage, of course. Say, for instance, a large neck wound."

Courtney almost didn't want to hear any more. Talk of a cure was just stupid. Even if it was real, why couldn't it have been around when Gordon got bitten? Why *now*, especially after so many people were already dead? What was the point?

She figured most everyone else in the room felt the same way she did.

"*Look, I've had enough of this,*" Ervin stated, standing up and rolling his eyes. "Listen to me, people. With the promise of a cure we could start taking more risks. We can send people through the gate and take back what was ours. We can expand beyond these walls without running too great a risk of casualties."

"There's always going to be a risk," Courtney stated.

Ervin glared at her. She didn't intend to anger him, but she didn't care that she *had* either.

"Am I wrong to hope for better things?" Ervin asked. "Am I wrong to want the people in Eastpointe to stop living in fear?"

"I agree with Courtney," Vaughn said. "Dr. Doom here—"

"*Dane.*"

"*Dane, whatever*, hasn't really explained *anything*. We know corpses started getting up and eating people. Even if they didn't have the means to digest them or even *chew* them, all they can think about is: *us equals food*. We know they carry a disease of some sort and to become infected is to become one of them. We've lived with this knowledge for five years. So what the hell do you want from us?"

"I'll tell you what he *wants*," Leon interjected, "He wants us to go *get* it because he doesn't actually *have* it. Why else would we be here?"

"That's what I've been assuming all along," said Vaughn.

"And your assumption would be correct," stated Ervin. "Dr. Dane tried bringing several samples of the Cure with him, but they were lost in an attack as he was salvaging that jeep he used to get here. But there's more of the Cure aboard The Atlantic Princess. Isn't that right, Doctor?"

Dane nodded.

"Wow, he's a man among men," mumbled Vaughn.

"*The six of you have been given a free pass!*" Ervin shouted, startling the group of Black Berets. None of them expected such a loud voice from such an old man. "For two years you haven't had to lift a finger around here!"

"But there used to be more of us than what you see in this room now," Vaughn retorted. "The rest are dead so you could have your cows and chickens."

"And *no more* have to die," countered Ervin. "That's the point. An antidote exists. You saw the bite on Dr. Dane's arm. What further proof do you need?"

Vaughn smirked and chuckled some more. He stated, "Listen, *Grand Pooh-Bah* —Dr. Doom here is about five years too late. We would gladly oblige you and go fetch this *Cure* if it had existed a few years ago, but *now* it doesn't matter. The zombies are rotting away. We just have to wait them out."

"But the zombies are *not* rotting away," Dr. Dane chimed. "There will be enough to last until the *next* doomsday. Did you not hear me when I told you that whatever parts of them were not dead to begin with would go on functioning?"

Courtney, growing annoyed with the arguing, decided to speak up in a constructive manner. She asked, "Wait a second. Why can't you just recreate the antidote *here*?"

Dane turned to her and smiled, seemingly happy that she had spoken directly to him. He softly explained, "Because the process took me the better part of two years."

"Two years?"

"Yes. I worked under the postulate that an infection will continue to spread through the blood of a human until it reached the core of the brain. But what if there was no brain to reach? No ultimate goal? What would happen then?"

Courtney shrugged her shoulders and replied, "What is this, a science lesson?"

"No," he said. "I don't want to go into the gory details, but needless to say I was forced to use a replicated environment of a human body. I kept adding endless supplies of clean blood to blood that was already infected. The infection continued spreading into the clean blood, but since there was no actual *body*, there was no actual *brain*. For months and months I kept adding new blood for the infection to consume, testing its determination and persistence. I found that —after more than *two years* —the infection *gave up*. It went into a dormant state."

"And?"

"*And*, if new infection encountered any *dormant infection*, it would assume there was no brain to contaminate and it would therefore become dormant also. So, by injecting dormant infection —the *Cure* —into an infected human being, the infection process stops when it collides with any dormant area. The infection is then naturally flushed out of the system as a whole and the body recovers in a matter of hours."

"Which means it doesn't die and become another zombie," Ervin added. "It won't die at *all*."

"Correct," said Dane.

All was uneasily quiet in the conference room for the next several minutes. No one was sure exactly how this calm came about, but they figured everything that needed to be said had been said. Now they were all just waiting for something to happen.

The typist over in the far corner was sitting motionless with his fingers hovering above the keyboard, eagerly waiting for another syllable to be spoken so it could be documented. The Procurement Committee was sitting patiently with their legs crossed and their arms folded, perhaps waiting for a signal from the Superintendent. Ervin himself was silently drumming his fingers on the table and Dr. Dane was just watching the Strike Team meditate over what he had told them.

What was there to say?

Courtney exchanged glances with the rest of the people she had ventured out of the gate with years before. It was because of them that Eastpointe had become fully self-sufficient, with plenty of supplies and an endless chain of sustenance. Because of *them*, it was safe here and there was never again a reason to go outside into a world where they would be hunted for the very flesh on their bones.

But there used to be more.

There were seven Black Berets to start with. Now there were six. The seventh had had his visor snatched away by a particularly sneaky zombie and then a chunk of flesh eaten off his exposed scalp. A couple of well-prepared citizens of Eastpointe had been in the original Strike Team as well, but they didn't last long. Even a couple of honest-to-god soldiers had aided them in their endeavors, but they weren't here anymore either.

Now the remaining six were living fairly comfortably, given a free pass to live off the fruit of their labors without any more actual work, but that wasn't what was important. Two years had passed since any of them had been in any real danger —any real threat of losing another member of their group. *Before*, when the Committees were sending them through the gate at least once a month, there had been no desire to establish any kind of bond between them aside from the trust factor. After all, they knew there might come a time when one would have to shoot another to prevent them from joining the enemy ranks and there couldn't be any hesitation to do what had to be done.

But now there was supposedly a Cure.

Now they were hearing that when a member of their group had been bitten, there might not have been a reason to administer a lethal dose of drugs and put a bullet in their head. Why bother fetching a cure *now*, after all the things they had been forced to do to preserve the humanity of those who had fallen? Humanity as a whole prayed for a cure since the beginning —but just as Vaughn had pointed out, it may have come a little too late.

That wasn't even the half of it.

While Courtney had remained alone since arriving at Eastpointe, she knew what the rest were pondering over in their silence. Now, since the danger was gone and they could go back to being regular people again, an inner circle had formed in the group. Courtney knew Mike and Delmas were people Leon played badminton with and she was fairly certain the others had developed some kind of relationship as well in the time following their last trip through the gate. And now —especially *now* —when it seemed possible she herself might find friends here even after her years in hiding, she wasn't sure she would want to risk losing it.

Actually, she *knew* she didn't want to risk it.

Then again, what had been bothering her for so long was that she knew the world had ended. Even in her conversation with Alexis she had pointed out that hope just wasn't a possibility anymore. Human beings were no longer the dominant species on Earth. Now there was just the last bastion of survivors tucked away in a tiny spot on the globe with walls blocking out the true reality of the situation and giving the illusion that the world outside didn't exist. For all she knew, the last survivors —with their last operational power plant and their last operational water treatment facility —were going on pretending things could go back to normal.

But she knew the reality of it. She had not been so far removed from it like the others had —not with the nightmare of the corridor haunting her almost nightly and the memories of the life she once had still fresh in her consciousness. It was all part of the consequences of being so long removed from the illusion everyone else was sharing. The world on the other side of the wall was very real and it wasn't going away.

Maybe the Cure was just what everyone needed. Just like the Superintendent stated, with the promise of a cure, humanity could make an effort to fight back. It meant that one day maybe there would be Oreos and Cheerios and Spaghettios again, not to mention fresh Sprite. She knew it wouldn't happen right away, but if there was a Cure, then at least there was hope that someday things would be normal again.

So, after the long, penetrating silence had overwhelmed everyone else in the conference room at the Eastpointe Hotel, Courtney slowly raised her hand and stated, *"I'll do it."*

Every head turned to her.

She didn't lower hers. She stared right back at them.

After a moment, Leon raised his hand alongside hers and stated, "Same here."

Courtney showed him a silent, thankful nod, which he returned.

The Superintendent then looked expectantly upon the other four Black Berets. Mike Newcome's hand was next to shoot up, followed in a few seconds by the hands of Delmas Ridenour and Christopher Gooden.

They all looked at Vaughn Winters.

After a moment he told them, "Okay. I'll put my hand up on one condition: If I get bitten on this little escapade, you'll bring me back here so I can bite off Ervin's nose. That'll be the only 'Cure' I need."

He put his hand up.

A smile then began to become apparent on Dr. Dane's otherwise emotionless visage.

Getting Started

The alarm feature on the digital clock on her nightstand hadn't been used in ages, but the next day it was used to wake her promptly at six o'clock in the morning. After rolling over and shutting it off, she stepped into the shower. She then spent most of her time under the sprays of water not doing anything but staring at the little porcelain squares on the wall and tracing over them with her fingers. When she was finally finished she dried off and went back into the bedroom.

She opened the closet door and dug through all the items inside until she found a large black luggage case near the back. She yanked it out and closed the closet door, then placed the case on the bed and unzipped and opened it. She then stared at its contents for the longest time before removing them and laying them out neatly on the mattress.

She started with the uniform.

She fit her legs inside and pulled the suit up to her waist, then fit her arms into the long sleeves and shrugged her shoulders to squeeze her way into the rest. Though she hadn't gone through the routine to zip it in almost two years, she didn't miss a beat. The first step was to reach straight behind her and pull the zipper from her lower back up to the middle of her spine. The second step was to reach over her shoulder and pull it from the middle of her spine all the way up to the very top of the collar. The tight, clinging feeling of the suit on her skin was something that she was still familiar with. After sticking a finger down the front of the collar to loosen it a bit from her neck, she moved on to the next step.

She sat down on the edge of the bed and put on a pair of everyday socks, then worked her feet into the black boots that accompanied the uniform. They reached halfway up her calf. Except for the shiny metal heel portion, they were completely dark and solid.

Next came the thin, nearly weightless belt. It fit almost as tightly as the uniform. She wore it low on her hips, which made it more comfortable since it wasn't constricting her belly. A V-shaped strap fell across her hip on the left side and another square-shaped strap with an empty holster fell across her hip on the right side. This one had a belt that buckled around her leg to help keep it tight and secure.

She took the wakizashi from off the mattress and unsheathed it for a quick inspection. The blade was still sharp and shiny. She fit it back into the scabbard and fastened it comfortably on the tip of the V-shaped strap on her left hip.

Next she opened a small metal box and took the .45 from the recess within. She screwed the silencer onto the barrel, loaded a fifteen-round clip into the butt, then switched on the laser sight. She pointed the gun at the wall. Upon seeing a red dot on the wallpaper, she flicked off the laser sight and tested the flashlight pod. After seeing it shine a light on the floor, she shoved the gun into the holster on her right hip. She took three extra loaded magazines for the .45 and tucked them into pouches sewn onto the belt behind her left hip.

She then went to her knees and dug a long case out from under the bed. She placed it on the mattress, then unsnapped the hinges and opened it. She took the rifle from inside and pointed it at the glass in the window, viewing through the scope at a tree some fifty yards away. She flicked a switch on the side and the morning daylight outside turned from bright and shiny to a rather bland shade of green. A slight humming sound could be heard emanating from within the scope. She then flicked the switch off and the colors outside returned to normal and the humming noise ceased. She took five bullets from the case on the bed and loaded them into the rifle, then slung the rifle over her shoulder and her head, letting it hang comfortably across her back. She took five more bullets and fit them into slots on her belt just above the area where the wakizashi was dangling.

She took one last thing —a small white container less than an inch square —and tucked it into her boot.

Finally, after slipping her hands into black gloves and fastening the velcro tightly around her forearms, she picked up the copper visor and the black beret and made her way to the front door.

ROCK FORGE
Army Research Laboratory

FINAL OUTFITTING SCHEMATIC OF THE BLACK BERET
Submitted by the members of "Project Black Beret"
under authorization by Col. Franklin Darlington

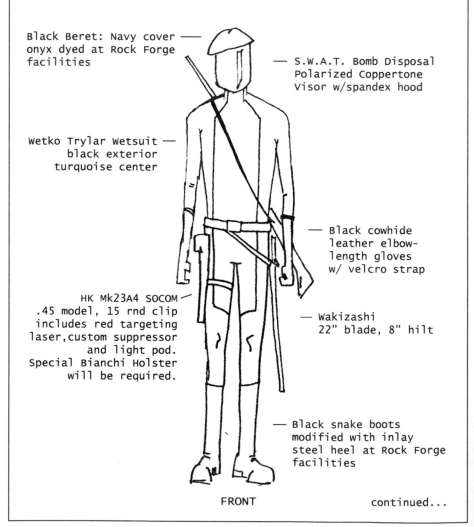

Black Beret: Navy cover
onyx dyed at Rock Forge
facilities

— S.W.A.T. Bomb Disposal
Polarized Coppertone
Visor w/spandex hood

Wetko Trylar Wetsuit —
black exterior
turquoise center

— Black cowhide
leather elbow-
length gloves
w/ velcro strap

HK Mk23A4 SOCOM —
.45 model, 15 rnd clip
includes red targeting
laser, custom suppressor
and light pod.
Special Bianchi Holster
will be required.

— Wakizashi
22" blade, 8" hilt

— Black snake boots
modified with inlay
steel heel at Rock Forge
facilities

FRONT

continued...

As the synthetic "trylar" was patented in the fall of last year, suits made of this material have been put into mass production only recently. Only one design scheme has been implemented. This may work to our advantage, in that all suits will be uniform and hopefully in time as easily recognizable as standard military cover.

Full parts list required to outfit a Black Beret will be forthcoming ASAP. We have found most locations of these parts are within a 100-mile radius and can be easily obtained provided the warehouses have been abandoned. If locations are still occupied, whether by rightful owners or reanimated dead, we recommend seizure of all necessary parts by any means necessary.

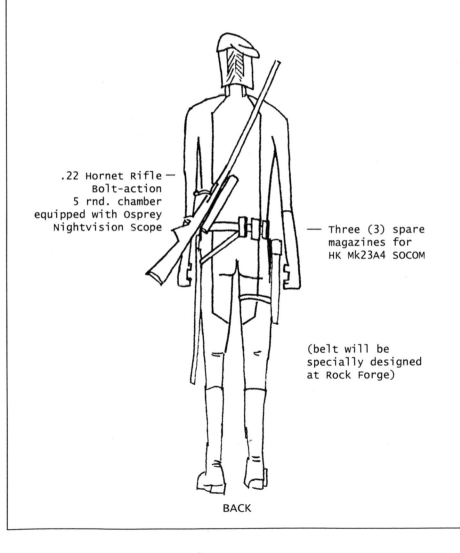

.22 Hornet Rifle —
Bolt-action
5 rnd. chamber
equipped with Osprey
Nightvision Scope

— Three (3) spare
magazines for
HK Mk23A4 SOCOM

(belt will be
specially designed
at Rock Forge)

BACK

Leaving

The Procurement Committee hadn't really told them much they couldn't have figured out on their own: The Atlantic Princess was beached on Point Judith, which meant Courtney and the others would have to travel past Snug Harbor and around the inlet. This road would take them through the town of Wakefield, which was an area they had had to go through during an earlier outing. It had been densely populated with the undead and probably still was. They would then have to venture to the very end of Point Judith Neck where the cruiseliner was said to be stuck on the shore.

Dr. Aaron Dane agreed to accompany them. He said he didn't spend the last five years of his life on a ship in the Atlantic creating a cure without being able to see it arrive safely to those who needed it. Besides, he knew the layout of the ship and could give them first-hand input on what directions they should take. He seemed very brave despite the isolation and hardship he had already suffered. It only made sense to bring him along.

Courtney was the first Black Beret to arrive at the garage that morning, but Dane was already there, sitting casually in a lawn chair and drinking coffee from a styrofoam cup. He was wearing only canvas tennis shoes, jeans, and a plain blue sweater. Courtney reminded him that he should have better protection and to go to the armory next door and ask for a shirt of chainmail to wear beneath the sweater.

He just looked at her and smiled. His reply to her concern, in his semi-elegant French-Canadian accent, was, "I'll be fine. I'll just stay behind the rest of you. Besides, *you* will be giving me something to look at, won't you?" His eyes then drifted lower.

She scoffed and told him, "*Don't be a pig.*"

He chuckled.

Apparently the poor guy lost most of his tact while he was adrift at sea, so she didn't worry about it too much. She just tried to avoid him as best she could as she inspected the humvees they would be taking that day.

One of them was the very same humvee she had used to drive to Eastpointe, which someone had taken and stored in the garage shortly after she arrived. When she realized this place was the best she could hope for she never gave the humvee another thought. She certainly didn't miss it either. Even now it made her uneasy to look at the seat she used to curl up on and go to sleep. She was never comfortable when it was one of the humvees chosen to be used on any particular outing.

Leon showed up within a few minutes suited up in his own Black Beret attire. He had received one of the later versions of the uniform, the only difference in his being the little waving American Flag sewn on just below his left shoulder.

She wished one of the other members had arrived before he did so she wouldn't have to deal with any awkward glances, but there were none exchanged anyway. She expected some kind of comment about the incident at Suds & Salutations, but he didn't say a word about it. Even after they nonverbally agreed to go to the armory and begin hauling supplies to the humvees together, any comments he would make were directed entirely to the business at hand.

She didn't like the quiet. Just to have something to say, she considered thanking him for backing her up at the meeting yesterday and raising his hand after she did, but for some reason it didn't seem like something she should thank him for.

They hauled some extra rifles and handguns and put them in the back of both humvees, along with spare wakizashis and ammunition. She even thought to get a shirt of chainmail to give to Dane despite his comment earlier. She thought about mentioning it to Leon to see what kind of reaction he would make, but she figured he might only say something along the lines of, '*Well, the guy's been on a ship with no one but zombies to keep him company, so his judgment might be a little off now. You know, like beer goggles.*' And she would tell him she hoped a thousand maggots infested his earlobes and that would be the end of it.

Both of them ended up hardly saying a word to each other.

The Superintendent arrived next, but didn't do much more than just stand back and watch while Courtney and Leon did the heavy lifting. Occasionally he would exchange casual remarks with Dane. Members of the Procurement Committee showed up to deliver road maps plotting the best course in red marker. They saw to it that both humvees had two copies, one in the middle compartment up front and one in the glove box. They also placed a short-range walkie-talkie in each vehicle. There was no way for a team outside the wall to communicate with Eastpointe, but at least the team could communicate with each other.

The Superintendent and the Committee left shortly thereafter, headed toward the front gate to finish preparations there.

Finally the rest of the Strike Team straggled in one at a time.

Mike Newcome, looking tired, went about giving the humvees a final once-over mechanical inspection. Delmas Ridenour proceeded directly to the fuel reserves and filled both tanks to the brim. Christopher Gooden brought two coolers of foodstuffs and Vaughn Winters, as was typical, did as little as he had to while pretending to look busy.

No one who was actually going on the trip talked a whole lot. Courtney was beginning to remember exactly what it was like on the mornings before the Strike Team ventured out the gate:

Solemn.

Aside from a few carts going here and there with the occupants on their way to whatever job they had to do, Eastpointe itself was very quiet. She wondered if any of them had been told exactly what the Strike Team was being sent out to recover this time. Certainly they had to suspect it was *something* important, but she was somehow sure they knew absolutely nothing. After all, knowledge of what was being brought back would have caused uproar throughout the entire community.

Finally, after all preparations had been completed and double-checked, the Strike Team divided themselves up into two groups and boarded the humvees. Though the vehicles were very similar, Courtney was pleased to not be in the humvee that was originally hers. However, this decision placed her in the same vehicle with Leon, Vaughn, and Dr. Dane. Vaughn decided he would drive the first shift through untroubled territory since he was not as practiced in handling a standard transmission. Someone else could then take over before they reached a known trouble spot. Delmas Ridenour steered the other humvee —the one that used to be Courtney's — and Mike Newcome and Christopher Gooden rode with him.

The humvees started up, sounding much louder and more menacing due to the exaggerated echoes caused by the confines of the Eastpointe parking garage. They immediately proceeded to the front gate, where Superintendent Ervin Wright and the Procurement Committee waved at them and told them to be safe.

A guard stationed on a scaffold near the wall fired off two shots from his rifle, putting down two zombies wandering near the gate. Then the siren went off as the gate guards hit the switch to open the inner gate, likely awakening everyone in Eastpointe who worked night shifts. The humvees ventured into the decontamination zone, then the inner gate was closed and the outer gate was opened.

Courtney counted eleven zombie carcasses here, including the one of the business-suited zombie she had no particular fondness of. Usually the bodies were given a dose of kerosene and lit on fire weekly. It seemed nobody had bothered to do it for some time. The wheels of the humvees simply rolled over them without a second thought.

Vaughn pulled their humvee in front and led them down the winding road away from Eastpointe. The outer gate closed behind them and the sirens ceased their deafening roar. The Strike Team then plunged forward into the world ruled by the living dead.

CHAPTER FIVE

The Road Less Traveled

"However did you come by *chainmail*?" asked Dane.

"*Knights of Yesterday*," Leon told him through a mouthful of sandwich. "Even the strongest zombie bite can barely dent it, so they took them out of Eastpointe Plaza and stored them in the armory."

"Oh, I see."

Dane fit himself into the ringed shirt and pulled his sweater down over top of it. He then wriggled his torso a bit, trying to get comfortable with the armor. Courtney saw that while he had his shirt off, it wasn't just his face that was pale —it was his whole body. The poor guy probably saw less sunshine on that boat than she did while hiding out in her house.

The humvees pressed forward.

Occasionally a blue-skinned person would appear and stagger after the vehicles, but Vaughn would ignore them. However, at one point Courtney looked back at the second humvee and saw that Delmas Ridenour swerved an extra couple of feet so he could ram one with the bull bars. It sent the zombie careening into the overgrown vegetation off to the side of the road.

She stayed mostly quiet as lunchtime rolled around and sandwiches were passed out. She wasn't hungry, so she chose to eat just one. Thankfully it was white bread and not wheat, as plain white bread was easiest to make and she still couldn't stand the taste of wheat. But she knew that if her father were here to hand her another of his sandwiches made out of wheat bread, she would gladly gobble it down. She sort of wished she wouldn't have given away those sandwiches he made before she was dragged aboard the deuce-and-a-half all those years ago.

Leon ate two and even Vaughn juggled one between his steering wheel hand and his gear-shifting hand, but Dr. Dane declined to have anything but another cup of coffee from the thermos.

He would glance out the windows once in a while to see the many houses that once had carefully manicured lawns, but were now reduced to nothing more than dilapidated shacks surrounded by lush jungles. There was foliage growing in the rain gutters and up through cracks in the pavement. Abandoned vehicles and corpses —both lying down and walking around —lined the hillsides. It was deadly quiet outside the humvees.

"It's everywhere, isn't it?" Dane commented. "In every nation on every continent."

Leon finished the last bite of his sandwich and rolled down the window long enough to toss out the empty ziplock bag and discarded crusts. He then answered, "As far we know, we're the last ones left."

"Has there been any contact with Canada though?" asked Dane.

"There hasn't been any contact with *anybody* until you showed up," Courtney replied. "We sure didn't think anyone else was alive out there."

He showed her an uneasy smile then took another sip of coffee. He swallowed hard. "It's just that I was on a ship while everything was happening on land," he explained. "How did things get so out of control?"

"Governments, armies, militias, religions, human rights activists —they all had a hand in it," Leon replied. "It's hard to pinpoint a single cause."

Dane nodded understandingly. He then asked, "But couldn't there be more places like Eastpointe? Walled-up towns with people like you?"

The eager expression on his face as he posed this question gave Courtney pause, but otherwise she didn't give it a second thought.

114

Later, however, she would wish she would have confronted him about his choice of words.

"There could be," she told him. "But there's no way of knowing."

"Hmm."

Courtney unscrewed the lid on a canteen of water and took several gulps. She handed it to Leon and he did the same, then he in turn handed it up to Vaughn.

"I heard some things about rescue stations," said Dane. "Government and police-funded areas citizens could go to be safe."

Courtney was almost tempted to laugh. Her experience at the Camp Rigero rescue station had been anything but safe.

Leon was the one to answer him. He said, "Most of the rescue stations got overrun from the inside out. Infected people were dying and then rising back up again."

"It was like being stuck in a barrel with a bunch of piranhas," Vaughn interjected, his tone implying first-hand knowledge. He peered in the rear-view mirror to eye Dr. Dane. "If we had been allowed to shoot the infected ones, all the uninfected ones might have gotten out of there alive. But *no*, our own humanity destroyed us."

"Vaughn's only quasi-human, Dr. Dane," Leon hastily added. "If it were up to him, he would shoot anyone who even caught a *scent* of zombie."

Vaughn laughed.

Courtney squinted her eyes and viewed the road up ahead. Houses were spaced closer and closer together now and the bouncing inside the humvee was softening as the tires found smoother asphalt. She opened the map and started comparing the landmarks to what she saw on the paper. After a moment she announced, "We should be coming up on Wakefield. Could be rough."

"Time to change drivers?" asked Vaughn.

Leon nodded, then squawked his walkie-talkie and said, "We're going to bring it to a stop and change drivers."

After a moment the walkie-talkie squawked back, "*Chinese fire drill style?*"

"Nope. Just over the seat."

The walkie-talkie replied, "*Darn. I like Chinese fire drills.*"

Vaughn slowly brought the humvee to a stop and pulled the

emergency brake. He sat up and started maneuvering his tall body over the seat, his black hair spilling messily across the cushions.

Leon sat up and prepared to exchange places with him.

Courtney put a hand on his shoulder to stop him. She said, "I'll drive."

"You sure?"

She nodded.

He sat back down and Courtney climbed over the seat and sat down in front of the steering wheel. She dropped the emergency brake, shifted into first gear, let out the clutch, and the humvee pulled forward.

Wakefield was approaching.

The New Atlantis

It had once been a mediocre town aspiring to receive its first skyscraper. It had a Main Street, a High Street, and even a catchy-sounding Silver Lake Road. It had the Commodore Oliver Hazard Perry Memorial Highway running to the south and the Cemetery of St. Francis of Azzizi to the north. The main stretch through town was typical of most mediocre towns —storefronts and apartment buildings crammed tightly together, all about five or six stories high.

Now, however, most of Wakefield was underwater. At some point in the last five years, the dam at the Indian Run Reservoir had been destroyed and the basin reclaimed the territory it lost when man decided to contain it long ago. The new lake engulfed the first floor of almost every building on every side street. Main Street and some of the area to the south was all that remained above water.

The fate of the town was similar to most places Courtney had seen while driving from Georgia to Rhode Island. Whole cities were flooded, fires were raging everywhere, buildings were crumbling, and she figured at least one or two nuclear bombs had been detonated somewhere in the world. (Surely at least one nation out there had tried using them.) She imagined that at one point Rhode Island was probably a very beautiful place. If circumstances were different, she would have loved to visit one of the many lighthouses she saw from the road. The blinding walls of Eastpointe didn't do South County any justice whatsoever. She felt kind of sorry for the rich folks who originally made their homes inside them.

She led the humvees cautiously through Wakefield.

Most of the zombies in the area were just lying around on the pavement and the sidewalks and it was hard to tell them apart from corpses that were actually dead. As the humvees went down Main Street, the functioning ones would sit up and listen intently to the approaching noises. Since they only drew oxygen when making one of their longer *I'm-gonna-get-you* moans and therefore didn't draw air to speak or otherwise communicate, it was impossible to tell what exactly was going through their heads. Therefore it was hard to tell why they chose to just lay around on their backs instead of stand and stagger like a bunch of drunken idiots. There weren't any more living people to chase after, so it made Courtney wonder if zombies felt fatigue and boredom after all.

This was where it was unavoidable and she had to start ramming them with the bull bars. The ghouls were spaced few and far apart and she knew it was best to get out of this man-made valley as quickly as possible. If she gave them time to cluster together it could mean trouble. Hopefully they would settle down again after the humvees left the area and by the time the Strike Team returned from retrieving the Cure, the zombies of Wakefield would start in prone positions once more.

Dane watched out his window and even made eye contact with one of the creatures. They stared each other down.

"Don't panic or anything," Leon told him. "We're safe."

"Oh, I'm not worried," said Dane. "It's not like they know how to drive a car and chase after us, right?"

And hopefully they never learn how, Courtney thought.

She was forced to swerve around a semi truck that had crashed into the front of a boutique and left its big silver trailer blocking half of Main Street. Several zombies were venturing around the other side, so she had to apply a little more pressure on the accelerator in order to ram them all at once. The hood of the humvee was high enough that she never had to worry about a zombie going up and over the windshield and leaving blood or formaldehyde all over the place. Instead they would fly backwards and off to the side as soon as they made contact with the bull bars.

The town was simply in shambles.

Shopping carts and miscellaneous debris were scattered all over. Broken glass littered the sidewalks. A fire had destroyed the Sunoco and three nearby buildings. Abandoned cars were smashed into parking meters. Streetlights dangled precariously from neglected poles and traffic lights were busted. Skeletal human bodies lay discarded in the gutters.

Out of the window of an apartment building up ahead, she saw, a corpse dangled from a noose tied around its neck. It was mostly just bones and bits of sinew now. A suicide letter was still pinned on its shirt, but it was too far away to be read. She knew that if the person had been infected before committing suicide then the body would have reanimated and been stuck in the noose for the duration of its existence. It didn't seem like it was moving now though —and if it reanimated then the decomposition would have stopped. It appeared the poor soul's neck would snap in two at any moment and send the body tumbling to the sidewalk forty feet below.

A perfectly healthy human who had been forced to abandon all hope.

She put her eyes back down and focused on the road ahead.

She occasionally glanced in the rear-view mirror to make sure the second humvee was keeping up. Delmas seemed to be having no problems, but the zombies were flocking together behind him and staggering after the vehicles in a big mob, all with hungry outstretched arms. She again hoped that they would settle down before her team had to return through this area.

Finally, when the buildings began to thin out and become spaced further and further apart, eventually being replaced with trees and houses, she knew Wakefield was behind them.

The two humvees pressed on.

It wouldn't be much longer before they would arrive at Point Judith.

ROCK FORGE
Army Research Laboratory

Addendum
By Dr. Allison Fischer (civilian status)
for the eyes of all civilians and military personnel
Under authorization from Col. Franklin Darlington

Title: Reminder

In the notes of Dr. Dalip Patel I found a crucial oversight that
I feel Black Berets and military personnel should be aware of.

As we know, decapitation will definitely immobilize a reanimated
dead. However, the head will continue to function until brain
activity has been terminated. This requires a bullet or a
powerful stomp to the cranium.

This is more of a mention. Dr. Patel did his work thoroughly; he
simply neglected to expound this important fact properly. I
recommend that this information be forwarded to M. Gordon Levi
and the members of the Black Beret Project for incorporation in
the Ad Hoc Black Beret Training Manual.

Further Addendum

Title: False Reports

Reports of mosquitoes transmitting this virus are totally false.

Since reanimated dead do not radiate heat nor their blood circulate,
they are not a target for mosquitoes.

Anyone who has come into contact with a mosquito has no reason for
distress. Rumors to the contrary should be stopped immediately, as
they are only spreading panic.

The Atlantic Princess

Leon squawked the walkie-talkie and said, "That looks like the last one." He then turned to Vaughn and asked, "Any more through your eyes?"

Vaughn lowered his binoculars and told him, "No."

Leon squawked his walkie-talkie once more and said, "Take it out and we'll get this show on the road."

The stoic reply came, "*Affirmative.*"

A rifle was pointed out the window of the second humvee and at the end of it was Christopher Gooden. He took careful aim through the high-powered scope and a moment later he pulled the trigger. There was a *bang* as a zombic shuffling along the beach about seventy yards away suddenly collapsed in the sand, a hole in its forehead spewing all kinds of coagulated gunk.

The disembarkation area was now free of undead opposition and there were no more walking corpses visible anywhere on the horizon.

Leon gave a nod to Courtney and she took the humvee out of idle and pulled out of the forest and onto the golden sands of Point Judith beach. The two-vehicle convoy crossed the shore in side-by-side formation, sending up clouds of dirt and exhaust in their wake.

They stopped when they reached the area by the fallen zombies.

It was in the shadow of the most behemoth ship she had ever seen —a millennium-class vessel with the words *The Atlantic Princess* scrawled along the starboard side. The majestic cruiseliner stretched almost four hundred yards into the distance and had a beam nearly sixty yards wide. Looking up, Courtney guessed that the very peak was some seventy yards in the air —and she wasn't taking into consideration how much of the ship was still buried beneath the sands. It appeared to have come to land very fast —she didn't understand knots or anything about ships —but now more than half of its mass rested lazily upon the shore and a mountain of sand crested along its bow. It was tilted slightly portside.

Seeing it there, disturbing the light of the midday summer sun, with waves gently lapping away at its sides and sea gulls swarming around and cawing noisily, the cruiseliner seemed as out of place as a city on the moon. Here at Point Judith was nature at its most basic level —and now there rested one of the largest manufactured

121

monstrosities ever seen. It simply didn't belong. It wasn't even like seeing the military in her backyard and the White House being overrun all those years ago —it was more like Mount Everest had erupted out of the peaceful plains of Kansas. No one was ever meant to see the wholeness of a ship. After all, less than half of it was supposed to actually be above water. Yet here it was, unnatural and imposing and disrupting the natural order of things.

Looking beyond the ship —and it was really hard not to be distracted by it —she could see the very familiar Atlantic Ocean. She knew the waters would be much colder here than they were on the north Florida coast, but it was still nice to see those waters once again.

One by one the Black Berets disembarked from their respective humvees and met on the beach in between. They slung their rifles over their shoulders and readjusted their belts carrying their sidearms and wakizashis. One by one they slipped the copper-toned visors over their faces and tucked their hair under the spandex hood in the back. Though seeing *out* of the copper visors was just as clear as not having any obstruction at all, it was very hard —if not impossible —to see *into* them and peer at the faces within. Finally they fit their berets on their heads and situated them slightly off kilter as they were meant to be. Aside from Dr. Aaron Dane and his casual everyday attire, they were all identical now, one and the same.

Courtney looked back at the ship. The rows of circular portholes along the lower portion were dark and empty, which prompted the question, "What kind of light are we going to have in there?"

"Emergency power is still on," Dane answered, tossing away the styrofoam cup his coffee was in. "It's not much. Mostly red lights."

"Then we'll be using our minilights," said Delmas.

"What else do we need to take into consideration?" asked Chris Gooden.

"Planning out some kind of route beforehand would be nice," Vaughn replied. "Just to get a general idea of where we'll be going. It's probably going to be cramped in there."

"It is," said Dane. "The sheer velocity of the ship as it came ashore and the sudden impact caused most everything —*including me* —to go tumbling towards the bow. There's going to be some obstacles in the way and some of the doors might be blocked from the other side."

"You're still going with us, right?" asked Courtney.

"Of course," Dane answered proudly. "I'm not chickening out. I'm going to see this through to the end."

"So where is the Cure?" asked Leon.

"In my lab." Then, almost as an afterthought, he added, "It's packed in a box with some excelsior. Don't worry, it's safe."

"Where's your lab?"

"Fortunes Casino. The military told us to set up our equipment on the tables there until they could find us something more suitable. But they never did find anything better. Maybe they didn't even bother trying."

"What's the fastest way to the Casino?"

"Probably to retrace the route I took getting off the boat," Dane replied. "I was in the lab when the collision happened. *Sleeping.* I had to dig my way into the elevator foyer and from there to the Conservatory hallway. Most of the doors wouldn't budge. Hell, it took me a long time to find a way out." He paused for a moment. "I can't remember the exact path I took."

"What about skin-eaters?" asked Vaughn. "Any roaming the halls?"

"No. They're still locked up. Most are in the crew cabins in the forecastle, some in the staterooms. I don't think any managed to get out."

"You'd better be sure."

"Yes, on that much I am sure."

Courtney looked away from the group to study the vessel. The main deck was pretty high up and there wasn't any visible means of getting to it. She asked, "How did you get down from there?"

"Emergency ladder," Dane replied, pointing. "Of the annoying rope variety."

Everyone followed his outstretched finger until their eyes focused on a rope ladder dangling off the starboard side of the ship near the bow. It was flapping against the 'tic' in the words *The Atlantic Princess.* It stretched from the railing of the main deck down roughly twenty yards to the mountain of sand pushed up against the bow.

"That's the way we go then," said Leon. "Once we get on deck we'll see if Dr. Dane can remember what path he took."

Everyone nodded in agreement.

They made their way across the beach and climbed the hill of sand in the shadow of the cruiseliner. It was pretty high, but not nearly as high as the main deck. Once at the top of the hill, Courtney grabbed the ladder and inspected it starting from the bottom and working her eyes slowly up each rung. It didn't look much thicker than clothesline rope and she didn't much like the thought of scaling it.

Leon told her, "You should probably go first."

She turned to him, trying to see his face through his visor, yet knowing he couldn't see through hers either. She then whispered, "Why? Because *ladies first*?"

"No," he answered. "Because you're the lightest."

She shrugged, then looked up the ladder one more time. She didn't like this at all.

Leon softly told her, "If you hear anything up there or see anything that might be trouble, get—"

"—I know," she snapped, cutting him off.

She put one foot on the bottom rung and slowly put more weight on it. The ladder grew more taut with each pound of pressure. She grabbed hold of one of the rungs further up and pulled herself on so all her weight was on the ladder. She bounced a little.

It seemed like it might be okay.

She put her other foot on the next highest rung and slowly began scaling the ladder. It was swaying side-to-side and if she didn't distribute her weight evenly it would twist and start to send her off balance. After scaling a few more rungs she looked down at the others and told them, "Hold the bottom."

One of them —she couldn't tell whom under their visor —put a foot on the bottom rung and added enough weight to hold the ladder perfectly vertical.

She then continued climbing.

About halfway up, after moving past the first row of portholes and just before reaching the words *The Atlantic Princess*, she heard a noise coming from inside the ship. It was a clanging sound, like metal on metal. She looked off to the side of the ladder and tried peering into the darkness behind the glass in one of the portholes. At first only her visor-covered reflection stared back at her.

Then, in an instant, a dead face was pressed against the opposite side of the window, snarling, biting against the glass. Its eyelids were gone and its grimy hands were massaging the edges of the porthole, wanting desperately to get at her.

She yelped and lost her footing. Only her hands tightly gripping one of the rungs above kept her from falling on the other members of her group. She dangled there for a moment before getting her feet back in place.

Leon called out, "What's going on?"

"A frickin' *zombie*," Courtney called back. "Its on the other side of the window staring at me."

Down below, Leon turned to Dr. Dane and asked, "What's the deal?"

"That's the forecastle," he replied. "I told you most of them were locked up in there."

Leon looked back up at Courtney and told her, "It's alright, doll. Keep going."

She grunted and continued climbing. She wanted to tell him to never call her 'doll' again, especially in his annoying New England voice, but she didn't want to make a scene in front of everyone else. Hopefully they hadn't paid too much attention to it.

Hello there? Concentrate.

She pulled herself higher, passing the last of the portholes and the words *The Atlantic Princess*, nearing the top. When she finally reached her goal, she slid over the railing and quickly hopped to her feet. The tilt of the ship was even more noticeable now that she was on it.

She pulled the silenced Socom from its holster. She flicked on the laser sight and flicked off the safety, then scanned the area from where she stood.

From down below, Leon called out, "What do you see?!"

She called back, "Give me a minute!"

There were two tennis courts in the vicinity with a rock-climbing wall erected between them. She could smell stagnant water somewhere nearby even over the smell of salty ocean water. She figured there was probably a pool on the other side of the big white divider. This theory was reinforced when she saw a sign that read, '*NOTICE - Clothing Optional Sunbathing Area.*'

She stepped away from the railing, keeping the gun pointed in front of her and highlighting everything she saw with the red targeting dot. Forward she went, sidestepping around the rock-climbing wall and checking to see what was on the other side. There was nothing —just discarded boxes and miscellaneous junk. She listened carefully for any stumbling footsteps or gaspless moans, but the only sounds she heard was the soft hum of the breeze as it sifted across the deck and the cacophony of seagulls cawing their displeasure at having a human disrupt their new territory.

There was a ramp leading up to the next deck with a wheelchair-accessible sign posted nearby. Above that was another sign. It had an arrow pointing upwards and the words '*To Promenade*' written next to it. Toward the middle of the deck stack was a sign reading '*Information Desk.*'

Further down on the starboard and port sides, lifeboats dangled from crane mechanisms. However, she noticed that most of the cranes weren't holding anything —there were simply empty ropes.

There were no dead bodies around, walking or otherwise.

She returned to the railing and peered over. She called down, "All clear!"

Leon nodded, then put a foot on the bottom rung and began his ascent, paying no regard to the zombie still looming in the porthole. When he finally reached the top he threw a leg over, straddling the railing, then brought his other leg over and put both feet down on the deck.

He immediately drew his gun.

Down below, someone else started coming up the ladder. From the groaning, it sounded like Delmas.

Leon viewed the area for a moment, likely taking in everything Courtney did, then turned to her and said, "This doesn't look too bad. Has to be easier than herding cows into trucks."

She snickered, knowing he was probably right.

Leon leaned over the railing again and called down, "Hey Delmas! What would you rather be doing? Climbing a shoddy rope ladder to get on an infested ship —or on a smelly farm somewhere herding cattle?"

The visor-outfitted person below looked up and replied, "Herding cows. You know me, I'm the ultimate cowboy."

Leon laughed.

Courtney could feel the sun hitting heavily on the main deck now and it was causing beads of sweat to form beneath her trylar wetsuit. It could be unbearably miserable if it got much hotter.

Leon seemed to notice the heat as well. He tilted his head side to side a few times, trying to catch a glimpse of the sign over by the big white divider. After a moment he commented, "Clothing-optional pool, eh?"

Beneath her visor she rolled her eyes and mumbled, "Don't even think about it."

He chuckled.

By now Delmas was hauling himself over the railing. Courtney and Leon helped get his brawny body onto the main deck, as it seemed he was having problems accomplishing this on his own. Once he got situated he gave them a thankful nod.

Courtney turned to Leon and said, "Dr. Dane should probably come up next and see if he can remember which way we need to go."

He replied, "*Sounds good*," then leaned over the rail and called down, "Let Dane come up next!"

A few understanding nods were returned, then Dr. Dane started negotiating the rope ladder. Courtney and Leon watched over the railing to make sure he was making it okay while Delmas watched the rest of the ship.

And, while she couldn't be certain, it seemed the zombie in the porthole paid no attention to Dr. Dane as he ascended the rope ladder. If it *was* still snarling, then the doctor certainly wasn't bothered by it. Maybe he was simply accustomed to the rotten creatures from having to live on a ship with them for so long. He made it up the rope ladder with no problems, but Courtney and Leon helped him over the railing anyway.

She told him, "Take a look around and tell us where we need to go."

Dane scratched his chin as he studied the deck. After a moment he pointed to the ramp going up to the next deck and said, "I remember coming across the Promenade."

"You sure?" she asked. "We can't just go opening doors at random, you know."

He nodded and replied, "I'm sure."

She turned around and watched Vaughn come up the rope ladder.

When he neared the portal with the looming zombie, he took a moment to very calmly tell it, *"Oh shut up you dead bastard."* He then continued climbing.

Dr. Dane commented, "I never expected to be crawling up that ladder again. I figured you people would be using grappling hooks or something of the like."

"We're not *commandos*," Vaughn replied as he crossed over the railing. "Jesus, you think this is *Mission Impossible* or some shit?"

Dane shrugged his shoulders. He said, "You're just zombie killers?"

"Well, *yeah*," Vaughn replied. "Who in their right mind *isn't*?"

Mike Newcome came up the ladder next, followed by Christopher Gooden. With everyone finally assembled on the deck, Courtney informed them, "Looks like we're going across the Promenade."

With their Socoms drawn and ready, they crossed the tennis courts and went up the ramp to the Promenade, which was something the likes of which none of the Black Berets had ever seen before.

Stretching proudly from one end of the cruiseliner to the other, the Promenade was a make-believe medieval town square and main street. The storefronts were composed of a multitude of different businesses, at least half of them themed to the times. There was Soccorsi's Pizzeria, Dragonslayer Theater, Gym of Olympus, King's Court Lounge, Fountain of Youth Spa, ShipShape Calisthenics, Chestnut Emporium, Captain Cook's Seafood, Ye Fine Art Gallery, Lord of the Joust Tavern and Sports Bar, and —to top it all off —an ice skating rink called *Princess On Ice*.

Some of the storefront windows were busted and a quick glance through the broken glass revealed that most everything inside had been looted, more than likely by the scientists and military that were onboard the ship. This included every liquor bottle behind the bar in Lord of the Joust Tavern. Also, surprisingly enough, X's were scribbled over the eyes of every painting in Ye Fine Art Gallery.

Courtney and the others didn't bother going inside any of the stores since there were no moans heard anywhere nearby, but the panicked destruction of the Promenade was easily evident. The street was covered with decorative stone tiles, but most of them were chipping away or missing completely. There was even a water fountain at the center of town that was probably quite remarkable when it functioned '*once upon a time.*'

The more Courtney saw of The Atlantic Princess, the more she began to believe that —given the proper circumstances —it could be much like a floating Eastpointe. The oceans could be its walls and there would never be a threat of them being breached. Provided there were enough rations stored onboard, a group of living people could survive on a ship at sea for almost a decade. It was a shame that the people on this cruiseliner had to go and ruin their good fortune.

They crossed the Promenade in two-by-two formation, keeping the seventh person, Dr. Dane, in the center where the highly efficient Black Berets could protect him.

With the crossing of the Promenade proving thankfully uneventful, Dr. Dane led them down to the main deck again, this time at the stern. He paused here for a moment before finally deciding to take them through a door on the portside of the vessel.

There was a French balcony here, along with a grand staircase spiraling down to a once-magnificent atrium. The walls crisscrossed between velure and beechwood veneer. Knights and dragons and damsels in distress were paid homage on the painted ceilings. There used to be a crystal chandelier hanging in the center, but now it was in pieces on the floor far below.

Just as Dr. Dane had warned them, there was only emergency power running throughout the vessel, and here the only illumination provided were the red backup lights mounted on the walls in a nonsensical sporadic fashion. The copper-toned visors everyone was wearing now reflected a menacing crimson hue.

The Team was forced to switch on the minilights on their Socoms.

Being careful not to inadvertently aim their weapons at another member of the group as they shone the lights in front of them, they descended the spiraling staircase to the dark and damp atrium floor. Only now were Courtney's feet finally getting accustomed to the crookedness of the beached cruiseliner.

There were two tall caryatids at the bottom. Both of the columns had been defaced; the eyes of the sculptured women were X'd over in red and there were circles drawn around the breasts. A constant, echoing *drip-drip* sound could be heard splashing from the statues. Courtney wondered what kind of emotions the people stuck aboard the ship might have felt as they began to lose contact with land while everyone around them was becoming infected.

She figured some of them probably went downright *insane*.

There were many exits from the atrium, all appropriately labeled by the signs dangling overhead. One, leading to another staircase going upwards, read, *To Conservatory*. Another, leading down, read, *Jacuzzi*. Yet another, leading up, read, *To Princess Suite*.

Dr. Dane opened a door with a sign reading '*Staterooms 001-142*'.

Being at the front of the group, Courtney and Leon shone their lights down the passageway. It was long and dark and narrow and lined with closed doors spaced in tight intervals. Red lights flickered on and off throughout the length of it.

With a deep breath, Courtney led the rest of the group down the hallway, keeping Dr. Dane secure in the middle.

Then the riotous thrashing began.

All at once all one hundred and forty-two stateroom doors began being bombarded with brutal, angry fists. Soulless moans and groans could be heard emanating from within. The ruckus was deafening, causing most of the members of the group to lower their weapons and cover their ears. The floor itself was vibrating from the physical abuse the ship was being subjected to. On top of that, Courtney didn't have any particular fondness for noisy corridors to begin with.

Someone in the rear shouted, "Sounds like the natives are restless!"

"See what I had to put up with?!" Dr. Dane shouted back, his face cringing under the red lights.

Leon nudged Courtney on the shoulder and motioned her to hurry along.

The group moved quickly down the hallway, still halfway covering their ears, and came out a door on the other side. Once every member was through, they closed the door behind them to muffle the noisy onslaught coming from the passageway.

Here was another sign: *To Elevator Foyer*.

"That'll take us to Fortunes Casino," said Dane. "My lab."

Mike Newcome, usually reserved and not very forthcoming, was this time the one to give voice to what everyone was thinking: "*Fucking finally.*"

With the minilights from the Socoms shining off at his sides, Dr. Dane confidently took the lead.

He guided them across the elevator foyer and through two sets of heavy wooden doors marked with the inscription *Fortunes Casino*.

It was humongous —nearly as big as the Promenade outside — and since there were no red emergency lights emphasizing the room's boundaries, there was no end in sight. Even with their minilights glowing, the Strike Team could not see their final destination from where they stood.

Dr. Dane informed them, "My lab's on the other side in the VIP room."

"Let's get moving then," said Leon.

Most of the gambling tables were knocked over and resting in the direction of the bow. Courtney knew they must be awfully heavy, so the impact of the crash must have been tremendous indeed in order to send them all sliding in one big lump. The impact and the sliding effect also caused most of the carpet to be ripped away, revealing bare hardwood below. The noise of the team's footfalls resounded through the hollow darkness, upsetting the calm, then echoed back to them from somewhere far away.

The team passed several more clusters of overturned gambling tables —mostly craps, blackjack, and roulette. Scattered in with casino chips and dice and loose playing cards were broken vials and electrodes and miscellaneous papers with a bunch of science jargon scribbled all over them. Discarded lab coats and military camouflage were buried underneath, some discolored with unrecognizable gunk.

And there was money —*a whole lot of money* —piles of bloodstained fifties and hundreds simply abandoned on the floor. Valued so highly in the world before, they were now nothing more than worthless slips of paper subtly reminding everyone just how drastically the rules had changed.

They walked for nearly a hundred yards before Dane put his hand up and said, "Over there. The VIP room."

The team then followed him to another set of heavy-looking wooden doors.

Opposite the doors was a long banister and another staircase leading down into more darkness. After shining her minilight down there Courtney saw rows upon rows of slot machines, most of which were leaning forward, yanked from their secure bases by the impact of the ship hitting the beach.

"Wait a second," Leon whispered, motioning everyone to stay put. "I hear something."

The team stopped and listened.

Courtney then heard the sound Leon was referring to: a guttural moaning of the undead type. It seemed muffled somehow —it wasn't just emanating from somewhere in the expansive darkness of the Casino.

"Well, it's definitely a skin-eater," said Delmas. "But where is it?"

Courtney peered over the balcony once more and shone her light into the darkness. She didn't see anything moving down there, nor did the moaning seem to be getting louder.

"There's nothing to worry about," Dane told them. "Like I told you, all the zombies are locked in the forecastle and in the staterooms in the hallway we already went through. Sounds carry much differently in a ship. That's all you're hearing."

Vaughn Winters and Mike Newcome directed their lights the way the group had just traveled to see if perhaps a zombie had broken out of a stateroom and followed them into the Casino.

But there was nothing —just the empty darkness.

Leon came to Courtney's side and with their combined lights shining over the balcony they were able to illuminate most of the area directly below. After looking for a moment he told her what she already knew: "Nothing down there."

They turned around and faced the rest of the group.

This was when they noticed Dr. Dane had strayed from them and was walking eagerly to the doors of the VIP room.

"Don't open those doors yet," Vaughn calmly told him. "We're dealing with a situation here."

Dane continued walking.

Vaughn told him again, louder and more firmly this time, "Don't open those doors."

Dane replied, "Don't worry," and kept walking.

"*Stop him*," said Leon.

Mike Newcome stepped towards Dr. Dane and prepared to put a hand on his shoulder, but he was too late. Dane had already reached the doors of the VIP room and with a simple triumphant tug he pulled them open.

No one was prepared for what came out the other side.

BLACK BERET ADVANCED GROUND TECHNIQUE

Modified Jiu-Jitsu Guard and Sweep

Diagrams are used only to illustrate progression of maneuver. As with all maneuvers discussed in this manual, your instructor will guide you through the exact steps and sign off once execution of technique has met satisfactory approval.

Step 1.

If target takes you to the ground, immediately form open Jiu-Jitsu Guard.

(outlined on page 14.)

Step 2.

Rest on shoulders and elevate legs.

Plant knees into the upper arms of target and firmly hold wrists. Teeth of target will not be able to reach you.

Known as the Safe Position, it can be maintained indefinitely provided there are no other targets nearby.

Step 3.

Sprawl out, keeping wrists of target firmly held.

Right leg should be out-stretched and flat on the ground.

Step 4.

Sweep target off by striking knees with right heel and follow through.

Step 5.

Return to standing position while target recuperates.

If target is still immobile, this technique can be followed with a heel stomp to the cranium.

(see page 274)

Rush

There wasn't just one. It was a mob of at least ten or twelve and something wasn't right about them. However, nobody was given enough time just yet to figure out what made them so different from all the others.

Events were simply happening too fast.

Dr. Dane was engulfed by the mob and was now gone from sight. The Black Berets heard nothing out of him —no screams for help, no cries of pain, *nothing*. Even though there hadn't been enough time to save him, they should have seen him struggling on his own and at least trying to put up a fight.

But there was nothing.

He was simply gone.

The Black Berets lifted their Socoms and aimed high, the spotlights below the barrels highlighting the ghastly faces of the enemy. Muffled gunshots then zipped through the air, but instead of hearing the satisfying sound of the bullets hitting skulls, they heard the clanking sound of bullets hitting metal.

The zombies continued advancing, spilling out of the VIP room and stepping in unnaturally fast strides and rapidly closing the distance between them and their prey. Bullets from the .45's were not even slowing them down.

In that instant Courtney began to realize that no zombie should be able to move as fast as these were, nor should any zombie be so invulnerable. She fired four more rounds at the head of one of the approaching ghouls and each shot was equally ineffective.

Then she noticed that the zombies' outstretched arms seemed to reach about a foot longer than they should. Something fastened at the end of their hands was reflecting the glare of the minilights, shimmering to a sharpened point.

Before her mind could interpret what exactly it was that gave them such an extensive reach, her eyes were discerning something else out of the ordinary. Instead of seeing rotting teeth in the snarling mouths of these creatures, she saw a silver glimmer running across the surface of the enamel. There was obviously something laced over their choppers —something sharp.

Her magazine spent, Courtney dropped it out of her gun and

quickly locked and loaded a new one in its place. All around her the rest of the Black Berets were doing the same. One of them —Delmas by the sound of the voice —shouted, "What the hell?!"

Courtney aimed high once more.

The zombies, getting closer now, compelled her to continue stepping back until the railing on the balcony behind her stopped her from moving any further away. The other members of the team were fanning out as the advancing creatures forced them to break formation. More shots were fired, but each bullet was still met with metal instead of skull.

It was then —with a zombie less than ten feet away —that she finally realized why her shots were ineffective. What at first glimpse she thought was hair or a hat or something else normal that a person on a cruiseliner might have been wearing when they died and reanimated, turned out to be some kind of helmet shaped over their scalp and forehead, around their eyes and past their jaw. The metal was thick enough to stop bullets.

Without understanding why these zombies were so equipped or even who equipped them, she shouted, "Go for the eyes!"

A bullet fired from Leon's gun finally felled one of the creatures with a shot through the eye socket and into the brain. It dropped backwards and hit the thinly carpeted floor of the casino with a resounding *clunk*. Courtney therefore knew that somehow the metal armor wasn't just limited to their heads —it was all over their bodies.

But only one zombie was felled. There were at least a dozen more.

Bad things started happening then. Shouts and screams echoed through the darkness. She lost sight of the other members of the team as she tried to focus on directing her shots into the eyes of the zombie approaching her. With most of her magazine already wasted simply trying to find their weakness to begin with, she ran out of ammunition before she could train the decisive bullet. She dropped the clip and reached into her belt for another one.

It was too late.

The zombie was already on her.

Up close, she could see that the extensions on its hands were actually bayonets welded into place on steel wristbands. Though the creature had no cognizance to efficiently wield them, this still meant that its fumbling arms were weapons of their own. It wasn't just the teeth she had to worry about now.

She ducked under the blades as the zombie lunged forward and forced her backwards against the railing. She then fell to the floor, landing hard and awkwardly on the rifle strapped across her back. The zombie fell on top of her, showing its metal-laced teeth as it snarled and drooled all over her visor. From her back, she quickly maneuvered out of the strap so she was free of the hindrance of the rifle, then she rolled onto her shoulders and elevated her lower body in order to plant her knees on the insides of the creature's elbows.

It was a Jiu-Jitsu technique Gordon had thought relevant to teach her. It was meant to prevent flailing claws, but in this case it worked to prevent the bayonets from reaching her. She knew the zombie didn't realize it was equipped with blades, so she was able to prevent the uncoordinated creature from slicing into her. There was some kind of thick plating on its chest, legs, and arms and as a whole it was the heaviest zombie she had ever wrestled.

Keeping her knees planted against its arms to hold them still, she reached into the back of her belt and took another magazine. She loaded it into the .45 Socom, then put the point of the silencer against the zombie's exposed right eye.

She pulled the trigger.

The gun discharged with hardly a sound and the bullet ricocheted several times inside the zombie's skull armor, most definitely destroying enough of its brain to terminate it.

The zombie then collapsed, its dead helmeted face pressed against the other side of her visor and its motionless mass pinning her against the balcony railing. She tried sweeping the zombie off, but it was too heavy and since there was no space between them to gain leverage, it wouldn't even budge. With her legs spread beneath the creature in a Jiu-Jitsu guard, this compromising position would have been embarrassing if it wasn't so grotesque.

Another armored zombie was quickly approaching.

Still pinned and feeling suffocated, she lifted her Socom and fired off five shots at the approaching zombie. The first four shots bounced off the zombie's helmet, but the fifth bullet went into the creature's eye and through its brain. The zombie then fell, motionless in its exoskeleton.

The glow of the minilights from the handguns was sporadic now and not many of them were still elevated. Even with silencers, Courtney knew she should still be able to hear muffled gunshots, but instead all she could hear was the grinding sound of metallic teeth chomping together. She realized that the trylar suits probably couldn't withstand a bite from the metal teeth in this mob of modified zombies and somewhere in the darkness other members of her team were learning for sure if this was true.

A voice, sounding like Vaughn, yelled, "Who's still with me?!"

"I'm here!" she shouted. "Get this frankenstein off of me!"

She heard Leon answer, "Hold on!"

Courtney forced her head away from the monster on top of her and peered into the darkness of the casino. Fallen Socoms with their attached minilights were casting beams across the floor. Everywhere she looked black and turquoise uniforms were covered in liquid crimson. Most of the people in those uniforms had already fallen and were now being assaulted by at least three pairs of greedy undead hands.

There were only two still standing.

She saw Leon, bleeding from the shoulder, attempt to decapitate a zombie. However, the blade of the wakizashi simply met with more metal at the base of the creature's skull. The zombie, still moving forward, forced Leon backwards so quickly that the railing on the balcony snapped under their combined weight and sent them both tumbling onto the slot machines below.

There was a loud thud and then there was only silence.

She saw Vaughn —the last one standing —with his wakizashi reeled back and ready to strike as he waited for an approaching zombie. His beret and visor were gone, probably discarded sometime during the melee. His rifle wasn't on his back and his handgun was also missing, all ammunition probably already expended. Courtney lifted her own Socom and fired the remaining rounds at the zombie's head in an attempt to take it out before it could reach Vaughn.

Her aim was too unsteady in her prone position. None of the shots hit where she wanted them to. She reached for her rifle, but it had been pushed too far away during the scuffle with her own assailant.

Vaughn waited for the zombie and then thrust the wakizashi straight ahead in a technique she first saw performed by Gordon

Levi. The point of the blade penetrated the creature's eye socket and entered its brain. However, as Vaughn wasn't accustomed to fighting a zombie with an extended reach, the zombie's outstretched arms allowed one of the bayonets affixed at the end to reach his neck.

Vaughn let go of the sword, which stayed put in the ghoul's eye, then covered his throat with both hands. Blood spewed from between his fingers as he collapsed to his knees. He sat like this for a few seconds, staring into the darkness, until two more modified zombies fell on him.

Courtney knew that if even cold and calculated Vaughn Winters had been bested, then it was highly likely all the others were gone as well.

Delmas, Mike, Chris, and Leon —*gone.*

All around her more armored zombies were lurching forward, the splints along their knees giving them greater support and mobility. She struggled to reach the last clip remaining in her belt, but since she was on her back with almost two hundred pounds of weight on her, this attempt proved futile.

She didn't want to get eaten.

So with no hesitation she lifted her right leg and reached for the little white container in her boot. However, the bulky body of the zombie on top of her prevented her from obtaining it.

The other zombies continued advancing.

But then they stopped.

The terminated zombie resting on her was slowly rolled off. With her view now unobstructed, she looked up to see Dr. Aaron Dane standing over her. He had a satchel bag over his shoulder. In his left hand he held a small handbox with an antenna jutting from the top. In his right hand was a revolver, magnum style.

He pointed the revolver at her and stated, "Do what I say and you'll keep your skin."

CHAPTER SIX

Fallen

Dane told her: "Lose the visor."

Ignoring him for now, Courtney put her palms on the floor and pushed herself up into a sitting position.

The minilights on the fallen Socoms illuminated the grisly scene in Fortunes Casino. The bodies of her teammates were scattered around her, bloody and broken and partially devoured. However, the armored zombies that assaulted them were all standing in place now, wavering and looking drunk. Dr. Dane stood with them, holding a button on the handbox as he aimed the revolver at her.

Finally she uttered, "What's going on here?"

"Don't ask questions and don't get up," he replied. "Just lose the visor. I won't tell you again."

Trembling and taking in stuttering breaths of air, Courtney removed her beret and slid the visor off her head. Her hair spilled out to her shoulders.

"Now the sword," instructed Dane. "Unsheathe it and toss it."

Courtney complied, pulling her last weapon from its scabbard and sliding it away. She stared back up at Dane.

"Don't give me trouble," he said. He motioned to the zombies at his sides and added, "Or I let my friends have at you."

He pushed down the antenna on the handbox and hooked it over the waistline of his jeans. He then stepped forward, keeping the gun trained on her, and put a foot on both sides of her legs. He loomed there for a moment before kneeling down on top of her and placing the barrel of the revolver on her forehead. It was righteously cold against her sweating skin.

He leaned in close and put his nose in her hair.

She remained still, staring at his finger as it hugged the trigger on the revolver.

After a moment he leaned to her ear and whispered, "Your hair smells like apple blossoms." He pulled away and smiled a very creepy smile. "You're just a small thing, aren't you? What are you, about five-five?" He paused a moment to study her, then added, "Nice body though."

All at once he used his free hand to grab her left breast, then squeezed and twisted on top of her wetsuit until he forced her to cry out. He held on for quite a while, clenching more than fondling, seemingly enjoying watching her face scrunch up in pain, then slowly started to release his grip. When he finally finished he mumbled, "*Hmph* —Not even a handful. But I like the way you scream."

She wanted to tell the loony psycho to get the hell off of her, but the gun being shoved in her face reminded her to stay quiet.

"I've decided," he said. "I'm keeping you."

He took off the satchel bag and placed it at his side, then opened it and rummaged through the contents, eventually pulling out a syringe. He eyed it over his nose and tested it by depressing the plunger a smidgen and squirting out some of the liquid inside. He whispered, "These suits you murderers wear can't stop a needle, can they?"

Despite the threat of the gun, she quickly squirmed to her side and tried to slither out from beneath him, but she suddenly felt the needle jab into her posterior.

Dane wrestled her to her back once more. He cupped his hand over her mouth and whispered, "It's just a sedative. You relax now."

She glared back at him, frightened yet angry. However, as the moments passed she began to feel lazier and lazier and almost wanted to close her eyes.

His hand slid down her stomach and began fumbling with the

buckle on her belt.

Through her drowsiness she mumbled, "Please don't."

Dane returned his gaze to hers and smiled. He said, "Don't worry. I'm not interested in the living."

He finished unfastening her belt and let it fall off. He then gathered her limp body in his arms and put her over his shoulder, then stood and carried her out of the casino.

Her eyelids fell shut shortly thereafter.

The Bridge

Her eyes opened in a brightly lit room. She was in one of the corners, curled up with her knees against her chest. There were control panels everywhere, but none of the buttons were lit up. Big windows all around the room let in endless amounts of sunlight. Though she could see only the sky from where she was sitting, a sea gull perched on a post outside reminded her where she was.

The cruiseliner. The bridge maybe?

The setting outside didn't look too different than when she was actually out there, so she guessed three hours had passed at most since she first got on deck of The Atlantic Princess.

She tried to stand, but still felt too dizzy and drowsy and her muscles weren't cooperating.

There were a dozen or so girly posters hastily taped to the far wall near the door. Every girl on every poster had their eyes X'd over in red paint and —where applicable —their breasts were circled. She remembered the paintings in the art gallery on the Promenade and the caryatids in the atrium and realized that *that* is what Dane must have done with all his free time while alone on the ship.

She hurriedly inspected herself. She was somewhat relieved to see she was still in the trylar wetsuit, so if Dane had decided to accost her again while she was sleeping, then he had only done so outside her uniform.

But he said he wasn't interested in the living.

Freak.

She tried to stand once more, even pressing her back against the wall and pushing with her legs, but still wasn't able to muster the energy. She sunk back down in the corner.

Then she heard the French-Canadian prick say, "Don't bother. The tranquilizer is going to be in your system at least another hour. So sit tight."

She heard footsteps and then saw Dane emerge from behind one of the control panels. He casually pulled up a nearby chair and sat down in front of her. He was smiling.

She tried to muster her energy again; maybe just enough to jump on him and get in a few punches to his face. However, all her body wanted to do was relax. She could roll her eyes and she could breathe and she knew she could talk if she needed to, but everything from the neck down was rebelling.

It left too many possibilities —unlimited tortures he could inflict on her while she was utterly defenseless. In her fear and uncertainty, she was sort of wishing he had gone ahead and shot her when he had the revolver pressed to her head outside the VIP room. She should have died with everyone else, yet here she was on the bridge, doped up on the floor while Dr. Aaron Dane loomed at her from his chair.

Gathering her anger, she snarled, "You killed them all. You slapped armor on a bunch of zombies and you led us here to get slaughtered."

He nodded and replied, "You noticed that, did you?"

Tears started to form on her lower eyelids. She wanted to wipe them away, but even her arms were refusing to move. She stuttered, "*Why*? Why would you do that?"

Dane didn't answer right away. He took a moment to watch her weep, then reached into his pocket and pulled out a lighter. He flicked it a couple times, letting a flame ignite, then letting it go, then flicking it again —all the while staring her in the eyes and smiling.

He then casually commented, "I had to quit smoking. All the cigarettes went stale a long time ago, but there are still plenty of working lighters. It's kind of sad they don't really serve a purpose anymore."

"You're a psycho," she countered.

And he replied, "You're so observant."

She gritted her teeth and tried moving again. She envisioned knocking him off the chair and choking him, watching his face turn blue and his eyeballs bulge from their sockets.

He had killed Leon.

He had killed *everybody*.

"I know you think I'm crazy," said Dane. "I know you think I lost my marbles from being stuck on a ship with only dead people to keep me company."

"Something like that," she snapped.

"Well, I'm sane," he said. "Before the apocalypse, I was just starting to get my life in order. I was on speaking terms with my wife again and we were talking about me moving back to Canada.

Our boy was going to be taken out of foster care and live with us. Things were looking up."

Courtney took a deep breath and let it out slowly, then let her groggy head fall to the side so she wouldn't have to look at him.

Regardless, he continued, "Then the bodies of the recently dead started rising from autopsy tables and funeral viewings and scaring the *bejesus* out of everyone. Eating them too. They increased their numbers with a simple transference of blood and saliva. One becomes two, two becomes four, four becomes eight, *yada-yada-yada*. Worse than that though —not even like the goddamn Fibonacci sequence or anything else that makes sense. Plagues can never be solved with math." He paused his rambling a moment as he toyed with his lighter, shaking it to listen to the fuel swishing around inside. Once he was satisfied, he went on, "I never got to say goodbye to Lilly or Bobby. No, the last thing I remember before the *American Army* came and ripped me out of my apartment wasn't a picture of Lilly or Bobby, but rather the garbage cans overflowing outside. The sanitation crews went on strike because of unsafe working conditions. Who'd have thought that the first thing to go after an apocalypse would be cleanliness? *That's* what's insane. But me? I'm still all there in the head." He put a forefinger on his temple and added, "No insanity here."

Courtney scoffed.

Without another word, Dane got off the chair and kneeled down in front of her. He then gently resituated her head so she was facing him.

She raised her upper lip in a sneer. She'd have spit on him too if she were able, but manipulating her facial muscles was the most she was capable of at the moment.

He looked down and took her limp left arm in his hands. Before she could wonder what this was about, he unfastened the velcro on her glove and pulled it off her hand. When he was finished he nonchalantly tossed the glove over his shoulder.

She asked, "What the hell are you doing?"

"I'm going to show you something," he replied.

Softly, as though he were caressing a newborn, he took one of her limp hands and curled up all her fingers one by one, leaving only her pinky outstretched. He held the digit firmly in this position while he brought the lighter up next to it.

Her eyes grew wide. She knew his intention and tried to pull her hand away, but under the effects of the sedative she wasn't even able to defend herself.

Dane then ignited the lighter and let the flame lick her finger, seemingly relishing the torment as her head fell back and she let out a silent scream.

Long forgotten memories returned to her in a flood. She could remember a time when she was a naive little girl and stuck her finger in the cigarette lighter in her father's car just to see what would happen. It had only been for a second, but the blister lasted for a week. She remembered crying because the pain wouldn't stop.

What was happening now hurt a lot worse. The tranquilizer had not numbed her tactile senses, so her nerve endings were able to detect every millimeter of skin on her finger burning and bubbling and sent signals of pain shooting up through her forcibly relaxed arm and straight to her brain where these signals could be recognized and exacted.

After almost five whole seconds he finally pulled the flame away. Courtney wanted to cradle her hand and maybe pinch her finger to prevent some of the pain signals from reaching her brain, but once he let go all she could do was stare down at her hand and see the black, peeling, blistering skin above the last knuckle on her pinky. Her whole arm was twitching involuntarily. Her face was wet with tears and she felt like throwing up.

Dane simply smiled and told her, "Pain is something you still feel."

He then outstretched his own pinky finger and put the lighter to it, letting the flame lick at the skin freely. He was smiling the whole time and didn't wince at all, even as the flesh began to bubble and peel away. When he was finished he displayed his mutilated finger to Courtney, stench and all.

She gagged and let her head fall to the side once more.

"I don't feel pain," Dane explained. "The nerve endings in my body no longer function. I feel nothing. My cells have ceased all stages of mitosis. By rights, I should be decaying, but my skin and muscles have stabilized. My heart beats but my blood runs cold. I breathe but I don't require oxygen. I am technically *dead*."

Courtney turned her head to face him again and mumbled, "Are you trying to say you're a zombie?"

Dane nodded.

"You're not a zombie," she sneered. "You're just a loony tunes masochistic misogynist."

"Those are some big words for a little girl," Dane countered. "But I already explained to you that I'm the sanest person you'll ever meet. Why, you ask? Because I accept what's happened to the world."

Gritting her teeth to ward off the pain in her finger, she asked, "What are you talking about?"

He stood long enough to return to his chair and sit down again. He shoved the lighter back into his pocket. Then —making Courtney gag once more —he put his burnt finger in his mouth and started nibbling on it. But it wasn't like he was simply chewing his fingernail —he was chewing the seared flesh.

She told him, "You're *sick*."

"No," he replied. "I'm *hungry*."

He rolled up the sleeve on his sweater and lifted the chainmail underneath, displaying the bite wound on his forearm that he had used to impress the Superintendent and the Procurement Committee at Eastpointe. He then lifted his arm and put his open mouth over the bite wound to show her that the teeth marks were at the perfect angle and perfectly matched his own.

She realized now that the wound was *self-inflicted*.

"God, you are a freak," she said.

He rolled his sleeve back down and replied, "God? No, I'm an atheist. I'm a man of science. You call the dead rising an *apocalypse*? An apocalypse is something out of the Bible. What happened to the world wasn't an *apocalypse*. It was an occurrence in *nature*."

"What are you talking about?"

"Evolution," Dane replied. "It was the theory for the longest time that evolution occurred so slowly that it wasn't noticeable in a single lifetime. But then the theory was advanced that evolution occurred in leaps and bounds. Many believed the next phase of our evolution would be to grow wings so we could fly through the air. Others believed that the next phase would be to grow gills so we could breathe underwater. Both ideas are incorrect. The next natural phase of evolution would be —*obviously* —to beat death. To be *immortal*."

"You're not immortal," Courtney told him. "You're just loony."

"*Au Contraire*," Dane replied. "I am proof of the success of evolution."

"No, you're just a crazy *bastard* and I hope you rot in hell."

Dane chuckled. "Of course *you* wouldn't understand," he said. "Just look at how quickly you abandoned your own species once they evolved beyond you. You call them zombies. You don't refer to them by name or even by male or female. They're all just zombies to you. They're *immortal* and you're jealous."

Courtney scoffed. She knew there would be no reasoning with this psycho, so she decided to stay quiet and concentrate on anything but the pain in her finger. It was making her nauseated and combined with the dizziness she was already feeling from the sedative, the idea of throwing up didn't seem so farfetched anymore.

Despite her detachment from the conversation, Dane continued, "Evolution made a slight mistake in that it didn't allow zombies a large mental capacity to solve problems nor the means to procreate. But being stuck here on this boat —searching for a cure —I was forced to use *myself* as a guinea pig most of the time. My evolution didn't occur naturally. You wouldn't believe all the things I had to inject into my own skin."

Courtney couldn't resist commenting, "Heroin junkie?"

"No," said Dane. "The serum of the reanimated dead. It was all part of finding some mythical *Cure*. Instead it had the opposite effect. It made me one of them —Except I maintained my mental faculties."

"That's what *you* think."

"But it changed my diet," Dane continued, unfazed by her interruption. "You have no idea what its like to feel true hunger — hunger that can't be tamed with the food from outdated military rations. No, a very specific sustenance is required to satisfy me."

Courtney's eyes grew wide. She gulped and softly asked, "Is that what I'm for?"

Dane formed another smile and replied, "Do you think I'd bother explaining all this to you if all I wanted to do was *eat* you?"

He stood then and proceeded to one of the nearby control panels where he picked up the satchel bag she had seen him carrying earlier. He opened it and pulled out a syringe. He placed the syringe on the chair he had been sitting on before and hung the bag over his shoulder.

He stood in front of Courtney and gazed down at her.

He said, "Since my cells have stabilized and my body doesn't radiate heat, the zombies consider me one of their number. In case you haven't noticed, they don't attack me. I walk with the dead."

She let her head fall back so she could look up at him. She asked, "So what? Does that make you their leader or something?"

"No," he replied. "I'm their *messiah*. And I'm going to deliver them into the new world."

"What new world?"

"A world where the old products of evolution are washed away —a world where *your* kind is gone. I'm taking my army to Eastpointe and I'm going to destroy the last remnants of you."

Courtney scoffed. She wanted to laugh, but her immobility wouldn't let her. Instead she asked, "And you plan to accomplish this *how*?"

"Using equal parts physiological psychology and equal parts sensory stimulation using modern technology. The reanimated dead are a lot more complicated than you think. When there's no food around, they operate with a pack mentality. And as you noticed earlier, I've equipped some of my shipmates with blades and armor. I only need to send electrical impulses to the pack leader and the rest will follow. I'm going to march my army to Eastpointe and pick up thousands of stragglers along the way, all willing to join the pack. Once I'm there —and since your city leaders were kind enough to give me a tour —I'm going to direct my army straight to the power plant. And from there, straight to the central housing."

"You'll never get past the wall."

"The wall is nothing a pipe bomb won't eliminate."

Courtney struggled once again to move. Now more than ever she wanted to push her thumbs through his eyeballs.

Dane motioned to the needle he had placed on the chair and said, "That syringe will allow you to evolve like I have. It contains the serum of the reanimated dead. And then you and I together can procreate and give evolution the boost it so desperately requires."

Courtney scoffed, "You and me? Don't hold your breath."

He chuckled. "You keep forgetting that I don't require oxygen."

"Whatever."

"I'm going to leave you here while my army marches to Eastpointe. I advise you use the syringe before I get back. You'll either be my Eve or you'll be my dinner. It's up to you."

"Go to hell," she snarled.

He chuckled again, then motioned to the small cooler against the far wall below the girly posters. He told her, "You'll be hungry after you use the syringe, so I took the liberty of chopping up your teammates. You'll find a leg or two in the cooler over there."

She wanted to scream. She wanted to shout and yell and curse him into the ground, but her lungs didn't give her ample energy to do so. All she could do was tell him in a loud voice, "I'm gonna kill you."

He smiled and replied, "Good luck with that. I'm *immortal*."

He then turned away and exited the bridge. Once the door was closed behind him, she could hear something metallic being propped up against it on the other side. She heard his footsteps go down the hallway, then she heard nothing.

She looked out the window and traded glances with the sea gull perched there. She stayed this way for some time, trying to fight away the tears and the pain still burning on her blackened finger.

ROCK FORGE
Army Research Laboratory

ADDENDUM TO FINAL OUTFITTING OF BLACK BERET
from Col. Franklin Darlington

<u>Title: Means of merciful death for a Black Beret</u>

Every Black Beret will carry with them a lethal dose of barbiturates that can be used to euthanize himself/herself after infection or under dire circumstances.

The drug should be stored in a container small enough to fit inside the lining of a boot yet readily obtainable. Furthermore, the drug must be able to quickly and painlessly end the life of a Black Beret if he/she judges it to be the best course of action.

This matter is non-negotiable. I will allow no more brave men and women to suffer.

See Dr. Dalip Patel for further briefing.

Motionless

Starting small, at first she concentrated solely on trying to wiggle the index finger on her right hand. She focused all her attention there, both body and mind, refusing to cry another tear.

It took at least an hour but finally that finger started moving, twitching at first, then curling from every knuckle much to her satisfaction. She moved her other fingers after that, enjoying the sensation of being able to ball up a fist, even if it was weak at first. She worked her wrists next, then her elbows, then her shoulders.

None of it was easy.

As soon as she could she cradled the burnt finger in her other hand and pinched the area below the scorched skin. It looked messy —a gigantic blister bigger than her fingernail was pushing up through the peeling, blackened tissue. She was taking deep breaths now and exhaling hard and fast, attempting to make the pain go away.

The hurt was still there, however, lingering even as she concentrated on moving her legs. She bent her ankles first, then her knees.

She fell forward on the sun-warmed tile floor of the bridge. She planted her forearms and brought her legs underneath her chest, then pushed herself into a crawling position. She struggled to the nearby chair, then reached up and put her hands on the cushion, immediately smacking away the syringe Dane had left for her. It clattered to the floor and slid to the base of a nearby control panel.

She lifted herself into the chair and sat down.

From there she lunged at one of the big windows lining the walls.

Holding fast, she peered through the glass and viewed the main deck of The Atlantic Princess from up high. A lot had changed since she had last seen it.

Now there were dozens and dozens of armored zombies moving rather rapidly across the bow, and —like a tide of lemmings —they each in turn fell over the railing and onto the golden sands below. From there the long line of them disappeared into the woods beyond the beach, with plenty more still following.

There had to be at least a hundred.

The passing of time had shifted the shadow of the cruiseliner off of the humvees her team had left parked on the beach. Squinting her eyes, she saw Dr. Dane standing next to those humvees, controlling the same handbox she had seen him utilizing during the ambush in the casino. She knew that somehow the antenna sent simplistic commands to the helmeted zombies, perhaps telling them which direction to go.

He had revealed that much in their conversation earlier.

She also noticed how the zombies simply walked right past him without a second glance. Either he really was technically dead or his delusions were real enough to fool even the mindless automatons surrounding him.

He had mentioned physiological psychology and sensory stimulation and something about electrical impulses. She had no clue what he was talking about, but regardless of the jargon he had used or the absurdity of the idea, Dane had had plenty of time to himself aboard the ship to pursue and perfect this insane vision.

And now he really was leading an army.

Courtney watched for several minutes as the last zombie fell over the railing and joined the rest of the storm troopers marching across the beach. They were walking with long, fast strides —moving quicker than any zombie she had ever seen before.

Once the last of them disappeared into the woods, she saw Dane push down the antenna on the handbox and climb inside one of the Black Beret humvees. She then saw exhaust come out the tailpipe and the vehicle pull forward.

The sight of this was enough to ignite the rage brewing in her gut.

Mustering her strength, she picked up the nearby chair and flung it against the window as hard as she was able. However, instead of glass breaking there was just a weak-sounding *boink* as the chair bounced off and hit the floor. The window hardly wobbled. Snarling, Courtney picked up the chair again and held it by the legs. She beat it against the glass over and over, resulting in nothing more than her own fatigue.

She dropped the chair and smacked her palms against the window.

"Dane!" she screamed. "I'm gonna kill you!"

But the humvee disappeared into the woods. Dane was gone.

She collapsed, her back sliding down the wall until she was sitting on the floor once again. She gasped in breath after breath, her entire body trembling. Her face —which had only recently been dried of the tears she cried —was now soaked with sweat. Her hair was sticking to her cheeks and forehead.

She brushed it away.

Struggling for air, she put her fingers down the collar of the wetsuit to pull it from her throat. As she did this she became even more aware of the pain in her scorched finger. She pinched the knuckle again, trying to make the pain stop.

It wouldn't.

She screamed long and loud, "*GODDAMNIT!!!*"

As soon as the last syllable left her mouth, she fell forward and started gagging, dry heaves collapsing her stomach and sending ripples of tension up her chest and neck. She wanted to throw up as long as it would make the pain stop, but nothing came out. It was just one dry heave after another.

She lifted her head and saw the cooler against the wall beneath the girly posters. Dane said he had chopped up her teammates and put pieces of them inside for her to eat after she used the syringe.

This was the trigger.

She puked. It spilled to the floor in a gross splash, relieving her of some of the pressure in her gut.

Breathing hard and unsteady, she brought herself to her feet and picked up the glove Dane had taken off her hand before burning her. She used it to wipe her lips, then tossed it away again.

She then staggered to the big metal door —the only door on the bridge —and tried to turn the handle. She could get it to go halfway, but something on the other side was preventing it from completely turning. She tried yanking on the handle in the hopes that somehow the door would open both ways and Dane had been too stupid to know, but gave up when she realized it was to no avail. She then took a couple steps back and gave the door a hard front kick, but it didn't budge at all.

It didn't even *react*.

She clinched her fists and let loose a cry of pure despair, then turned around and put her back against the door. She slid down and returned to a sitting position with her knees against her chest.

Her eyes were turning red as wetness formed once again across her lower eyelids. Tears came, rolling freely and indiscriminately down her cheeks. Her face fell into her palms soon after. She seized several strands of her hair and tugged them violently between her tense fingers.

She didn't want to take her hands away from her face and she didn't want to open her eyes again. She knew that if she did she would see the syringe on the floor where she had flung it earlier. Some kind of green gunk was swirling inside the casing. She knew there was no way in hell she would ever use that syringe. She knew there was no way she would *ever* give herself to Dane, even if it was the only way to stay alive.

And the others were all dead —Leon and Chris and Delmas and Mike and Vaughn.

Slaughtered.

Eastpointe was doomed too. Her new friend Alexis was going to be Dane's dinner and Courtney was powerless to stop it. The same went for Superintendent Wright and all the Committees and the rest of the five hundred or so people living within the walls. All they had wanted was a Cure, but instead all they got was deception.

So, with her decision made and her eyes closed, her right hand found its way down her leg and maneuvered into her boot. Her fingers wrapped around something inside, then brought it out.

She opened her eyes, but focused only on the new object. It was a little white container about an inch wide.

She popped it open.

Inside were dozens of little white pills. She had seen them used by others. She knew that once she swallowed them she would be dead within moments.

Sniffling, she wiped her eyes with her forearm and dropped the pills out of the container and onto her open palm. She then opened her mouth and prepared to place the pills on her tongue.

That was when there came a light knocking on the other side of the door she was resting against. A voice then asked, "Courtney? Is that you? Are you in there?"

The pills fell from her hand as she stood up and faced the door. She didn't believe it at first, but the voice on the other side had been instantly recognizable.

She uttered, "Leon?"

"Yeah," the muffled voice replied. "Are you okay?"

She sniffled long and hard and wiped her eyes again. She said, "No, I'm pretty far from okay. Get me out of here."

"Hold on."

She heard something get pulled away from the other side of the door, then saw the handle turn freely. A moment later the door swung open.

Standing there was Leon Wolfe. His beret and visor were gone, as was his handgun and rifle. Blood was leaking from the scabbard where his wakizashi was held. His hair was clumping together and his face was paler than usual.

She asked, "How did you find me?"

"I used deductive reasoning," he replied, attempting to show one of his cocky smiles. "You know, like Sherlock Holmes and Jessica Fletcher. Maybe even Matlock."

She showed him a confused expression.

"You were making enough noise to wake the dead," he said with a sigh. "Pun intended."

Despite his arrogance and his annoying accent, her only reaction was to embrace him. She wrapped her arms around his torso and put her face against his neck. She had thought the worst when she saw him fall over the balcony in the casino and assumed Dane had dismembered him like he did the others.

Leon seemed to hesitate for a moment before returning the hug, but he winced and pulled away before he got his arms completely around her. He took a step back and all of a sudden his cheery attitude was gone.

She asked, "Leon, what's wrong?"

"I've had a really bad day," he replied.

He turned around, showing her his back.

Courtney could see that his suit was ripped below his left shoulder and there was blood running from a gash there. At first she thought it was just a puncture wound from the bayonets the armored zombies were wielding or maybe an injury he received when he fell off the balcony. However, neither scenario was the case. She could see, very clearly now, that there were two rows of indentations surrounding the bleeding hole in his shoulder.

Teeth marks.

ROCK FORGE
Army Research Laboratory

INTERNAL MEMO
For the eyes of all civilians and military personnel
From: Col. Franklin J. Darlington

Ladies and gentlemen, civilian and soldier alike, we have worked together to a common goal and I feel we have done our best with the means provided us. Do not despair. Though we have found no immediate solution for this world crisis, we have accomplished a great many things during our time at Rock Forge.

Black Berets have been dispatched to several rescue stations this side of the Mississippi and though most have fallen in the line of duty, those trained under them will remain vigilant.

The notes and records of our research will prove that we are an intelligent species capable of studying the minutest detail of our enemy, no matter how uncanny that enemy may be. While we were unable to take advantage of our findings, I am certain future generations will benefit from our studies. I promise you that humanity as a whole will not suffer their world to be conquered by this undead threat.

As many of you are aware, as I write this Rock Forge is under siege by zombies both outside and inside.

Tomorrow we fight back. I myself have been infected, but I promise to fight alongside you until the bitter end. Though we may perish, we will be remembered as brave and strong. Our last moments on this earth were not without purpose.

These are the times that define us.

I will see you tomorrow.

Col Franklin Darlington

Semper fi

CHAPTER SEVEN

Life and Death

They returned to the beach.

Luckily there were still no zombies roaming around. Any of them in the vicinity probably followed Dane's storm troopers into the woods.

Courtney and Leon opened the rear hatch of the remaining humvee to obtain the supplies stashed there. It had been *her* humvee —the very same one she had used to go from Georgia to Rhode Island. However, this fact wasn't what was foremost on her mind at the moment.

As she tended to the wound on Leon's shoulder, she explained all the things that had happened to her after the ambush in the casino. Leon took several minutes to contemplate what she told him, then commented, "So this psycho put metal choppers on the zombies' teeth?"

She replied, "Among other things."

Leon shook his head and rolled his eyes.

Courtney finished cleaning and bandaging the bite wound on his shoulder, then grabbed a roll of duct tape from the back of the humvee and began patching the tear on his wetsuit.

She was sniffling the entire time.

It was growing late in the day now. She guessed it to be about five o'clock or so. The sun was still high in the sky and the sea gulls were still swarming around the cruiseliner nearby. It was actually quite a beautiful setting; it was just too bad that circumstances didn't allow Courtney to enjoy it.

After applying the last patch of duct tape, she patted Leon on the back and said, "All done." She then grabbed a canteen from the cooler in the back of the humvee and took another swig of cold water. It was somewhat refreshing.

Leon peered over his shoulder as best he could to inspect the first aid work Courtney had performed. His face was pale and his lips were turning white.

After a moment he whispered, "I appreciate you playing Betsy Ross, but—"

"—Betsy Ross created the *flag*," Courtney interrupted. "You're probably thinking of Clara Barton. She founded the American Red Cross."

"*Whatever*," said Leon. "All I'm saying is that we both know it's a waste of time. We've been through this routine before."

Courtney snapped, "Just shut up, okay?"

She handed him the canteen and let him take a drink while she crossed her arms and stared off at the ocean. She had forgotten the smells and sounds of the beach. It reminded her of Florida. She wished she wouldn't have taken it all for granted when the world was normal.

After Leon capped the canteen and returned it to the back of the humvee, he motioned to her left hand and asked, "Want me to help you with that?"

Courtney gazed down at her pinky finger. It was looking even more grotesque now. Puss was seeping from the blister and the skin around it was black and peeling. However, since finding out Leon was still alive, this was the first time she noticed how much her hand trembled on its own.

She asked, "What do we have?"

He paused a moment to think, then replied, "There's Neosporin in the first aid kit. Should be cold wraps too."

She nodded and said, "Alright."

Leon leaned inside the humvee and retrieved the first aid kit she had used to clean his bite wound. He fished out the Neosporin and the cold wraps.

He said, "Okay doll, give me the finger. And I don't mean that in a vulgar way."

She smiled a bit, then turned her head away long enough to sniffle and wipe her eyes just in case emotions were getting the best of her. Then she turned to face Leon again and extended her scorched pinky finger.

He squeezed some Neosporin out of the tube and onto his index finger, then dabbed the cream lightly on Courtney's pinky. When he had it covered he tore off a piece of cold wrap and put it over her finger, making certain the adhesive was sticking only to the healthy skin near her bottom knuckle and not on anything tender. Finished, he returned the unused supplies to the first aid kit and put the box back in the humvee.

She inspected the bandage on her finger, realizing the skin would be scarred forever. After a moment she softly stated, "This sucks. My finger's gonna be deformed for the rest of my life."

"Maybe, but it's just your finger," Leon replied, taking her hand and examining it. "The rest of you will still be beautiful."

She grunted and pulled her hand away. She stammered, "Don't."

"Don't *what*?"

"Don't flirt with me. Not now."

"Not now? Why?"

She turned away and faced the ocean again. She mumbled, "I'm sorry. I'm sorry about *everything*."

Leon exhaled deeply and then leaned against the fender of the humvee.

Courtney watched the sea gulls for a while as they went about their routine, all of them oblivious to the happenings in the human world. Her body trembled as she thought about Eastpointe and the army of zombies marching there to attack it. If Dane used a pipe bomb to blow up the wall as he mentioned —and if he did so where patrols where few and far between —then it was quite possible everyone in Eastpointe would be devoured before they even figured out what the explosion was.

The worst part was that she knew she could never make it to Eastpointe in time to warn them. Dane would be taking his army via the most direct route, so even if she somehow got past them or went around them and beat them to their destination, she knew precious moments would be wasted trying to explain to the Superintendent and the Committees about the danger headed their way. It would be hard to convince them she was serious, that this wasn't a joke, and that Dr. Aaron Dane had really assembled his own undead army and was currently leading them to conquer the last bastion of living humans.

Courtney gritted her teeth and smacked her palm against the side of the humvee. Too many thoughts were going through her mind to allow her to stop and focus on any of them.

She remembered Dane mentioning a pack leader and that zombies worked in a pack mentality when there wasn't any food nearby. She knew the handbox Dane used somehow sent signals to the zombies, but what if it only sent signals to *one* zombie? That sounded right. Dane would only need to send signals to the pack leader and the rest would follow. Not only that, but other zombies the army met would also fall in line and follow the pack. Courtney realized that could add up to at least a thousand if Dane led his army through Wakefield.

There may be even more. If zombies just lying around somewhere somehow sensed that a large herd was moving, they may get up and follow even if it was from miles away. She wasn't totally sure how far away a zombie's senses could work, but she knew she had to factor it into her reasoning.

She turned to face Leon again.

He had his head down and his arms crossed. He didn't look very healthy at all. She knew it would only be a couple of hours before he got too sick to move. He would be coughing and vomiting and then several hours after that he would be comatose. He would then die and reanimate.

However, a Black Beret never got that far. Usually they swallowed their barbiturates long before now. Leon was setting some kind of record.

She said, "Everyone at Eastpointe is going to die unless we stop Dane before he gets there."

Leon lifted his head and gazed at her. He replied, "We?"

She nodded, pulling her hair back and tucking it behind her ears.

She explained, "Yeah. If we can take out the lead zombie and then take out Dane before he creates a new leader, the zombies will just stop marching and lay down. They won't migrate unless they're being led. We don't have to fight them all. We just have to kill Dane and the pack leader. We can do it."

Leon shook his head side-to-side and weakly stated, "I'm sorry, doll. But this beach is really nice. I think I'm just going to lay down and take my pills."

"No," she said. "I need you. I can't do this alone."

Leon sighed and looked away, appearing to stare at the reflection of the sun on the calm ocean waves. He kicked at the sand at his feet. "I think I understand why Black Berets take their pills so quick after being infected," he said. "It's because they know the inevitability of death. They want to die before that fact really hits home. That's what I want too. I don't want to sit here and cry. I don't want to be depressed about it. I want to keep my pride and die quietly. If you were me, you'd understand."

Courtney stepped in front of him and looked into his eyes. She softly said, "Leon, I need you. We have to do this together or everyone's gonna die."

"What do you care?!" he snapped. "Since when do you give a damn about anybody at Eastpointe?!"

"Of course I care," she stuttered. "What, do you think I'm totally heartless or something?"

"You live in your own world anyway," he continued, glaring. "Why don't you just find a nice little island someplace where you can be alone for real? Swim to Martha's Vineyard or Block Island for Christ's sake. Clear out a house and spend the rest of your life dreaming about James Spader. What the hell do you want from me?!"

Without hesitation or anger, Courtney replied, "Your *help*."

"But what can I do? I already feel this gross stuff building up in my lungs and I'm gonna start hacking and coughing like an eighty year-old smoker. I'm not going to be much help. Just let me die."

Courtney crossed her arms and told him, "I'm not exactly stopping you. What you mean is that you need me to put a bullet in your head after your heart stops."

Leon nodded.

"Well, *fine*," Courtney said. "Help me kill Dane and I'll make sure you don't reanimate after you swallow your pills. Fair?"

Leon sighed and shrugged his shoulders. A throbbing red vein was visible beneath the pale skin on his forehead. The color in his blue eyes was fading a little. His hair was falling messily across his ears and one of his eyes and altogether he looked very weary.

He said, "Fine. Let's kill that psycho."

Courtney looked away and sniffled, then replied, "Glad you're with me."

Leon started digging through the supplies in the back of the humvee. He said, "No more visors or berets, doll. We've got another sword and a couple rifles here, but not much ammo. There are a couple Socoms, but they're not assembled. I'll have to attach the laser sights and load up some magazines. I'm pretty sure they're in a box back here somewhere." He paused a moment as he reached deep to retrieve something buried under the cooler, then added, "And here's another belt for you."

She took the belt and fastened it around her hips, taking the time to secure the lower holster strap around her right leg. She took another wakizashi and scabbard but held on to it for now instead of fastening it to her belt right away.

She said, "Let's get moving."

Leon grabbed a couple of handguns and laser sights, along with a couple of rifles and scopes and a box of ammunition for both. He walked around the humvee and climbed onto the passenger seat. He immediately started attaching the laser sights to the handguns and loading bullets into magazines.

Courtney walked around to the driver's-side door, but stopped halfway. She leaned with her back against the humvee, then lowered her head and closed her eyes.

It was hard not to be overwhelmed.

She sniffled and wiped her eyes —just in case there was any emotional residue —then opened the driver's-side door and climbed onto the seat.

She held her breath as she turned the ignition, thinking that Dane might have taken the time to somehow booby-trap it or something. Despite her fears, the engine started without a hitch. She shifted into gear, let out the clutch, and the humvee sped forward down the sandy beach.

As the tires met the gravel on the road leading through the forest, Leon looked up from the magazines he was loading and commented, "Do you ever miss fiddling with the radio?"

She turned her head long enough to glance at him, then faced the road again. She asked, "What do you mean?"

"It's just that every time I ride shotgun I'm still in the habit of wanting to cycle through the radio stations. Kind of stupid, huh?"

She shook her head and softly stated, "No, it's not stupid."

BLACK BERET ADVANCED UNARMED TECHNIQUE

Judo Hip Toss with Heel Stomp

Diagrams are used only to illustrate progression of maneuver. As with all maneuvers discussed in this manual, your instructor will guide you through the exact steps and sign off once execution of technique has met satisfactory approval.

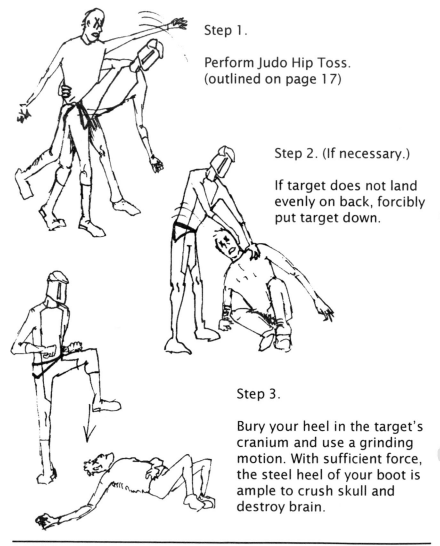

Step 1.

Perform Judo Hip Toss.
(outlined on page 17)

Step 2. (If necessary.)

If target does not land evenly on back, forcibly put target down.

Step 3.

Bury your heel in the target's cranium and use a grinding motion. With sufficient force, the steel heel of your boot is ample to crush skull and destroy brain.

Return to the Dead City

Dane's trail was easy enough to follow.

Despite being the very same road the Black Berets had traveled originally, everywhere she looked zombies were being pulled out of hibernation and drawn to the pack like a magnet. She simply went in the same direction the walking corpses were going.

There were all kinds —men and women and children zombies, plainly-dressed zombies, formally-dressed zombies, policemen zombies, postal worker zombies, even a zombie in full football gear, minus only the helmet. However, no matter what gender, race, occupation, or age they were before becoming infected and reanimating, they were all pretty much the same now.

—Wrinkled, with blue skin.

Some of them had wounds that would be fatal to a living human. One had an exposed ribcage, another was missing both its arms, and another had a large gash running from its ear all the way down to its waist. These injuries might have been received when they were still alive and could have been what killed them, or the injuries might have been sustained after reanimating, which meant they didn't feel the pain at all. Either way, it certainly wasn't slowing them down today.

And Courtney didn't bother slowing down either. Any dead person getting in her way was promptly rammed with the bull bars. This humvee was very familiar to her, after all, so handling it felt much more natural than any of the others she had driven.

The further she went the more tightly packed the zombies became. Eventually she had to forsake ramming them in favor of simply going around. It was quicker than climbing a pile of disfigured corpses.

The trail eventually led back to Wakefield. The sun was only shining through the narrow alleyways now, highlighting the heads and shoulders of the zombie citizens and proving that the day was coming to an end. This was what she had feared; that Dane would take his army down Main Street and amass hundreds of more recruits. None of the zombies here were lying down anymore. All of them were on their feet, staggering after the more nimble armored zombies Dane had previously outfitted. Courtney could see the vanguard about fifty yards up the road, but the ordinary zombies following them were packed shoulder-to-shoulder on Main Street. It would be impossible to ram her way up to the leader.

Leon pointed and said, "I don't believe it. Look at that."

Courtney's eyes followed where his finger was pointing until she saw what he was indicating. She couldn't believe it either —parked off to the right of the street in downtown Wakefield, out of the way of the undead parade, was the second humvee —the same one Dane had stolen.

Leon screwed a silencer onto his handgun and started rolling down his window. He said, "Get alongside it. Let's get this over with."

Courtney steered their humvee past the masses of walking corpses and slowly pulled up next to the other humvee. Leon had his Socom aimed out the window. She could see the red targeting laser pinpointing a dot at the approximate area where someone's head would be if they were sitting normally on the driver's seat in the other vehicle. However, once she got fully in line with the second humvee, they both could see very clearly that no one occupied it.

"What the hell?" said Leon. "Where could he have gone?"

By now they had drawn unwanted attention from a few dozen zombies in the procession, and these zombies were currently straying from the herd to come pound on the windows on the left side of their vehicle, trying to get at the humans inside.

Courtney gave them a glance, then again focused her attention on the second humvee and the missing messiah. Besides, she knew from experience that the windows of her humvee were shatterproof. The worst those zombies could do was hold the vehicle under siege.

"Would Dane be walking?" asked Leon.

Courtney looked over the hood of their humvee and beyond the heads of the mob of dead people migrating down Main Street. She knew zombies didn't look upon Dane as a viable source of food, so she figured maybe he had decided to play George Washington and lead them into battle himself. However, she could still see the armored zombies at the vanguard and Dane wasn't with them.

She then realized he would probably want to be someplace where he had full view of the procession. He would need to guide the pack leader with his remote control and make sure it didn't lead the herd into any crashed semis or flooded areas caused by the dam break at the Indian Run Reservoir.

Peering through the windows of both humvees, Courtney caught sight of a fire escape in the alleyway next to the building beside them. The stairs went back and forth up several flights, then a ladder at the summit went the rest of the way to the rooftop.

That must have been where Dane went.

Courtney pointed and said, "There."

Leon looked and saw the winding fire escape for himself. He followed it up with his eyes, gulping when he reached the very top. He uttered, *"More heights."*

She asked, "Are you ready for this?"

"Now or never."

He handed her a Socom modified with the laser sight and silencer she was accustomed to. She slipped it in the holster on her right leg, then attached the scabbard containing the wakizashi to the V-shaped strap on her left leg. She slid three extra loaded magazines for the handgun into the slots in the back of her belt. Finally she grabbed another rifle and slung it over her shoulder. All she lacked was a visor and a beret and a glove to replace the one missing from her left hand and she would once again be perfectly outfitted as a Black Beret was meant to be.

Ready to go, she glanced out her window and saw the hundreds of hungry corpses waiting for her on the other side. Some of them were trampling the others so they could press their faces to the glass and stare at her. They hadn't yet ventured to the area between the two humvees on Leon's side of the vehicle.

She said, "I think we'll go out through *your* door."

He solemnly replied, "Good idea."

Leon readied his weapons, then lifted the handle and threw the door open. Courtney followed him out and they immediately dashed around the second humvee and into the alleyway. The mob of zombies that had strayed from the herd staggered after them, but the ones in front were put down with a single shot each from Courtney's silenced handgun, the red dot on their foreheads replaced with a gaping bullet hole. As they fell it caused the ones behind them to trip and stumble, effectively slowing them down.

A lone meter-maid zombie was blocking the fire escape. Rather than waste a bullet, Leon tossed the ghoul over his hip. Once it landed on its back, he planted his metal heel in the creature's skull, then scraped off the gooey residue on the stairs. Courtney figured it must have been like therapy for Leon for everything he had already been through.

They ran up the noisy metal fire escape, leaving the streets behind.

Like so many dead cities, gaspless moans and the stench of decay were everywhere in Wakefield. It certainly wasn't the most pleasant place to fight for humanity's right to live. Nevertheless, Courtney knew that in the event of an apocalypse any field of Megiddo would have to do.

Heights

Vastly outnumbered yet having the advantage of greater mobility and higher ground, Courtney and Leon surveyed the town of Wakefield from the rooftop. There were a string of zombies stretching back as far as their eyes could see —*thousands* —and all of them were scampering to join the herd. On the other side of the building, stray zombies could be seen emerging from the flooded areas of town. Thankfully none had scaled the fire escapes to join them on the roof.

Now they just needed to find Dane.

Courtney took the rifle off her shoulder and pointed it into the distance, using the scope to view the rooftops far away. Most of the buildings in downtown Wakefield were the same height. None of them seemed to rise above six stories tall, so there was only about a ten-foot difference in some places. Most had a shack or a trap door with a staircase or a ladder that would lead down inside. She knew if she didn't take care of Dane fast enough he might retreat into one of the buildings and hide, in which case she would probably never find him again.

She figured he would be near the vanguard of his army, but the rooftops in that direction were bare. She then turned her rifle in the direction she and Leon had traveled, towards Point Judith Neck.

That was when she discovered Dane.

He was hiding behind a small greenhouse erected on top of a building five rooftops away. Though she couldn't see him directly due to the translucent panes of glass, his shadow betrayed him. The sun was beginning to fall from the west, so its light was concentrated to the east —right through the glass panes of the greenhouse, casting a long silhouette of his figure across the rooftop. It had to be him — the shadow of the antenna on the remote control he was holding gave it away.

She knew she would need to be much closer to fire an effective shot. Dane's position was simply too far away and she couldn't judge where exactly his head would be on the other side of the greenhouse.

An old piece of rusty iron grating was situated between her rooftop and the next, forming a makeshift bridge over the alley. It was only three feet wide and it was hard to tell how long it had been there. It didn't look very secure, but that must have been what Dane used to cross over.

She lowered her rifle and turned back to Leon. "I know where he's at," she said. "He knows we're here. He's hiding from us."

"No, he's probably setting a *trap*," Leon replied. He covered his mouth to suppress a cough, his face tensing up from the pressure in his lungs. He painfully continued, "If he's smart enough to organize an undead-pride parade, then he's smart enough to bait us into something."

"Won't happen," she told him. She pointed to the rooftops in the other direction, past the vanguard of the mob, and said, "I'll take Dane. You get the pack leader. Get in front of them where you can get a clear shot through the eyes of its helmet. Don't go back down to the street. Stay up high."

"You think I'm an action hero or something?" Leon scoffed, motioning with his arm to the gaping chasm three buildings away. "There's an alley to jump over."

"You can do it, stud. Just get the pack leader. It'll be the only one that doesn't look so damned aimless. You'll recognize it."

Unable to hold back any longer, Leon turned away from her, leaned over and put his hands on his knees, then began a coughing fit so hard and fierce that it startled even her. It sounded wet, like he was on the verge of vomiting.

Courtney put her hand on his shoulder and tried to comfort him. She whispered, "We're almost done. The pack leader is probably the only zombie Dane equipped with a receiver to collect the signals he's transmitting. If we stop the pack leader and Dane at the same time, it'll be over."

Leon continued coughing, eventually spewing droplets of gross yellow saliva. After taking a few moments to get his lungs under control again, he mumbled, "I'm trying, doll. I really am. I just don't feel too good right now."

She stepped in front of him and lifted his head so she could see his face. Though his physical appearance hadn't worsened since the beach, she knew the infection inside his body was multiplying and consuming his organs. He was obviously trying to hide this pain from her, but his legs were noticeably trembling.

Through pale, chapped lips he uttered, "I bet you don't think I'm such a pretty guy anymore, do you?"

She forced a slight grin as she replied, "You're still a pretty guy."

"So you finally admit it?" he asked. "You sleep with me, but you have to wait until I'm dying before you pay me a compliment?"

"You're not *dying*."

"Save it for the tourists," he replied, bringing himself fully upright again. "Let's get this over with."

She took a step back and nodded her head with finality.

"Be careful with Dane," said Leon.

"I will," she replied. "You be careful too. We'll meet back here when we're finished."

He nodded, though they both knew that meeting again might not be possible.

Leon took the rifle off his shoulder and held it at ready as he walked to the other side of the rooftop. He threw a leg over the short wall and put his foot on the adjoining building, then continued in the direction the zombies were headed on the street below.

Confronting the Messiah

The wind rippling calmly through her hair, Courtney carefully balanced her feet on the grating that spanned across the alley between the two buildings. It was wobbly and made all kinds of noises under her weight, but she knew it had to be what Dane used to get to where he was. If the bridge supported *his* weight, then she knew it could support *hers*.

Several zombies had flocked to the area below. Some were ascending the fire escape she and Leon had used to access the rooftop, but she knew it would take them a long time to reach the summit. When they did, they would then have to negotiate the ladder extending from the top floor to the rooftop. Zombies weren't known for their outstanding coordination, but they *were* known for their persistence. They would be able to climb the ladder, but it would take even more time than climbing up the stairs on the fire escape.

She wasn't too worried about them, even as their moans and groans echoed up the alley and haunted her ears.

She finished crossing the bridge, then hopped down on the adjacent rooftop. She took her rifle off her shoulder and slid the bolt lever back then forward again to load a bullet into the firing chamber. She hurried across the rooftop, heading to where Dane was hiding. Luckily there were no more alleys to cross. Every building between her and her target was flush.

As she stepped over to the next rooftop, she found a fully clothed human skeleton in a sitting position against the wall. Its biker-style leather attire suggested it was male. A large hole erupted out of the top of its head. A rusty discolored shotgun was positioned vertically across the chest, the barrel situated below the jaw and the butt planted between the corpse's legs. A bony index finger was still stuck in the trigger guard.

Unlike the corpse she had seen dangling from the noose over Main Street on her first trip through Wakefield, this body had no suicide note. The person probably figured it was a waste of time to write a letter. After all, the city was populated only by the undead and they weren't known to be heavy readers.

This corpse, however, was a likely candidate to have been the one to place the metal grating over the alleyway. She wondered if the person ever considered that someone else would be using the makeshift bridge all these years later.

She passed the corpse and continued across the rooftop.

There were only three buildings separating her and her target now; a distance of about fifty yards.

She figured this was close enough.

She lifted her rifle and took aim.

Dane's silhouette had changed somewhat. Now instead of the shadow of the remote control in his hands, there was a shadow of a revolver —probably the same one he had had pressed to her head on the cruiseliner.

She squinted her left eye and peered through the scope with her right eye. She took a few moments to judge where his head might be on the other side of the greenhouse, then situated the crosshairs in that area.

She steadied her shoulder and pulled the trigger.

These .22 Hornets didn't give off much noise when fired and since they were for distance shooting, silencers weren't necessary. The unmuffled sound of the gun was quite satisfying for Courtney, especially when the fired bullet burst through the panes of the greenhouse and sent shards of glass crashing to the rooftop in a fantastic display of lights and colors.

Dane's silhouette was moving sporadically, showing panic. She could see some of the area on the other side of the greenhouse through the broken glass, but none of Dane's body was visible. She waited for a moment, hoping he might come out of hiding, but he didn't.

She cocked the rifle and took aim again, situating the crosshairs in the area where Dane's head might be.

She pulled the trigger.

Another satisfying firing sound came from the rifle and an even more satisfying crashing sound of glass breaking followed. The entire frame of the greenhouse was beginning to crumble now, losing stability due to the missing panes that used to help support it. As more and more of the structure fell, more of the area beyond was becoming visible. Soon she saw a most promising sight:

Blood.

It was sprayed against the glass on the far side the greenhouse.

She knew now that she had hit her mark —hopefully fatally.

She saw the revolver fall and clatter to the rooftop, then Dane emerged from behind the greenhouse, blood spilling from the shoulder where his familiar satchel bag dangled. He appeared to be heading to the stairway shack on the other side.

Courtney quickly fired her rifle again, missing. She cocked it and took aim once more, trying to keep up with the moving target.

Her next shot sent a bullet into Dane's arm, spilling more blood across the rooftop. However, he appeared unfazed and hardly lost his stride. When he reached the door to the stairway, Courtney cocked the rifle and put a bullet into the door.

This was enough to finally deter Dane. Instead of opening the door and running inside, he dashed around the shack and hid on the other side.

All of her rifle ammunition depleted, Courtney laid it down and pulled the Socom from its holster. She knew she had expended most of the magazine shooting zombies on the street, so she dropped it and loaded a new one.

She held the handgun at ready as she hurried across the rooftops to get closer to Dane. She cast occasional glances at the revolver he had dropped, making sure he didn't try to retrieve it.

As she got near she heard him yell, "You shot me!"

"Well, *duh*, asshole!" she replied. "Does it hurt?!"

"Of course not!" he called back. "It's just annoying! You should have stayed locked up on the ship! Now I'm going to catch you and I'm going to eat you!"

Courtney didn't return a taunt. She slowed down as she stepped over the short wall separating the rooftops and then sidestepped around the shack Dane hid behind, staying far away so he couldn't get a jump on her. She kept the red dot from the laser sight at the approximate height of his head, waiting for him to appear so he could eat a bullet.

"I bet you'll be soft and tender!" Dane shouted from the other side of the shack, laughing maniacally. "You'll taste good with ketchup!"

From the direction of his voice, she realized he was circling around the shack the opposite way, keeping the obstruction between them. She fired three shots into the rotting wood in one-foot intervals, hoping maybe they would go all the way through and hit him.

None appeared to. Dane was still laughing like the whole thing was a joke. If he had been shot again he certainly didn't care.

Courtney continued sidestepping, then dashed back the way she came, hoping to cut him off. However, Dane predicted her movement and stayed away.

Frustrated, Courtney shouted, "C'mon, Dane! I'm tired of playing ring around the rosey! Come out and I'll make it quick!"

"But I can keep this up forever!" he retorted. "I'm *immortal*, stupid girl."

"I'm *twenty-two*, dumbass!"

"And you could have been twenty-two forever if you'd have used the syringe I left for you! Now you're going to be naked on a platter with an apple shoved in your mouth!" Then, in singsong, he added, "*I'm-gonna-eat-you-uuuuup!*"

Having enough of this game, Courtney sprayed the shack with bullets from her Socom, keeping them all at head level and sending splints of wood flying through the air.

Dane simply laughed during the entire onslaught. When it was over, she could see one of his eyes peeking at her through one of the many holes the bullets left in their wake. She dropped the magazine from her gun and quickly locked in a new one. If she had to bring down the whole shack to get to him, then so be it.

However, just as soon as she locked the new magazine into the butt of her gun, Dane seized the opportunity and dashed from around the shack and lunged at her. She hurriedly lifted her gun and fired two rounds, one hitting him in the shoulder and the other missing entirely.

She didn't get a chance to fire again.

He was already on her, latching on to the barrel of the gun with both hands and aiming it away from his body. She tried forcing the silencer towards his head, but he was too strong.

They went to the ground, both struggling for control of the gun. Courtney instinctively went to her back and used her legs to form a Jiu-Jitsu guard, preventing him from gaining leverage by keeping her feet planted on the insides of his hips. While he wasn't able to move up on her, he was able to slip a finger into the trigger guard of the Socom and force her own finger to squeeze off the remaining rounds in the magazine.

Every bullet flew into the air unanswered until there were no more bullets left and the gun made only a clicking sound when the trigger was pulled. Both Courtney and Dane gave up on the gun and allowed it to fall to the rooftop.

He tried punching her, but his fists swung like uncoordinated sledgehammers and he was grunting before each one to add extra impact. He may as well have been sending a telegraph to announce their arrival.

She ducked her head left and right and dodged them all. The closest one got was barely nicking her ear.

He then reached forward with both hands, spreading his fingers, making it obvious he was going to attempt to choke her.

She elevated her legs and rolled onto her shoulders to prevent him from grabbing hold. She then shifted her hips, putting her body perpendicular under his, and swung one leg around to try trapping his right arm so she could lock it between her legs and break it with a thrust of her pelvis, but he was too strong and he easily pulled his arm free.

She seriously doubted he knew Jiu-Jitsu —much less the maneuvers she was attempting —but despite his sissy temperament the pansy was actually pretty tough.

None of her tricks were working.

As she struggled beneath his weight, she could hear another .22 Hornet being fired in the distance. It meant that Leon had caught up to the pack leader and was putting bullets into its brain.

There were three shots, then silence.

Leon had done it.

"You know what that was?" Courtney gritted, staring up at Dane and catching her breath. "That was the sound of your army being put down. How's it feel to be a *loser*?"

Dane snarled and reached out to try to choke her again.

Courtney trapped his arms against her chest and grabbed his sweater with both hands, feeling the chainmail underneath, then pulled him forward as she kicked his knees out from under him, causing him to lose his balance. She swept him off and quickly stood up.

She drew her wakizashi.

Dane scurried away on his hands and knees to the remains of the greenhouse about twenty feet away. He picked up a long shard of glass and then stood up and pointed it at her in a threatening manner.

His crude weapon didn't stack up too well when compared to her sword. Courtney could tell Dane understood this. She could see the fear growing in his eyes.

"You know it's not just me you'd be killing," Dane uttered, almost stuttering. "You'd be killing evolution itself."

"What happened to the world wasn't *evolution*, you psycho," Courtney replied.

"It *is* evolution!" shouted Dane, throwing his arms in the air and waving the shard of glass like a baton. "You know how I know? Because zombies attack and feed only on warm flesh! They don't kill *each other*! Before the dead began to rise, all we humans did was make war and rape and pillage and plunder like a bunch of goddamn pirates! Zombies are beyond that! They're *above* humans! Can't you see it?!"

Courtney raised the wakizashi and started to step forward.

"Wait! Just wait!" Dane shouted. He removed the satchel bag from his shoulder and displayed it to her. It was covered with blood from the many times he had been shot. He said, "Don't kill me. I'm going to get something out of this bag. It's not a gun or anything. Just let me show you."

Before Courtney could reply, he slowly opened the bag and reached into it. When he pulled his hand out —*slowly* —he had another syringe gripped in his fingers. This one had pinkish liquid swishing around inside and the capped needle was almost six inches long.

It wasn't another tranquilizer and it wasn't the green gunk he left with her on the bridge of the cruiseliner. It was something else entirely.

He whispered, "*Do you know what this is?*"

She answered, "Should I care?"

Dane rolled his eyes and said, "Use your head."

"What?"

"Your head! It's that useless lump three feet above your ass!"

Having quite enough of this standoff, Courtney readied her wakizashi and stepped forward again. However, she stopped in her tracks when Dane casually tossed the syringe at her feet.

It laid there on the rooftop, shining under the setting sun. She gazed down at it for a moment, then back up at Dane.

He informed her, "That's the Cure —The one and only. I saw your boyfriend in the humvee when you drove into town. He's infected, isn't he?"

"He's not my boyfriend," Courtney solemnly replied. "But *yes*, thanks to you, he's infected."

"Then take that syringe and leave me alone. Stop interfering with evolution and the natural order of things. Take him and find an island somewhere and spend the rest of your lives making wild, passionate love. Just leave me alone."

Courtney could admit that Dane's somewhat romantic French-Canadian mannerisms almost made him sound convincing. He probably would have made a very good spokesman for some expensive brand of cologne.

Then again, she knew there was no such thing as a Cure.

"I'm not stupid, Dane," she said. "Why would a freak like you carry a cure around when you just want to kill every last living human?"

"The reasons should be obvious," Dane replied. "I locked you up and left you a serum so you could be immortal like me, but I knew there was a chance you wouldn't use it. If I found another attractive lady after the attack on Eastpointe, I could save her if she had been bitten and bring her back to you. If you used the serum, we could dine together. If you didn't, the other lady surely would and we would dine on *you*."

Courtney gulped and gazed down at the syringe once more. No matter how creepy his explanation was, it made sense in its own diabolical little way.

She knelt down to pick up the syringe, keeping her wakizashi pointed toward Dane.

As she did this, Dane tucked the shard of glass under his arm and pulled a very familiar lighter out of his pocket. He then took something else from the satchel bag —a cylindrical aluminum pipe about five inches wide and a foot and a half long. It was capped at both ends.

Courtney stood up once more, syringe in hand.

Dane was smiling as he put the lighter to the end of the pipe where a fuse was sticking out. He held this position, threatening to ignite it as he calmly explained, "I never lied about finding a Cure. I never lied about using a pipe bomb to destroy Eastpointe's walls either. It would be a shame to use it here and now, but I will if I have to. *Leave.*"

Courtney tucked the syringe into her belt where extra rifle ammunition used to be stored. It fit nice and snug. She then gripped the hilt of the wakizashi with both hands, getting a firm hold.

She reeled back the blade and stepped forward.

"You don't have time to fight me!" Dane shouted, hurriedly lighting the fuse. "This'll go boom in thirty seconds!"

Courtney replied, "Thirty seconds? I only need *one.*"

BLACK BERET ADVANCED WAKIZASHI TECHNIQUE

Two Step Decapitation

Diagrams are used only to illustrate progression of maneuver. As with all maneuvers discussed in this manual, your instructor will guide you through the exact steps and sign off once execution of technique has met satisfactory approval.

Step 1.

Target approaching.

Wakizashi drawn and ready.

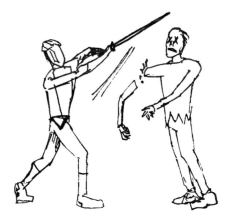

Step 2.

Remove arm of target with fast upward stroke.

Basic knowledge of wakizashi use is required.

Step 3.

Spin on <u>left</u> heel, moving to undefended zone of target.

This step should be fluid.

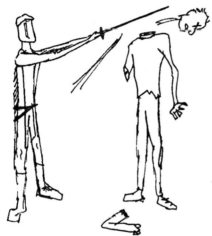

Step 4.

With arm removed, there is no obstruction.

Using momentum gained from spin, decapitate target with hard stroke left to right.

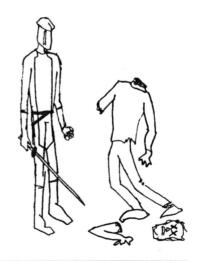

Note: Execution of entire technique should be fluid and require less than one (1) second. Your instructor will time you.

One Second Later

Had she been a lip-reader, she might have realized what Dane was trying to say were the foulest obscenities a man can throw at a woman. It proved that —just like zombies —Dane's head would continue to function when severed as long as the brain was undamaged. However, since he no longer had access to his vocal cords, he couldn't give sounds to the curses his mouth was forming.

It didn't matter though. He wasn't going anywhere.

Next to his head was his severed arm, chainmail sliced cleanly in two. Though the arm didn't move, it still held the pipe bomb in a tight grip between its fingers. Courtney kneeled down and pulled the bomb loose, then pinched the fuse between her thumb and forefinger of her gloved hand. To her dismay, the sparks continued to burn down the fuse from the inside out.

Panicking, she flung the bomb off the roof where it fell six stories down to Main Street. It bounced off some random zombie's head, leaving a large dent in its cranium, and landed on the pavement amidst hundreds of shuffling feet.

Covering her ears, Courtney peered over the edge to watch the result.

It was magnificent really. There was a thunderous boom and a fiery explosion that sent every zombie in a thirty-foot radius sailing through the air in little bits and pieces and dominoing many others, showering them with blood. When the dust settled and the smoke cleared, there was a large crater in the middle of the road.

Courtney uncovered her ears.

She picked up her wakizashi and sheathed it, then picked up her Socom where it had been lost during the struggle with Dane. She reached into the back of her belt for another clip and loaded it into the gun. Finally, she situated the red dot on Dane's forehead and pulled the trigger. His existence ended rather awkwardly in mid-swear with his tongue dangling out of his mouth.

Courtney dashed back across the rooftops.

Leon was on the other side of the bridge across the alley, putting bullets into the heads of all the zombies who had followed them up the ladder. There were at least thirty walking around on the rooftop now, with many more already terminated and lying face down.

Courtney began highlighting their heads with the red dot and pulling the trigger. When her clip was exhausted, she dropped it and loaded the final one. With five more shots and Leon's help, they cleared all but one of the zombies. Deciding to save her last few bullets, Courtney gave the final zombie —some horrendously ugly dead guy with wire-frame glasses —a hard front kick to the ribcage, sending it head over heels off the roof and down to the alley below.

However, it landed on something a lot softer than concrete.

Peering down there, Courtney could see that every zombie in Wakefield was gathering around the building, shoulder-to-shoulder as they clawed at the bricks. She could not even see the actual street beneath their bodies. Hundreds more undead were in line coming up the fire escape and negotiating the ladder. They had also engulfed the two humvees parked below. Everywhere she looked, wrinkled blue faces were staring back at her.

In her hurried plan to eliminate Dane, this was something she had forgotten to factor in. Since there wasn't a pack leader herding the zombies anymore, the entire undead army was coming after the food stranded on the rooftop above.

The odds were not in her favor.

Twilight

Leon staggered across the makeshift bridge to the rooftop Courtney was on and then collapsed, sitting weakly with his back against the wall. His arms hung lazily at his sides and he let go of his gun.

He started coughing.

Groaning and gritting her teeth, Courtney grabbed the sides of the heavy metal grating and lifted it enough to drop it down into the alley. It whistled as it fell, then came down hard on the skulls of several zombies, crushing them upon impact. Now it didn't matter how many ghouls came up the fire escape —they still wouldn't be able to cross the chasm and get to their meal on the other side.

Courtney went to Leon and knelt in front of him. She said, "They're all over the humvees. They're *everywhere.* But we might be able to cross the next rooftop and find a way down somewhere else."

He lifted his weary head, eyelids halfway closed, forced a cough to stay in his chest by swallowing it back down, then muttered, "You can, but I'm just going to stay *here.* Sorry."

She reached into her belt and pulled out the syringe Dane had given her. She displayed it to Leon and said, "You're going to be okay. This is the Cure."

He forced his eyelids open and replied, "Says who? Says *Dane*?"

"Yeah," she said. "I think he was telling the truth."

"And what if he wasn't? What if it causes me more pain?"

"Leon—"

"—*No,*" he interrupted. "I'm *dying,* Courtney. I don't want any more complications. I just want to go easy."

Courtney dropped the syringe and put her palms on his cheeks, forcing him to look into her eyes. She sternly told him, "Leon, *yes,* you are dying. And you *will die* unless we take a chance that Dane was telling the truth."

Leon weakly shook his head side-to-side.

"Leon, *please,*" Courtney begged, "Let me do this. Let me at least *try* to help you."

Leon, seeing wetness forming across her eyelids, asked, "*Why*?"

She swallowed hard. She knew there were a lot of reasons why

186

she didn't want him to die and she knew she didn't have time to discuss them all. For starters, it would take both of them working together to even have a *chance* of escaping this dead city. If one died the other would probably end up like the leather-clad corpse on the next rooftop who had swallowed his own shotgun. Besides that, she wanted to tell Leon that maybe he wasn't such a bad guy after all and that she thought he died once already and she didn't like it. On top of that, there weren't many decent guys left in the world to pick from. She didn't want him to simply fade away.

So she stated, "*I don't want you to die.*"

He sighed and turned his head. He mumbled, "It might be too late anyway."

"But it might *not*," she quickly replied.

"And suppose it *is* the Cure," he pointed out, "Are you sure you want to use the last of it on *me*?"

She gently turned his head so he was looking at her again and very sincerely replied, "*Yes.* Every drop of it."

He stared into her eyes and she stared back.

After a moment he whispered, "Okay, we'll give it a try."

With a breath of relief, Courtney pulled the cap off the needle and —after seeing how long and thick it truly was —commented, "I think it has to be injected straight into your heart."

"*What*?!"

"Your *heart*," she repeated. "You know, like an adrenaline shot?"

"You're using a lot of guesswork here."

"But it makes sense. By injecting it directly into your heart it would spread the dormant infection through your bloodstream a lot faster. Don't you remember Dane's lecture?"

Leon weakly shrugged his shoulders and mumbled, "Dane was full of shit about a lot of things."

Courtney motioned for him to lean forward, then she unzipped his wetsuit in the back and pulled it off his shoulders, minding the bandaged bite wound, and tugged it off his arms.

His torso was no longer just pale —it was turning blue.

Courtney ran her finger over his chest, using it to feel for the area where his heart was beating. When she found it she memorized it before pulling her hand away.

She hoped it wasn't too late.

She sniffled and wiped her eyes, clearing her vision. Her breath was beginning to flutter. She forced herself to stay strong just a little longer.

She took aim with the needle and reeled it back. She knew she would need a lot of force and momentum to pierce his breastplate.

She whispered, "Are you ready?"

He nodded.

With one powerful stroke she drove the needle into his chest and pushed the plunger. Leon's head fell back and his mouth opened and he screamed long and loud —so loud he drowned out the moans and groans of the dead city.

His body startled convulsing.

She pulled out the needle and tossed it, then wrapped her arms around him to hold him still. His body shook for several more seconds, then gradually the shaking subsided.

She let go and studied his face, almost expecting him to be dead, but he was still very much alive. Actually, nothing seemed to change at all.

She asked, "Do you feel any different?"

He paused for a moment as he evaluated his condition, then replied, "I can't tell."

Courtney sat down beside him and leaned against the wall as zombies on the adjacent rooftop started moaning and hollering even louder, angry that they could no longer see their would-be meal. She situated herself close to Leon and let her head rest on his shoulder. She brought her knees up to her chest and wrapped her arms around them, locking her fingers.

They had a nice view of the setting sun from here.

After a moment Leon said, "If I'm still alive in the morning we'll see about getting out of here."

"And we'll know the Cure works," Courtney added. "We can go back to the ship and search for more. *Later*, of course."

"Oh, hell with that," Leon tiredly replied. "Somebody else can do it."

"Good idea."

He turned his head to face her and softly added, "But if it doesn't work you're going to have to shoot me. You know that, right?"

Courtney sniffled and nodded slightly. She whispered, "I know."

Together they watched the sun go down. Aside from the riotous noise of all the moaning and groaning and shuffling feet of the thousands of undead surrounding them, it was a perfect twilight.

And she didn't take it for granted.

BEFORE TWILIGHT
GLIMPSES OF THE PAST

NΛSΛ

NATIONAL AERONAUTICS AND SPACE ADMINISTRATION
FREEDOM OF INFORMATION ACT REPORT
REGARDING VENUS PROBE "SOJOURNER IV"
PURSUANT TO CODE 03-AEX-14

1. Cosmos ███

   Two additional mentions:

   Series: ███████
   Purpose: Interplanatary spacecraft for mission to Venus
   International Designation: ████████████
   Launch Date: ██████
   Re-entry: █████
   Notes: Failed to achieve correct orbit

2. Fragology
   1 citation exists to ████████ Master List of the
   Washington National Records Center. The transferring
   agency, as the legal custodian, controls access of the
   records. A written request and authorization must be
   obtained from the transferring agency before the records
   can be used.

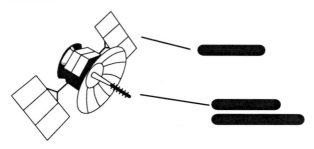

3. Space Debris which re-entered the Earth's atmosphere
   Instrumentation indicated probe contaminated with high levels of
   unspecified radiation; tentatively titled, "Type ████"
   ████████ destroyed at time of re-entry. ████████████

FOUNDING FATHER

THERE WAS A dead man in the barbed wire.

Kurt Garrett was too curious not to pull over and investigate. After all, despite the bombardment of images of them on every news channel, he had yet to see a zombie in person. The desolate rolling hills of West Virginia were the perfect natural deterrent for a catastrophe of the sort the world was currently experiencing, and the calamities of more heavily-populated states had not yet reached Appalachia quite as profoundly.

He let his motorcycle engine idle, then lowered the kickstand and dismounted, leaving his helmet dangling from the handlebars.

Deep, thick forests lined both sides of the road. Every ten trees or so, someone had posted signs reading:

PRIVATE PROPERTY
No Hunting, Fishing, or Trespassing
Violators will be Prosecuted to
the Fullest Extent of the Law

A scribbled landowner's signature accompanied every message.

The zombie was just past the drainage ditch at the edge of the trees, trapped in a portion of long forgotten, long-neglected barbed wire fencing. The fence posts, spaced roughly fifteen feet apart, were termite-infested and whole chunks of them were missing, rotted away and returned to the soil. The actual strands of iron thorns were rusty with age and almost completely camouflaged by the overgrowth of weeds that were permitted to grow uninhibited.

—A cross-country runner would be in for quite a surprise if he didn't notice them in time.

Garrett approached slowly, keeping watch on a bunch of hornets buzzing around a nest in the upper limbs of a tree not twenty feet away. They didn't seem intimidated by him, but they weren't being forceful either.

The zombie, however, hissed and snapped at him the entire time. It had its hands outstretched, clawing and grasping at the air, but Garrett stopped a foot short of its reach.

He stood there for a moment and watched.

It was a man, definitely. He was wearing a green cap and an orange vest. Beneath that was a full suit of hunter's camouflage. An ammunition pouch was slung around its left shoulder and a toothpick knife was in a sheath on its right hip.

But the zombie didn't reach for either of these, and instead kept snarling and probing with its hands. The barbed wire was lodged in the pit of its stomach, buried at least six inches deep.

Garrett guessed that this foul thing had stumbled out of the woods and directly into the three vertical strands of barbed wire, and hadn't had the cognizance to negotiate around it. Instead it had kept pressing forward, waging battle with the fence —and *lost*. All of its struggles succeeded only in worsening its predicament. It was evident that the zombie had turned around at least once, burying the barbed wire even deeper.

It continued to thrash about. It certainly wasn't feeling any pain, and was focused only on Garrett.

Garrett nonchalantly lifted up on his leather pants so he could comfortably kneel down and study its face.

The dead man had a neatly-trimmed mustache and goatee much like Garrett's, but it was obvious this man was much older. The skin was wrinkly and pale and hinting at turning blue. Yet there was a layer of dirt all over the guy —some still in chunks, especially under the fingernails —as if it had clawed itself out of a shallow grave.

Garrett studied closer.

He then saw a hole in the zombie's orange vest, surrounded by a telltale stain.

—*A bullet hole.*

Then, looking up at the zombie's face, disregarding the unpleasant snarl and glazed-over eyes, Garrett saw another bullet wound, this one in through the right cheek and out through the left, taking several teeth along with it. At first Garrett had thought all this to be mere decay.

"So what happened to you, huh?" Garrett whispered.

The zombie didn't answer, and in fact seemed even more peeved by Garrett's attempt at communication. It rasped and clacked its teeth together repeatedly, trying to maneuver its head closer to Garrett's warm skin, in the process unintentionally coughing up an earthworm that slithered over its bottom lip and dripped to the ground.

Garrett reached out his right hand, watching the zombie follow it with its eyes and teeth. He slowly waved his hand back and forth like a policeman giving a sobriety test, and the zombie kept pace.

"Can you really not understand what I'm saying to you?" Garrett asked it, raising his eyebrows to appear sympathetic.

The zombie let out a hissing, *"Ghhhaaaaaaaaaa!"*

It was viciously chomping its teeth, turning and stretching its neck in a way that would be most uncomfortable to a normal human being, persistent to somehow reach Garrett's skin.

"C'mon," Garrett uttered, scoffing in disbelief. "You can't really be this stupid. You guys are taking over the world."

The zombie gave no response.

Garrett stood and walked to the barbed wire, keeping out of the zombie's reach. He raised his left hand and let it hover above the zombie's head, keeping it distracted, while he used his right hand to reach around and feel at the zombie's posterior.

He lifted the back of the orange vest and reached into one of the camouflaged pockets.

The zombie quit snapping at Garrett's left hand and tried turning to reach the even closer right hand, but couldn't. It looked very pathetic then, like a man tied over a table and being sexually assaulted and unable to do anything about it except bitch and moan.

Garrett found what he was looking for.

From the zombie's back pocket, he pulled out a pristine, mock-leather tri-folded black wallet. He took it and stepped back, stopping several feet away.

He opened the wallet.

There wasn't anything of value inside. If the dead man had had money or credit cards, then they had already been taken by someone else.

But Garrett wasn't interested in that. He wasn't a thief.

He pulled out the dead man's driver's license and held it at arm's length, keeping it in his sight right next to the snarling face protruding from the barbed wire. He studied the picture on the license and compared it to the one in front of him.

The faces were similar, but at the same time seemed a world apart.

Garrett said, "So this is what you looked like, huh?"

The zombie didn't reply.

Garrett examined the monospaced text below the picture and read aloud, *"Michael Abram Browning. Seventy-one Highland Avenue, Kingston Falls, West Virginia."*

Below the text was a signature. Garrett compared it to the signature on the *'No Trespassing'* signs on the nearby trees.

They didn't match.

He situated the driver's license back in its original place in the wallet and tossed the whole thing back at Dead Michael. It hit him on the forehead and fell to the ground.

Dead Michael didn't even flinch.

Garrett looked away and meditated, still waist-deep in the weeds. His motorcycle engine continued idling in a pleasant purr alongside the road. The hornets were swarming in the trees, and somewhere not too far away, a turkey gobbled.

After a moment he turned back to face the dead man.

He asked it, "Did somebody take issue with your trespassing?"

The zombie opened its mouth wide, damn-near breaking its own jawbone, and snarled.

"Another hunter shoot you by accident?" Garrett added.

Still, the zombie didn't give any hint of a coherent reply.

Garrett decided that *yes*, someone had indeed shot him, whether by accident or intention, (probably by intention, since he *was* shot twice,) and had then hastily buried him.

Then, all across the world, the dead rose.

Who would have expected that?

Garrett wondered, with the condition of the world being as it was, if there would ever be an official investigation into this. Then, almost as quickly as the thought popped into his head, it was replaced by another: *Probably not.*

He nodded farewell to Dead Michael, then started walking back to the road. Dead Michael waved his arms frantically, almost pleading with him not to go.

You're lunch, the gesture seemed to indicate.

Garrett retrieved his helmet from its perch on the handlebars and placed it on his head, then strapped it.

His bike was a beautiful restored Indian motorcycle, circa 1969. He didn't care for the loud, modern Harleys that flooded the preferences of his peers. No, Kurt Garrett was old school. As a matter of fact, he had an equally beautiful restored Triumph, circa 1962, and it was a hard choice which one to take with him, especially since he had considered that if the national crisis worsened, he may never again be able to go home and retrieve it.

In the end it came down to a coin flip. The Indian won.

He straddled the seat and maneuvered the kickstand up with his right foot and locked it in place. He pulled in the clutch and clicked down into first gear, fed his machine some gas via his shiny silver throttle, eased off the clutch, and went forward.

The road was particularly empty; a small, single lane that snaked through the hills. It originally veered off the main stretch in some unincorporated town between Kingston Falls and Timberlake. It was immaculately paved and obviously well cared for, unlike nearly every other road in the state that was pockmarked with potholes from excessive use by coal trucks, or just downright neglect.

He was accustomed to the hills, and therefore negotiated the winding turns with ease and a certain amount of grace. There were no signs indicating what the road led to, but Garrett knew.

He had been born and raised in West Virginia, currently residing in nearby Kingston Falls, the county seat. Outside the hustle and bustle of the growing city, there was an unending sequence of hills and valleys, with an almost infinite sequence of other mountains in the distance. Over the mountains and valleys was a wilderness of shrubbery and trees, so genuinely lonesome and devoid of human life that a lot of it could very well be uncharted.

All of this area just south of the Mason-Dixon line had been sacred hunting ground for ancient Indians. Even now, if a person was lucky enough, he could discover an authentic arrowhead in the dirt or lodged in a tree.

When Garrett thought about it, he wondered if hundreds —or even *thousands* —of ancient Indian ghosts could gather in the hills or wail from the treetops and if any living soul would be the wiser.

However, aside from the healthy purr of his motorcycle engine, all was quiet.

It was for all these reasons —the lonesomeness, the isolation, the silence —that a group of high-ranking people decided the area was perfect for their intentions. Away from prying and curious eyes, a military installation in the West Virginia hills could accomplish a lot, in secret.

One such installation, Rock Forge, lay just over the hill, where the twisting road came to a rather abrupt and sobering end.

* * * * *

Kurt Garrett had received an invitation to come here, and by the tone of the message there seemed to be considerable urgency. However, he was used to the Army's *hurry-up-and-wait* mentality, and got there only as fast as he felt like going. It turned out just being a couple of days, but he was still glad he could make his point that he wasn't on the *Army's* time anymore —he was on his *own*.

When he reached Rock Forge's main gate after the final series of deliberately-placed speed bumps, he expected to simply state his name and the guard would push a button and he would be allowed right in.

But that wasn't the case.

The guard —some young punk with a Texas accent —restated his name several times, rolling it off his tongue as if he was trying to coax the last bit of flavor from a stale piece of gum, followed by, "And what is your business here?"

"Actually, I have no fucking clue what I'm doing here," Garrett told him, staring him down through the diamond-shaped holes in the chain-link fence. "I was invited. By *Colonel Franklin Darlington*."

"I'm not aware of any Colonel *Darlington*," said the guard.

"Yes you are," Garrett replied, calling him a liar in as few words as possible. "Stop beating your peter, go in your little shack there, and get him on the fucking horn. *Pronto*."

"Oh, I'll get *somebody* on the horn," the guard snapped back, "but you may not like it."

The guard turned and walked to his octagon-shaped shack fifteen feet away. He entered.

Garrett then took the time to notice how much Rock Forge had grown in the last few years and how it was now nearly bursting at the seams with activity. The road through the gate (if it would ever open to him) disappeared a hundred yards up, where an assortment of barracks, buildings, and landing strips rose up in its place, like a long fuse burning down to several sticks of dynamite. Camouflaged military vehicles stopped appropriately at stop lights and foot traffic hustled over crosswalks in front of them.

It was like a small city nestled away from the world.

—*And every citizen carried a gun.*

The young guard returned to the gate, showed an apologetic face, and said, "I'm sorry sir... *Sergeant*. You aren't wearing stripes. But Colonel Darlington is coming to meet you. He's on his way."

Garrett raised his upper lip, showing him a look in return that said, '*Yeah, don't judge a book by its cover, you little E-1 prick.*'

He didn't have to wait for long. Darlington showed up on the other side of the main gate in less than a minute.

Garrett had a lot of preconceptions. He expected that he'd be allowed in then, that he and Darlington would return to his private office and close the door behind them, (one of those heavy metal doors so common in military bases, the kind that closed loudly no matter how hard you tried to close it quietly, with floor-shaking reverberations and echoes down the narrow hallways,) then Garrett would sit across from Darlington, separated by his lavish desk, and drink coffee while they spoke in confidence.

That all happened, of course, but Garrett wasn't allowed inside right away. He had to undergo an interrogation first, him on one side of the fence and Darlington on the other.

The Colonel had aged just as Garrett expected: now in his late forties and gray around the edges. His voice was bland and monotone, neither Appalachian nor city-dweller, completely non-regional and utterly unidentifiable. In other words: *boring*. He was wearing camo pants and a dark green sweater, proudly displaying his stripes.

Darlington started with: "Good to see you again, Sergeant. How are you enjoying your *civvie* status?"

Garrett chuckled almost sickly as he replied, "Actually, *I'm loving it*. Did you know there's no grenades in the civilian world? Amazing, huh?" He noticed Darlington glance down at his feet, regardless of how much he tried to hide the move.

Once Darlington lifted his eyes again, he said, "You got yourself an honorable discharge. It's not all bad."

"Maybe," Garrett replied. "But I'd trade it in an instant for a better one of these..."

Here he lifted his left foot and rapped on his boot with his knuckles. Beneath the leather, there was hard plastic. It made a very discernable sound when knocked.

He then put his foot down again and stood completely erect.

Darlington turned his head when he noticed the young guard step a little too close. He waved him off in a *shoo-shoo* fashion, making it clear he wanted privacy.

He turned back to Garrett and said, "Well, all extremity-abnormalities aside, we could use your assistance."

"How so?"

Darlington cleared his throat, and then began, "Certainly you're aware of all these reanimated dead people up and walking around?"

Garrett nodded.

"They're eating us," Darlington continued, in a matter-of-fact tone. "We can send in the biggest guns we have against these people, and still they get us."

Garrett thought about the barbed-wire zombie. He had had a head wound, right through the mouth. But it didn't go through the brain. So, Garrett reasoned, it must be the brain that matters. Destroying the brain will destroy the body. The speculation on television had been correct.

He informed the Colonel: "They have to shoot them in the head. That'll bring them down."

"It's not that simple," Darlington replied.

"What's not simple? These dead people are *dumb*. I saw one down the road there that probably couldn't find its way out of a wet paper bag."

"You're in West Virginia," Darlington explained, motioning with a nod at the expanse of uninhabited mountains all around them. "You're not thinking about *numbers*. You're not thinking about whole armies of these things flocking together in large populations, because we haven't seen it yet out here in *Bumfuckt*. But we've got men out there who are dealing with it right now, and they're getting *slaughtered*. I'm afraid it's going to be bad."

"How bad?"

"*Real bad*. Could be the end of civilization."

"And where do I play into all of this?"

Darlington shuffled his feet. He took a moment to glance behind him at the isolated compound of Rock Forge, as if to form a reference point from which to make his case.

He explained, "It's been decided that Rock Forge is the ideal research hub. If the crisis truly does get out of hand, there'll be a good chance this place will still be standing unmolested. We're bringing in all the top minds in the world, whether they be Army, Navy, Coast Guard or civilian. Doesn't matter. We've got doctors Dalip Patel and Allison Fischer leading the research. They'll find out what's causing this problem and a possible solution—"

"But *I'm* no scientist," Garrett interjected.

"Didn't say you were," Darlington replied. "Scientists can only accomplish so much. We still need a way to fight the problem."

Garrett gleefully boasted, "I *was* one hell of a Ranger. First in my regiment, first place in five out of seven ten-mile marches, and first place in the only *Best Ranger Competition* I participated in. How do you like *them* apples?"

"Yes," Darlington replied. "I know all this."

"But now I've got this fake foot."

"Yes, well," Darlington began, choosing his words, "You're not here because you were a Ranger —or even enlisted for that matter."

Garrett's eyes narrowed in confusion.

Darlington continued, "Like I was saying, you could be one-hundred percent civilian for all we care. You're here because you're a ranking instructor in *Krav Maga*."

Garrett scoffed, "You want a *seminar*?"

Though he knew teaching Krav Maga had been good to him —it was where the money came from to restore his vintage motorcycles —he didn't see any use for it in this situation.

"No," said Darlington. "We want you, along with others of various specialties, to help us develop a practical fighting system to deal with the reanimated dead. Something that can be *taught*."

Garrett got suspicious. He asked, "Who are these *others*?"

"Right now we've confirmed Zhang Wu and Milton Levi. Other names are pending."

"Milton Levi?"

"Yes. Instructor-level black belt in Jiu-Jitsu."

"I *know* who he is," Garrett said. "I worked with him at a self-defense seminar. A word of advice: Don't call him *Milton*. He goes by *Gordon*."

"Point noted."

Garrett leaned against the fence, wrapping his fingers around the links and resting his head as he meditated.

He spit.

"So what say you?" Darlington asked.

Garrett didn't raise his head as he uttered, "You want to develop a brand new hybrid fighting system in —*what*, a matter of days?"

"As quick as possible. You'll have every resource at your disposal."

Garrett let out an audible chuckle, then lifted his head and showed a disbelieving grin. He said in a low voice, "You know, I've heard a lot of rumors about Rock Forge —about how its got nuclear silos hidden in the hillsides —about how its got a mile-long underground complex reserved for the President in the event of an invasion —about how maybe, just maybe, you might even have UFO's hidden here."

Darlington laughed. Perhaps it was practiced, but he was able to very solemnly reply, "I assure you those rumors are not only *not* true, but completely ridiculous. Our desks may be a little bigger here, but that's it."

Garrett made it a point to watch his eyes as he spoke, but still wasn't able to tell if he was lying or not. However, he knew at least the UFO rumor wasn't true. *That* was civilian conspiracy-theory rhetoric bullshit. The *rest*, on the other hand, was still plausible.

He had wanted to see the Colonel squirm, but didn't get the reaction he had hoped for.

After a moment he continued, "When you invited me here... well, I guess maybe I pictured something on a grander scale."

"Sorry to disappoint," Darlington replied. "It is what it is. Take it or leave it."

"*I'll take it*," said Garrett. "Just let it be known that I'm not calling you *sir* and I'm never going to join a chant of *hoo-wah*. I'm finished with all that shit."

"Understood, Sergeant," said Darlington. He motioned to the young guard at the shack, and a moment later the main gate began to open, propelled along by rails and motors. He met Garrett with a handshake and said, "Welcome to Rock Forge."

ROCK FORGE
Army Research Laboratory

INTERNAL MEMO
To: F. Darlington
From: K. Garrett

Frank,

While waiting for the other members of this project to arrive, I've taken the liberty of testing some of the proposed theories of Dr.'s Patel and Fischer.

THEORY #1= A reanimated dead person doesn't require its internal organs.

Using one of the test subjects provided me, I wrestled it to the ground and after hyperextending the arm I was able to puncture the soft flesh in the armpit area with my fist. I dug in and grabbed hold of its heart. I yanked it out. (It doesn't beat or anything.)

The zombie was still functioning.

Next I wrestled it back down and locked my arms around its neck from behind. I modified an existing Krav Maga maneuver here. I squeezed and twisted and pulled its head clean off. Once the spine was out far enough the zombie's body stopped moving.

But I still had to crush its skull with my heel to finish off the head.

I almost got bit. I suggest that from now on the zombies be wrapped in airtight black rubber suits from head to toe and have masks over their mouths.

--K. Garrett

Sgt. Garrett,
#1) Rock Forge is NOT your personal playground. Take this report, shred it, burn the pieces and bury the ashes. I don't need this bullshit ever coming back to haunt me.
2) In official documentation you will address me as "Col. Darlington", NOT "Frank". Thank you.
3) Don't use the term "zombie". You're in the real world, not science fiction.

BROKEN BUTTERFLY

IN SEVERAL HUSHED talks with his best friend Tyrell, Creyton casually expressed interest in running out, but he was never really adamant about it until his superiors seized all of his nine millimeter parabellum rounds for "reallocation and redistribution," even though he himself hadn't fired a single shot. And when the reallocation was supposed to come back around, lo and behold, none of the peons were reallocated *anything*.

Yet strangely enough, even then it hadn't been *him* that gave the final word. It had been Tyrell.

"We gotta vacate, bro," he had said.

Creyton knew Tyrell to be responsible to a fault, so hearing him insist on desertion was somewhat unexpected —*seizure of his ammo notwithstanding* —but at the same time, he knew it was coming. Tyrell had left his family at their home outside city limits, probably under the assumption that the problems of the city would end in a few days or so. He was like everyone else, thinking that it was only temporary, like a flood disaster or something of that sort.

At first, nobody *really* thought the world was ending.

But Creyton played it sheepishly. He got Tyrell to elaborate and say all the things he wanted to hear, like how they were both young —in their mid-twenties —and not about to die because of other people's fuckups —Like how they were smart enough and strong enough to outlast the cookie crumbs that fell out of the box first, but not if they had to take orders from the big cookie idiots that continually forced them into perilous situations.

Hadn't *containment* ever crossed the higher-ups' minds? Why were they still treating it as a traditional plague, but then allow healthy people in the same rooms with the dead and dying? What were they *thinking*?

"You're saying you want to hop the fence?" Creyton asked.

And Tyrell replied, "Damn straight I do."

Creyton was then reminded, after all, that they wouldn't be the first. Several sheriff's deputies, police officers and national guardsmen had fled already. Some made it, but some were shot by their own or eaten by the cannibals not fifty yards from the fence. Added to this the fact that many doctors and nurses had fallen ill after receiving bites or scratches from infected refugees, and all they were left with was a bare-bones skeleton crew that was in control of *nothing*.

With its exterior milky white and its interior bathed in blood, the rescue center at Canonsburg General Hospital was nearing the zenith of its downward spiral.

People were leaving.

People were dying.

And Creyton had always hated sitting on his hands. Besides, he wasn't even really a cop.

Not anymore.

Tyrell told him that he knew of a place they could go —someplace north —and Creyton agreed that any place was better than here.

Together they swiped the luggage of an expired refugee, then slipped out of sight and crept up to the second floor, through one of the out-patient dormitories, and exited onto the adjacent balcony.

There they changed from their sweat-soaked uniforms into clothing found in the refugee's suitcase —dorky-looking clamdiggers and tropical button-up shirts. Still, by looking like civilians they might not be hassled as much by the remaining national guardsmen patrolling the fence.

There were several down below, but not nearly as many as there were starting out. Now there was just one guardsman per forty yards of fence. Creyton figured it shouldn't be too difficult to hustle past one of them.

On the other side of the wrought-iron fence erected around the perimeter of the hospital grounds, there were still at least a hundred scattered refugees hollering to be let in. The soldiers were shouting back that it wasn't safe here any more, but —*like true idiots* —they were using bullhorns to get their message across, and therefore attracting more and more plague-infested citizens of Canonsburg.

Plague infested? Creyton mused. *Infected?*

He was in the habit of using these terms ever since the mandate that '*zombie*' shouldn't be uttered, as it was spreading undue panic —as if '*plague*' wouldn't cause panic enough. Even the emergency broadcasts on television channels and radio stations avoided use of the Z-word. And these same broadcasts were supposed to be informing the Washington County population that it was no longer considered safe to go to Canonsburg General Hospital.

But were the stations still broadcasting?

Creyton wasn't sure.

All the same, people continued showing up and demanding protection from the cannibalistic wilderness the city had become. Several attempted to scale the fence and get inside, spikes and razor wire notwithstanding, but warning shots fired in the air from the soldiers' M-16s quickly sent them scrambling back down.

Really all that these unnecessary shots accomplished was the migration of more dead people.

Zombies.

Occasionally one would stroll up to the fence and bite a chunk of skin off of a refugee or two before the guardsmen recognized them and gunned them down.

—When *everyone* was dirty, smelly, and hungry, it was some-times difficult to tell the difference.

Outside on the balcony, the air reeked of junkyard and was filled with screaming and howling. Creyton was hearing it as if he was underwater. It was an ambient sound, constantly there, but tuned out almost to the point of being muted entirely.

He took his personal items from his uniform and shoved them in the pockets of his new clothes. He then discarded his uniform pants and started fitting himself in the clamdiggers from the stolen suitcase. They were a perfect fit, mostly.

"So where is this place you have in mind?" he asked.

"Up north," Tyrell repeated.

"*North...*"

When he thought of north he thought of New York, and that didn't sound too appealing.

Creyton and Tyrell both ducked down then as they heard the sound of approaching footsteps emanating from the hallway inside, squeaking loudly on the polished floors. Swallowing hard, they retreated to opposite sides of the balcony and pressed their backs to the wall.

They held their breath.

The footsteps sounded coordinated, so Creyton guessed that it had been another officer making his rounds, and not a shambling dead person. He knew the barricaded hospital morgue was full of them.

The footsteps came and went.

Creyton and Tyrell left their positions against the wall and peered over the balcony. The grassy front lawn was roughly twenty feet below, and Creyton knew dropping that far was a good way to break an ankle. However, there was a myriad of modern architecture jutting out this way and that, and it looked to provide a means of getting down to the ground level.

He scouted a path with his eyes. Across from the balcony was a marble gazebo with a pinnacle resembling the Statue of Liberty's crown. And directly below the balcony was a narrow beam that would take him to it, leaving him only a hopscotch jump away from the crown. If he negotiated all of this architecture to the very end, the furthest he would have to drop would be eight feet.

Tyrell saw the path as well. He chuckled uncomfortably and said, "Now *this* is going to be one treacherous bitch."

Creyton threw one leg over the balcony, then another. He pushed off and dropped onto the first outcropping. Tyrell followed.

They crossed the beam heel to toe like clowns on a tightrope.

It occurred to Creyton then that they weren't exactly camouflaged. And with their blueberry shirts and lemon yellow shorts, it was no wonder they were spotted.

Fifty yards away, one of the guardsmen glanced over and caught them.

"*Aw, hell, Ty,*" Creyton grumbled. "We got made. Watch out."

Creyton tensed up, certain he would soon have to dodge bullets or leap off the beam. But the guardsman did nothing. And after a few seconds, Creyton saw him shake his head indifferently and switch back to studying the fence.

It seemed nobody gave a damn anymore. If Creyton had had any guilty residue about running, then at that moment those qualms vanished entirely.

He finished traversing the beam, then hopped over onto the gazebo. From there he shimmied down until he was hanging by his palms.

He let go.

He landed on his feet, bending his knees and squatting to absorb the impact. He moved out of the way to allow Tyrell to drop next.

Once they were both down, they crossed the lawn and leapt the curb, ducking behind stray ambulances parked here and there, and jogged across the parking lot.

They took positions near the perimeter fence.

Directly on the other side was a family of four: a father, a mother, two daughters. Their clothes were wrinkled and worn. Their suitcases were being used as makeshift furniture. It appeared they hadn't bathed in days.

The father stared at Creyton, but said nothing.

Thirty feet away, the soldier who had seen Creyton earlier was also staring at him, but he was saying nothing either. After a moment he gave a nod and showed the slightest of smiles.

It showed regard.

It showed *understanding.*

The soldier turned about-face and marched the opposite direction —merely going through the motions, it seemed.

Creyton grabbed the vertical, wrought-iron bars and started climbing. At the top of the fence the bars sharpened to spikes, with arrowheads welded on for emphasis. The whole thing appeared to have been salvaged from a cemetery —*or stolen.* Some of the dirty concrete anchors were still intact. At the base on the exterior side of the fence, the military faction had laid out a long row of coiled razor wire. It would shred the legs of anything that tried to go through it.

Getting *in* was a problem, getting *out* was not. Whoever placed the razor wire probably hadn't considered there'd be desertion.

When Creyton reached the top of the fence, he placed his feet on the horizontal bar supporting the spikes, then carefully rearranged his legs so they were on the opposite side. He then climbed halfway down and leapt off, intending to miss the razor wire.

It still managed to cut him a little. It sliced his clamdiggers on his right side from the bottom all the way up to the middle of his boxer shorts. There was a trickle of blood where it nicked his skin.

Tyrell climbed next.

Creyton knew there was no real damage to his leg, but he was nursing it anyway, mostly so he could ignore the family that was so close by they were practically breathing down his neck. It made him feel antsy to look at them or even think about them.

"Why won't they at least give us water?" the father asked, his voice hoarse and weak.

Creyton glanced at him, then turned away again when he caught the children looking at him too. Their clothes were filthy and their skin was sallow. He had only ever seen children like that on infomercials for charity organizations —*never in person* —especially considering that the family appeared to have been middle-class, and not completely destitute.

Tyrell finished crossing over the fence and jumped off, missing the razor wire completely.

"Let's get rollin'," he said.

Creyton nodded and took two steps, preparing to jog.

Then, from behind him, the father spoke again.

"What should we do?" he asked, obviously trying to raise his voice louder than he was able. "We haven't eaten and my girls are thirsty. Nobody is *helping* us."

Creyton couldn't bring himself to turn around.

The father continued: "*Please, guys.* You're *deputies.* I saw you in uniform. Tell me... What's it like in there? Should we stay? Will they let us in?"

Creyton noticed Tyrell pause, but he didn't face them yet.

"*Please,*" the father added. "Can't you see what we're going through? Don't you have family?"

Finally Tyrell half-turned around, but like Creyton, he couldn't face them entirely either.

He said, "Yeah, I've got family. I'm going to them now."

The father whimpered, sobbing.

"I can't tell you what to do," said Tyrell, "—because *I don't know.* I don't know what's best for you and your family. I'm sorry."

With that, Tyrell grabbed Creyton by the arm and ushered him to move. It was Creyton's final indication that all was not right in the world: Tyrell was finished being *responsible.*

They ran.

"We'll need guns," Tyrell panted. "I've got a sidearm at my house."

Creyton almost laughed as he replied, "I think it's safe to say guns are overrated. They only draw attention. But I've got a regular *hand-cannon* at the bar if you're interested."

Tyrell got the joke and chuckled despite the situation.

They sprinted to the knoll that divided the main parking lot from the distant, over-crowded employee parking lot. The breeze was nice and steady now, and the junkyard smell was fading.

Creyton dashed to his little Volkswagon punchbug, painted pinkish-orange like the color of fish guts, peeling in places.

Tyrell went straight for his family-style Jeep Liberty. Creyton could remember his reason for buying it: It was the only vehicle that was even remotely cool while still being able to act as a grocery-getter.

"Whoa, hang on!" Tyrell shouted. "We don't need to take two cars. We can all fit in this." He motioned to his Jeep.

Creyton hesitated, swallowed hard, and uttered, "*There's someone I want to bring with me.*"

Tyrell rolled his eyes and put his head down. He let out a deep exhale.

Creyton pulled his car keys from his pocket and fumbled with them until he found the one for the door. He shoved it in and twisted.

"Crey, *don't do this,*" said Tyrell. "Let's not complicate it."

"I don't like thinking I won't ever see her again," Creyton mumbled, feeling even less like a man with every syllable. "I want one last chance."

Tyrell growled as he fumbled with his own keys. However, unlike Creyton's old beat-up bug, *his* vehicle unlocked with the push of a button. He pressed it and the doors unlocked with a roadrunner-like *beep-beep.*

"Give me thirty minutes," Creyton said. "I'll meet you at our spot." He paused, then added, "You *do* remember our spot, right?"

"Yeah, man, I remember our spot."

"Then give me thirty minutes."

Creyton opened his door and climbed into the driver's seat. He shoved the key in the ignition and turned it, tapping on the accelerator to help get the old bitch going. The engine stuttered a moment, then started with a frail roar.

In the driver's seat of his Liberty, Tyrell rolled down his window and shouted out, "Crey, if she doesn't want to come along, *leave her*! She was never worth the trouble!"

Creyton had barely heard him, but his facial expression and lip movements were readable enough.

He nodded.

Tyrell led them out of the parking lot and onto Medical Boulevard. But after that they went their separate ways.

* * * * *

Creyton Hathaway was *red*.

Partly of German descent, but mostly Irish, he was red from head to toe. He still had freckles and his hair was the color of strawberries. It got curly if it grew out, so he kept it cut short. Otherwise Tyrell would call him *Raggedy Andy*.

They had been friends since kindergarten. Even when Creyton's minister father took a temporary position at a new church fifty miles away, forcing his family to move, the two never really drifted apart. Eventually Creyton's family moved back, and he and Tyrell went about their routine like nothing had changed.

They grew up together and even had their own inside jokes.

For example, Tyrell had been cursed with a slight stuttering problem until he hit puberty, and Creyton would tell him, "Would you please stop reverting to your African roots? I'm not fluent in clicks and grunts." And Tyrell would fire back with: "The ventriloquist with his hand up your ass is a real funny guy," —a reference to pre-teen Creyton looking a lot like Howdy-Doody.

Everyone knew that if Creyton and Tyrell weren't ribbing each other, it meant they weren't getting along.

And they rarely didn't get along.

212

They had trouble finding what they wanted to do after high school. They both went to college in an attempt to obtain degrees in Information Technology, which seemed like a wise move at the time. But when they found computers to be excruciatingly boring, they tried something with a greater degree of manual labor: *welding*. They took classes and got pretty good at it. However, they soon found that —despite the money they could earn if they ever went union — the black gunk that contaminated their nostrils and the flakes of molten metal constantly sinking into their forearms wasn't very rewarding. In fact it was downright painful.

Tyrell went to straight-up construction work.

Creyton took a job bartending.

He got pretty good at this as well, even being able to add a little flare to his performance. It was nothing too fancy, just a bottle flip here and there, and occasionally filling shotglass mountains. Bartending was fun and he loved the attention. Besides, he was instantly attractive to female patrons.

He lived the lifestyle. He put a piercing in both his ears and labret, along with a stud in his tongue. He used drugs occasionally, but found alcohol to be more rewarding. But he always kept himself in check.

So it surprised him the day Tyrell called him up and said, "Guess what we're going to do?"

"I give up. What are we going to do?"

"Law enforcement, my man. We're taking the test to be sheriff's deputies. They have positions open. We'll get free training, benefits, the works. I can get us in."

Creyton was flabbergasted.

What surprised him so much was that he and Tyrell had a running joke: When they would pass a policeman doing speed checks alongside the road, they would roll down their windows and Tyrell would shout, "What are old pennies made of?!" And Creyton would shout back, "Dirty copper!"

So, yes, law enforcement was the absolute *last* career he thought Tyrell would choose for them.

But it made sense. They were both smart and fit and didn't have any strikes against them. Plus they had an ongoing hatred for dirtbags. What better way to show it than to be the exact opposite?

Creyton agreed to it and they passed the tests, both mental and physical, quite easily. They went on to train at Penn State University *—pre-paid by the city* —and graduated from the Academy within a year.

But his job moonlighting at the bar went downhill.

When the owners —who would often lock themselves in the women's bathroom with select patrons so they could snort coke like madmen —found out he was "switching sides," they promptly canned his ass.

But it didn't matter. He was a cop.

But that only lasted two years.

* * * * *

After exiting Medical Boulevard, Creyton drove straight down North Central Avenue.

His hometown of Canonsburg was a medium-small city about twenty miles south of Pittsburgh, but its narrow roads in the downtown area were often just as congested as its big city neighbor's. However, the closer Creyton got to his destination, the more he noticed that the streets were absolutely bare. He had only ever seen them this deserted on major holidays.

Occasionally he heard gunshots in the distance, and at one point saw a blood-soaked man being pursued by a group of twenty or so shambling dead people. The man cut across the street right in front of him, tripping over the curb and falling face-first onto the sidewalk. He pried himself up and threw open the door in a nearby toy store, then slammed the door shut behind him.

Creyton steered his Volkswagon up to the door and honked the horn, but when the group of dead people turned their attention to him, he floored the accelerator and continued down the road.

He decided then that he had to stop trying to help people, otherwise he would only end up dead.

When he arrived at the junction of North Central Avenue and West Pike Street, he realized what happened to all the cars:

They were here.

The busiest intersection in town was a mess of smashed automobiles, all abandoned. The traffic lights dangling above were all without power, clouded by billows of gray smoke rising from shattered engines. The horn on one of the vehicles was blaring incessantly, but it was noticeably waning.

Four or five vehicles into the mess, a reanimated dead person was trapped in the collision of two pickup trucks. Its legs were thoroughly stuck between two bumpers, but it was still very much active. It was snarling and hissing and clawing at the open air.

On the other side of all the wreckage, Creyton could see even more dead heads trying to negotiate the maze of smoke and twisted metal.

He steered his Volkswagon onto the sidewalk with a teeth-gritting jolt and into the adjacent parking lot. From there he parked directly in front of Crossroads Saloon.

He knew he had to do this fast.

*   *   *   *   *

It was funny how life quite often screwed him over.

A year or so ago, a film class at the local junior college made arrangements with the Canonsburg commissioner to make a documentary about the Sheriff's Department. Creyton's understanding of it was that it was to be part of a much larger piece —the ups and downs of a mediocre town in general. There was no telling how bad Canonsburg would end up looking after the film was finished and edited. It was all a matter of what gimmick the final product would be given, and whether or not the students themselves were better than what their amateurish demeanors presented.

Nevertheless, the film crew got the action they were looking for, and it was all caught on tape.

A deputy —*not Creyton* —pulls over a car. The driver refuses to turn off the engine. There is subtle arguing for almost two minutes, but the driver is using *yes sir's* and *no sir's*. But he's also very, very high. He makes a move for the gearshift. The deputy sprays his face with mace, but the driver floors it and takes off, blinded.

There is a brief chase and other deputies are called in, including Creyton and Tyrell.

The driver eventually wrecks on his own accord. There is an arrest and high-fives are traded back and forth, all for the benefit of the camera. The icing came when a decently-sized stash of heroin was found in the trunk.

Therein lay the problem: Too many people wanted to be seen.

Too many people wanted to be interviewed. Too many people ranked above Creyton, who was the lowest man on the totem pole, and too many people were giving him orders.

Nobody wanted to do the piddly stuff. Instead they wanted to look important by doing important things. Everything was different because the camera was there.

In the confusion, nobody frisked the driver —or, at least —nobody frisked him *good enough*.

Creyton could recall someone off-handedly telling him to pat down the driver, who by then was lying on the pavement in handcuffs. But his head was spinning from so many people barking orders that a moment after he was told to frisk the driver, he was told to lay road flares by someone who ranked even higher in seniority.

So he laid road flares.

The suspect was taken to jail and put in a holding room. His handcuffs were removed. He asked for a glass of water, which he received. He was left in the room alone.

The surveillance camera caught the rest: He took a sip of water, set down the glass, then very calmly pulled a small pistol from deep within the nether-regions of his jeans, put the barrel to his head, and shot himself.

They later found him slumped in his chair, quite dead.

Accusations were thrown around, and in the end they were all directed at Creyton. *Somebody* had to be blamed. Somebody had to be *fired*.

And fate decided that that somebody would be Creyton.

He wasn't too heartbroken about it. He had never really found his stride in law enforcement, and really thought of the job as just a gig —a temporary thing. Unlike Tyrell, he had never learned cop-speak very well, always calling men *gentlemen* or *individual* and the women *lady* no matter how big of a dirtbag they were.

But he was given ten thousand dollars severance to go out quietly.

With the money he bought *Crossroads Saloon*, his old workplace. The former owners had long since run the business into the ground by being a little too coke-happy. Creyton was able to pay all the security deposits, the first month's rent, buy a liquor license, restock the alcohol, and give the establishment an entire makeover.

Only the name stayed the same, but below that he proudly declared, "UNDER NEW MANAGEMENT."

Creyton the cop was now Creyton the nightclub owner. Of all the occupations he had had, he knew mixology was what he was best at. It was also the most fun.

He made it evident, right from the start, that he wouldn't tolerate dirtbags —scummy, vulgar, wife-beating dirtbags. In Creyton's opinion, they were a step below rednecks and hillbillies. Canonsburg had its share of them.

He even made saying "dirtbag" an art form. It would roll off his tongue: *dirt-bag*, with emphasis on *dirt* and an expression of total disdain upon utterance of *bag*.

Dirtbag.

He could have called them many things —*much more vulgar things* —and they knew that, but the method in which he pronounced 'dirtbag' showed that they were the lowest of the low and there were no better terms to define them.

Just because you give me a look that might put your wife in line, he would growl between his teeth, *doesn't mean you scare me one bit, DIRTBAG.*

He freely used the word when ejecting someone from his establishment. He wasn't a big guy though; he was even on the skinny side. However, he was wiry and knew how to scrap. He had learned that he could take on bigger guys just by letting them punch themselves out. (The fatter and drunker ones usually got tired after throwing only two or three.) When that happened, Creyton would repeatedly aim for the jaw until they were out cold.

He made a lot of enemies this way. Part of him was glad that the world was ending. Otherwise one of them would probably end up traipsing into his nightclub and capping his ass.

Though he knew Canonsburg's population had a lot of dirtbags, he also knew it had its fair share of young hipsters.

And, over time, that was the crowd he brought in.

Everything was actually pretty simple after that, and he was making money.

But then things got complicated again when he met the girl upstairs.

* * * * *

Creyton threw open the outside door, which he never bothered locking, and stepped into a dark entrance area where one of his bouncers would check ID's and stamp hands on busier nights. The walls were covered in layers of flyers for upcoming and locals bands, and business cards for karaoke and DJ services, all held in place with pushpins.

The inner door, however, he kept sealed with two padlocks and a deadbolt. He constantly checked over his shoulder as he adjusted his keyring to catch the miniscule ray of midday sun that seeped through the crack in the outer door.

Most of the keys he knew by feel.

He found the one for the top padlock and used it.

The next immediate key unlocked the lower one.

Then, on the opposite side of his *My-Weiner-Does-Tricks* keychain, was the key to unlock the deadbolt.

He inserted the key, twisted it, and yanked open the door.

He flicked the light switch hiding behind the mirrored Budweiser sign, but after a few tries it became evident that there was no power. Even the jukebox in the corner, which was usually always abuzz with flashing lights and spinning discs, was totally lifeless.

However, there was enough indirect light to get by. It caused ominous shadows to appear behind racks of pool cues and cashew vending machines, twisted and distorted into the forms of jagged claws and salivating fangs sported by hunchbacked boogeymen.

He maneuvered around the dance floor to get behind the bar.

He hunkered down, slid open one of the cabinets, and reached deep inside, pushing aside stacks of receipt books and old martini glasses. His hands eventually rubbed against a heavy black case. He pulled it out and placed it on the bar.

He opened it.

Inside, floating snugly on ribbed foam padding, was a tiny .22 semiautomatic pistol. He pulled out the box of bullets lying alongside, then slid out the clip and began loading it.

It held ten.

It was just a snub-nosed purse gun and not very threatening at all. It only cost him a hundred and fifty bucks. But those weren't his reasons for buying it.

Though he had never had to use it, he knew that this style of gun in particular was less powerful than higher-caliber guns, but bullets fired from it would often cause more damage by staying inside the body rather than making a clean exit wound.

That meant some doctor would have to fish it out. Wounds were rarely lethal if emergency treatment was provided fast enough.

—If he had ever had to use the gun, it meant some dirtbag was going to be in a lot of pain, and live to experience every moment of it.

He finished loading the clip, shoved it back inside the butt of the gun, and slid it into the right pocket of his newly-inherited clamdiggers. He took the box of bullets (there were still at least twenty remaining) and put them in his other pocket.

He opened the door of the nearby cooler and pulled out a bottle of Jager. The power hadn't been off for more than a day, which he surmised by there still being some chill to the bottle.

He unscrewed the cap, then put the mouth of the bottle to his lips and tilted it back, taking several good chugs.

When he had enough he allowed the bottle to fall to the floor and shatter, expensiveness of the liquor be damned.

He wiped his mouth.

He asked himself, "You ready for this?"

*　*　*　*　*

Her name was Mizuki.

Mizuki Sakuraba.

She and her husband Hideko owned and operated the Japanese restaurant on the second floor, aptly titled, "Sakuraba's Japanese Cuisine." Before opening the bar every night, Creyton would eat a quick dinner there from the buffet.

Mizuki, who served as waitress while her husband served as chef, was very nice and very pretty. She never crossed over into open flirtation, but after Creyton's thirtieth visit or so, she began showing him interested —if not merely curious —glances. They were easily translatable.

She would attempt to make conversation with him as he ate, but her Engrish was horrible and his Japanese was even worse —practically nada. A lot of the time he couldn't even understand what she

219

was saying. He would just nod and smile.

He wished she came equipped with subtitles.

She had a beautiful voice though, a good body, and a sweet demeanor.

It made her a worthwhile prospect to look into.

So he learned certain Japanese words, having purchased an instructional cassette that he listened to every day while he mopped the floors of his nightclub. Still, he never got good enough to put together a complete sentence.

He could say *Bi, yokkyuu,* and *pa-fekuto.*

It turned out that these words were satisfactory to get his message across, and —*surprisingly enough* —she had practiced her English and was beginning to put sentences together, regardless of how discombobulated they were.

Their communication increased.

He gestured to her and uttered, "*Bi.*"

"Beautiful," she replied, smiling.

To impress her further, he cleared his placemat and scribbled the character in crayon:

美

"Yes," she told him. "Correct."

Next he pointed at himself, said "*Yokkyuu,*" then pointed at her.

"You desire me," she translated.

He nodded.

Then he pointed at her and said, "*Pa-fekuto.*"

With a laugh she replied, "Oh, I not *perfect.* Not close."

He nodded again and said, "Yes you are."

It went from there, their midnight trysts, secreting her away from her husband who couldn't speak a lick of English, mostly because he was too proud of his heritage to bother with such an inferior language. He was completely lost in American culture.

Actually he was downright clueless.

Creyton learned that their marriage was one of convenience —a way to escape overcrowded Tokyo with enough money to try their luck in Canonsburg, Pennsylvania, in the United States of America. Mizuki was Creyton's age, though Hideko was about ten years older, and both were doing well, considering even the language barriers they had to overcome.

He learned that she had an overwhelming fear of German Shepherds, and all big dogs in general, since where she was from all the dogs were only ankle-high.

"Okay, so we'll never own a dog," he told her.

But it never got that far.

Hideko eventually picked up on what was happening, and in the end Mizuki chose him over Creyton, severing all ties.

Creyton still ate at their buffet, but avoided eye contact and was quite often overcharged at the cash register.

He didn't have any master plan to get her back, but he wanted it to happen. He simply decided to play it slowly and see how things unfolded. He thought he had all the time in the world.

Then the zombie problem began.

The first reported sighting in Canonsburg was at a funeral, of all places. The deceased rose up out of his casket, tipping it over, and stumbled after his bereaved family members. He was able to eat a couple of them.

Then it spread. Walking dead people could be seen just about anywhere.

About a week after it became officially unsafe to travel, Tyrell called him on his cellular phone and said, "Hey Crey, we need you."

"*We* need?"

"Yeah," Tyrell replied. "You can get your job back. They want everyone who ever wore a badge to help out at the hospital. They're setting up a rescue center."

Creyton had never really wanted to be a deputy again. It was obvious by the way he went against regulations after being canned and had a psychedelic sun tattooed on the back of his left wrist. Certainly they would never let him in again with such a visible marking.

(And he really doubted he could ace a piss test.)

But it didn't take too much pondering for Creyton to decide to change back into his uniform. It would take his mind off of Mizuki, the girl upstairs.

He figured this disaster was temporary. After all, they were talking about *dead people* here. Certainly they would rot to the point of immobility within a few weeks.

But it soon became apparent that the zombies were not rotting, and that the world was indeed ending.

* * * * *

Creyton exited his nightclub via the front door, slouch-walking to avoid catching the attention of the two dead folks he saw plodding up the sidewalk. (One he thought he recognized as one of the drunken dirtbags he had barred from his establishment.) He hustled around the side of the building and ran up the wooden staircase there, which forked into two paths halfway up. An arrow pointing to the right had a sign below that read, '*Sakuraba's Japanese Cuisine.*' To the left was a door marked '*Private.*'

He had somehow known that Mizuki would never show up at the rescue center, though on the rare occasions he was given a breather from his duties, he would scour along the fence and make sure she wasn't among the refugees pleading to be let in, just in case. He knew her well enough to know that she would be in utter confusion about what was going on, even more so than the common American. Her husband was a non-trusting, non-confrontational coward, and would definitely try to hide them both from the problem.

There was one solitary four-foot by four-foot window next to the door marked '*Private*', and institutional green-colored curtains on the inside were blocking his view. He quietly situated his head back and forth, trying to discover a way to see inside.

When he found the gap where the curtains parted, he saw Mizuki sitting on the middle cushion of a sofa-mat laid out on the floor, (there wasn't an actual couch anywhere to be seen in the Sakuraba apartment,) her elbows on her knees and her face in the palms of her hands.

Creyton had once made out with her on that sofa-mat while her husband was out shopping. He wondered if perhaps she was crying now —that perhaps Hideko was bitten by a zombie and he would have to shoot him.

It would make things so much simpler.

He tapped lightly on the window with his index finger and Mizuki's head shot up to detect the source of the noise. Creyton then saw that she wasn't crying; she was just tired. Her face, though still beautiful, was heavy with sleeplessness.

She made eye contact with him. At first she showed uncertainty, (as if she didn't recognize him,) then she showed fear, (as she recognized him but wondered if he had turned into one of the *crazy people* rioting in the streets,) then she stood up.

She walked to the window and pulled apart the curtains.

Creyton gestured with a beckoning curl of his index finger and mouthed, "*Come with me.*"

She immediately let go of the curtains and they fluttered closed again.

Creyton almost panicked. Then he heard the deadbolt on the front door be unlatched. An instant later the door swung open about six inches.

He went to the door and pushed on it, but a security chain pulled taut on the other side was refusing to budge.

Mizuki's face appeared in the crack.

"Creyton, what are you doing here?" she asked.

"I'm here for *you*," he replied. "Come with me."

"Come where?"

"The hell out of Canonsburg."

"I go nowhere," she said. "People with sickness are outside. You be careful."

With that she attempted to close the door, but Creyton put his foot between the door and the jamb.

"Mizuki," he said, calmly, "You can't stay here. It's not safe."

She showed a touch of anger, but didn't get loud. It was obvious to Creyton now that not only was Hideko alive and well, but he was also within listening range.

She whispered, "I cannot see you anymore. I have husband."

"This isn't about you and me," Creyton told her. "I can't just leave you here. You'll *die*. It isn't sick people outside. It's *dead people*."

She still wasn't getting it; it was evident in her next statement: "You... you *whirlwinded* me, Creyton. You said I was your *butterfly*. I should stood by husband."

Creyton knew she was now saying things she wanted to say a long time ago, (they had never gotten to have their break-up argument,) but this wasn't the time for that. He repeated, "This isn't about *us*. It's about keeping you safe. You *and* Hideko."

"How we go? Where we go?"

"We're going with Tyrell and his family. C'mon, you've met Tyrell."

"Black man?"

"Yes, black man."

"Hideko will no like him. He is stubborn."

"Where is Hideko now?"

She thought a moment, then replied, "In room with *tee-vee*."

"Let me speak to him."

"No."

"Let me speak to him, Mizuki."

The door closed in Creyton's face. After a moment he heard the security chain unlatch and then the door swung open. Mizuki stepped aside and allowed him entry, then she pushed the door shut again and re-latched the chain and turned the deadbolt.

The room stunk of stale candle smoke. There were several still smoldering throughout.

She pointed to the long, narrow hallway. She said, "I go first. I speak. Do not provoke him."

Creyton nodded, then followed her down the hallway.

They emerged in another room, this one almost American in appearance, save for the two bonsai perched on two porcelain columns. Several framed Beatles and Elvis posters hung on the walls, and a giant flatscreen television was mounted between two large, six-foot windows, which were also covered in the same ugly, institutional green curtains.

Hideko was on his knees playing around with wires. He was wearing trousers and an old Steelers jersey, both disheveled. He was muttering to himself.

Looking at him now, especially, Creyton didn't understand at all why Mizuki went back to him after their affair. He looked fifty-five instead of thirty-five, and was downright *ugly*.

Mizuki announced her and Creyton's presence.

Hideko jumped up, growling and hissing, and at first Creyton almost went for the gun in the pocket of his clamdiggers.

Hideko pressed his forefinger in Creyton's chest, shouting, *"Deteke!"* then put both hands on his shoulders and pushed him backwards.

Creyton knocked his hands away, trying to be as passive as possible. He said, "You'll die if you stay here." He then put his palm around his own neck and stuck his tongue out, trying to impersonate gagging. He then said, "You can't stay here. If you stay," he pointed at the windows, hoping Hideko would know he meant what was on the other side, "...The monsters will get you."

Hideko showed only confusion.

Creyton tried putting it another way: "*Godzillas,* you non-English-speaking douchebag. Do you understand *Godzillas*...?"

Mizuki intervened and translated for Hideko, obviously leaving out the frustration-induced insults and obscenity.

Hideko then made a motion that was universally understandable by waving the back of his hand in disregard and mumbling, "*Bah.*" He went back to his knees in front of the television and repeated, "*Deteke.*"

Creyton approached Hideko again and knelt down beside him. He saw that Hideko had several batteries organized on the rug with wires connected to them. The other end of the wires disappeared behind the television.

"It doesn't work that way," Creyton said.

Hideko raised his head and appeared ready to shout more Japanese profanity.

Creyton hurriedly put his index finger to his lips, then pointed at the windows and said, "No more noise. No more arguing. They'll hear you."

Hideko showed more confusion. He went back to fiddling with the wires.

"*No,*" Creyton said, firmly. "The television isn't coming back on. There's no power." He pointed at the ceiling fan, then at all the lamps and light switches, then plucked one of the batteries loose from the concoction of wires Hideko had laid out. He shook the battery and said, "No good. This won't make the television work."

"*Teiden dakara muimi daga, nani mo shinai yori mashi daro.*"

Creyton gazed up at Mizuki and asked, "What's he saying?"

"He says he knows the television is not working because there is no power, but doing something is better than doing nothing."

"Then tell him to leave with me. The both of you. I can protect you."

Mizuki translated.

Hideko shook his head side to side and said, "*Iie.*"

"He doesn't want to," Mizuki said. She lowered her gaze and added, "And he is not going to change his mind. I tell you he is stubborn. Creyton, will we really die if we stay here? Things will not go normal again?"

"It's not looking that way," Creyton told her. "We have to go somewhere safe, and *this is not it.*"

Mizuki spoke to Hideko again in their native tongue, and this time her pleading tone was obvious. She was almost crying.

Still, Hideko only repeated, "*Iie.*"

By now Creyton understood that to mean, '*No.*' Or even: '*HELL NO,*' if this Buddhist bastard even believed in Hell.

Or was it Nirvana?

He had had enough.

He put his hand under Hideko's armpit and forced him to stand. On their feet, Creyton was easily a head taller.

He put a finger in Hideko's face and expounded, "*You ignorant stuckup.* If you stay here you'll die. And *she'll* die too."

He pointed at Mizuki.

Mizuki wept.

Hideko gazed at her, then at Creyton, then shrugged himself free. He went into a tirade.

"*Kore wa ore no uchi da. Haitte wa dame da.*"

"This is my home," Mizuki translated. "They cannot enter."

He added, "*Soto ni iro. Haitte wa dame da to wakatteiru daro.*"

Mizuki translated, "They will stay outside. They know better than to enter."

Seemingly to prove his point, Hideko stomped over to the rightmost of the big windows behind the flatscreen television and all at once drew back the curtain, revealing the outdoors in all its glory.

Creyton lunged, but hadn't had enough notice to stop him.

Then he froze in place.

Through the glass they saw that at least a dozen zombies had congregated near the back porch and were just standing there, wavering and bumping into each other. As the curtain revealed the living humans inside, all the dead heads turned, in unison, and snarled with open mouths.

Creyton screamed, "Hideko, you idiot!"

"*Monsutaa!*"

The three zombies in the forefront immediately lurched forward, heading for the window. Two were half-eaten, meatier parts of their bodies gone, blackened blood encrusted over the wounds. One had autopsy scars all over its naked chest.

Hideko stepped back, gagging, and the curtains closed.

Mizuki cupped her palm over her mouth as vomit rose from her throat in a painful spasm. She hurriedly exited the room, sidestepping half of the way, dashing the rest. Upchuck seeped from between her fingers and dripped to the floor.

Creyton grabbed Hideko by the shoulder and spun him around. He growled, "*Give it up. We're leaving.*"

Then the window shattered.

An instant later many unseen hands were pushing against the opposite side of the curtain, causing it to flutter as if there was a slight breeze. Distorted silhouettes of dead bodies cascaded across the ripples.

Hideko yanked himself free of Creyton and dashed to the window, shouting, "*Sutoppu! Sutoppu! Sutoppu!*"

He yanked the curtains open.

Shards of broken glass hung menacingly at the top of the frame like stalactites, ready to fall at any moment. Three zombies were already trying to pull their way inside, the stalagmites of glass tearing into their stomachs and splitting them open. Blood —and in one case, *formaldehyde* —spilled down the wall and onto the carpet like a leaking faucet.

In one of the dead hands was a foot-long portion of two-by-four. It was the likely candidate to have been the window-breaker.

Jesus..., Creyton thought, *They can use tools?!*

Hideko began trying to slap away the hands that were reaching inside. He shouted, "*Uchini hairuna!*"

Creyton pulled his 22. pistol from his pocket and released the safety.

Aim for the head, he remembered.

A hand grabbed Hideko's Steelers jersey and started pulling him near a foaming open mouth.

Creyton dashed forward, put the barrel of his gun flush against the forehead of the zombie that had grips on Hideko, and pulled the trigger.

The gun fired very weakly and there was a slight spray of blood around the barrel, but it was enough to make the zombie release its grip. Its eyes closed and it collapsed, impaling itself across the windowsill.

Creyton pried away the hand that gripped Hideko's jersey, but another took its place.

The window was now a vertical sea of dead arms and clacking teeth. More of them latched onto Hideko's jersey and were stubbornly trying to pull him through the window.

A pair of yellowed teeth was ready to clamp down on his neck.

Creyton filled the zombie's open mouth with the short barrel of his .22, feeling a certain satisfaction at forcing the deadhead to give his gun a blowjob. He then shot twice, the first bullet lodging in the spine and the second shooting right through it.

The dead hands were no longer molesting only Hideko —now they had grips on Creyton's ridiculously stupid shirt and were massaging at his scalp.

He shot another zombie in the head, and then another. Each one fell and was soon trampled underfoot by the others who were pushing themselves to the forefront and assaulting the open window.

Hideko managed to turn himself around and was no longer struggling to fight them back. The reality of it all had apparently wised him up and now he was simply fighting to get free.

With Creyton's help, he was almost there.

—But then Creyton stopped struggling.

—He stopped fighting.

He knocked away the dead hands that were assailing him and took two subtle steps backwards.

—But the zombies continued clawing at Hideko.

Creyton took another two steps back.

Hideko's eyes opened wider than Creyton thought their slant would allow, and both eyes were cursing him and damning him to hell.

They stared at each other for an eternity.

More dead hands clamped down on Hideko's shirt and in the

next moment his torso was pulled through the window, smothered in dead bodies, his legs dancing wildly in the air, the skin on his spine ripped apart by broken glass.

Several clawing fingers forced their way into the flesh on his right shoulder, blood churning around the knuckles like a penetrated volcano. In the next instant Hideko's arm was pulled from its socket and sought after like a bar of gold.

The rest of Hideko's body was then pulled completely through the window and disappeared in the swarm of dead bodies.

Creyton continued stepping away.

After that, the zombies started spilling inside, tumbling messily through the window frame like uncoordinated drunkards.

Creyton backstepped out of the room and pulled the door closed. He looked for a lock or switch on the doorknob, but there wasn't any.

"*Haitte kuru zo!*" he heard Mizuki shout. "They're in kitchen!"

Creyton heard more thrashing and banging coming from the other end of the hallway.

He darted back through the living room and found Mizuki scrambling on her hands and knees on the slick linoleum floor of the kitchen. Looking up, he saw that a zombie had torn away the air conditioner and was clawing through the open hole left in its wake.

Creyton went to Mizuki and lifted her up.

"We've got to go."

"Hideko!" she screamed, blasting his eardrums. "Where is Hideko?!"

"He's gone," said Creyton, tugging her along by the forearm.

"*Oh no, Hideko!*"

"It's just you and me now," Creyton expounded.

He saw that she had a half-full suitcase open on the floor, which he simply stepped over. He knew there was no time for her to finish packing.

He almost expected her to kick and scream, but she followed him without a struggle. They exited out the front door of the apartment, took the stairs two at a time, and made for his Volkswagon.

After he sat down in the driver's seat and Mizuki in the passenger, only then were the zombies beginning to pour around from the side of the building.

He started the engine, pumped the accelerator to help it along, shifted into gear, and got going.

* * * * *

Creyton was relieved to see that Tyrell had rescued his family, and was waiting for him at their designated spot —just off of Interstate 79, their old carpool rendezvous when they were taking welding classes together.

Tyrell was standing outside of his Jeep Liberty with his own gun. Three dead bodies, (previously zombies,) lay not twenty feet away. Creyton then figured that he hadn't been waiting long, or there would have been more carcasses and they would have been in piles.

He pulled his Volkswagon up alongside the Jeep and cut the engine. It was a good thing the vehicle was useless now.

—It was almost out of gas.

"We're here," he said. "That's Tyrell."

Mizuki, with tear-stained eyes, stared at him, but said nothing.

Creyton got out of the car, then walked around and opened the passenger door. Mizuki stumbled out, seemingly having trouble finding her footing.

Tyrell's wife Kendra was immediately at her side.

"Hello there, honey," she said in her typical sweet demeanor, placing two fingers underneath Mizuki's chin and gingerly raising her head so they could exchange gazes. "I'm *Kendra*. Creyton's told me a lot about you. Come on, let's get you in the car. You're safe with us."

Creyton watched them go, then caught a troubled glance from Tyrell.

Creyton immediately looked away.

Mizuki was situated in the back seat of the Young family's Jeep amongst several suitcases and Tyrell's five year-old son Terence.

Terence smiled and said, "Hello lady."

Kendra nodded to Tyrell, mouthed, "*Let's go, babe*," then climbed in the passenger seat and shut the door.

Creyton gazed down at his keyring, full of teethed metal he would never again have a need for.

He dropped them on the gravel shoulder like he would a used cigarette butt. And once they were let go, he was shocked to realize how noisy they had been and how much they had weighed him down.

He started walking toward the Jeep when Tyrell grabbed his arm and pulled him aside.

He asked, quite firmly, *"Where's her husband?"*

Creyton let his eyes wander away, coughed, and replied, "Zombies got him."

Tyrell let go, but his hand lingered in the air as if he wasn't sure he wanted to.

They climbed into the Jeep and, once everyone was settled in, pulled off of the crunchy gravel shoulder and onto the smoothly-paved Interstate 79, heading north.

There was only one occasion when they saw another vehicle in motion, and the driver inside looked deathly ill. He probably wouldn't last much longer.

Is it everywhere? Creyton wondered. *Is a fourth of our nation's population dead? A third? Half? More?*

After a few quiet miles, he asked, "So where are we going?"

Tyrell didn't answer. He was intently watching the empty road. Or maybe he had a lot of other things on his mind.

Kendra opened the glove box and grabbed something, then handed it around the seat.

Creyton accepted it from her.

It was a tri-folded pamphlet —an attractive full-color brochure advertising a golf resort in Rhode Island. Most of the attractions listed inside were labeled 'COMING SOON' or 'UNDER CONSTRUCTION.'

But Creyton didn't feel like reading. He asked, "All you know about this place is what you've read?"

"No," Kendra told him. "You remember the Turners? I babysat their kids Elliot and Alexis."

"Turners..." Creyton breathed, thinking. He remembered an older gentleman from his welding class who, like himself, just never seemed to be able to catch a break. His daughter Alexis would be in her late teens by now and had probably turned out very pretty, as Creyton somehow guessed she would. They deserved that much, because they were genuinely good people, just poor.

He said, "I remember Jim Turner. Family's down on their luck, but making the most of it. Right, Ty?"

Tyrell didn't answer, but Creyton could hear him breathing. He saw his eyes watch him briefly through the rear-view mirror.

—*Those eyes seemed all-knowing.*

Those had been the same eyes that had accompanied every disappointed comment about Creyton's not settling down, getting married, straightening out his life. Creyton hated looking at those eyes when they were like that, so he lowered his gaze to avoid them.

Kendra spoke up again: "Yeah, Jim got a job as maintenance man up at this place we're going."

"And what's so special about it?"

"It has walls."

"Oh."

Creyton exchanged a look with Mizuki. He showed her a smile.

And, after a sniffle, she showed one in return. Then she hugged him.

They held their embrace for several hours.

In the next five years, Tyrell would only ask two more times what had really happened to her husband. And each time Creyton wasn't swayed in his answer. He would say, very plainly, "Zombies got him."

And that would be that.

It surprised him, however, that he would hear similar excuses from a lot of other people.

They all knew no one was innocent enough to judge them.

RICK: Next we'll be speaking with two guests representing different views regarding the crisis spreading across our nation.

EARL: Right said, Face-For-Radio Rick. Please welcome Dr. Allison Fischer. She comes to us all the way from Rock Forge, West Virginia. And may I say I love your accent. Are you originally from Britain?

FISCHER: I don't see how that's relevant.

EARL: And may I add that you're a very lovely lady?

FISCHER: You're not nearly as charming as Howard Stern. Knock it off.

RICK: I think you're annoying her.

EARL: Maybe I have nothing better to do. Hey am I still getting paid?

FISCHER: What is he doing?

RICK: Earl are you leaving?

EARL: [expletive] right. What's the point of this [expletive]?

RICK: You're really leaving.

EARL: [expletive] right. [expletive] this.

RICK: Some of us have a work ethic.

FISCHER: How unprofessional. I'm here on my free time.

RICK: And we thank you for that, Doctor. On behalf of WKTT I apologize for Easy-Going Earl's behavior.

FISCHER: Let's move on.

MAXWELL: Yes. I believe I've been very patient as well.

RICK: Yes you have and we thank you for that. Let me introduce Reverend Wilfred Maxwell. He joins us on behalf of the Apostolic League. A division of the Moral Majority. How are you today?

MAXWELL: Much better now that I've been acknowledged.

RICK: Indeed. My apologies. Let me start with you, Doctor. Let's start with facts. The public needs facts.

FISCHER: Very well. I'll start by dispelling a rumor. The disease is not airborne. Of that we are certain. Nor is it transmittable through mosquitoes. I want to make that very clear. Remember this isn't malaria.

RICK: So it doesn't have the characteristics of a typical epidemic?

FISCHER: In some ways yes and in some ways no. I'm just trying to quash some of the rumors.

RICK: Tell us more. That doesn't make sense.

MAXWELL: Agreed.

FISCHER: The public needn't be fearful of mosquitoes. A poke from one of those buggers isn't cause enough to justify more flooding of emergency rooms. The virus which we haven't yet been able to isolate does not carry via mosquito. The blood of the reanimated dead does not circulate and their bodies do not radiate heat. Therefore they are not targets for mosquitoes. Basic. Simple. Let's move on.

MAXWELL: You talk circles woman.

FISCHER: Pardon?

MAXWELL: For the sake of argument let's say that a mosquito takes a nibble from a man who was just recently bitten by a zombie.

FISCHER: Reanimated dead.

MAXWELL: I'll say zombie if I so please. Let's say that a mosquito takes a nibble from this man. Okay? The man was just bitten by a zombie. Are you going to let me finish?

FISCHER: I haven't said a word you [expletive] ponce.

MAXWELL: Fine. Fine. Tell me. If this mosquito carries the blood of a man recently bitten and if this mosquito takes a stab at an uninfected human being will the uninfected human being then become infected?

FISCHER: There is no evidence of such a case on record.

MAXWELL: I see. So this is something science cannot solve?

FISCHER: I never said that.

RICK: Stay on topic lady and gentleman.

MAXWELL: I'm very on topic. This is further proof that what we are seeing is a calamity against man.

RICK: A calamity against man?

FISCHER: Oh pish-posh.

MAXWELL: Pish-posh? You've admitted yourself that this outbreak possesses no similarity to any virus mankind has dealt with before.

FISCHER: Do what? I never said that.

MAXWELL: You said as much. Would you like further proof? Take for example the fact that zombies feed only on mankind. The animal kingdom remains untouched.

FISCHER: That's not entirely accurate. It's been observed that in rare instances the reanimated dead will feed on birds, dogs, and what have you. It's been further observed that such things are not to the liking of the reanimated dead. A glitch, if you will. They will discard the remains almost completely intact.

MAXWELL: And do the animals reanimate?

FISCHER: No. They simply die. There have been no reanimated dogs or birds. In thousands of cases no animal has reanimated.

MAXWELL: Further proof that this is a calamity only against mankind. The Lord God is sparing the animal kingdom the punishment brought upon the world by the sins of man. We are witnessing the rapture.

RICK: The rapture?

FISCHER: Oh bloody hell. Religious speculation. Not this again.

MAXWELL: Six thousand years ago God created the heavens and the earth. Four thousand years ago he unleashed a flood to cleanse the earth of the offspring of unfaithful angels and the promiscuous women who slept with them. And two thousand years ago he sent his only begotten son Jesus Christ to die for our sins. Everything happens in two thousand year increments. You see? We are now two thousand years from the birth and death of our Savior. We are witnessing Wormwood. Thessalonians tells us that the dead in Christ shall rise up. We are witnessing the rapture. It's a wonderful thing. Soon we that are alive shall be caught up in the clouds to meet the Lord in the air.

RICK: Zombies are somehow involved with the rapture?

MAXWELL: Precisely.

FISCHER: Excuse me. I'm confused. Didn't Jesus raise Lazarus from the tomb after three days of interment? According to the Bible, and I use that phrase very loosely, didn't Lazarus resurrect with his soul intact? Well it appears to me that the reanimated dead have no soul. If anything I would think that this solidifies the fallacy of your logic. Not to mention your entire religion.

MAXWELL: It's evident the souls departed the body in the rapture and all that remains is a primal shell. A husk. You want to argue scripture with me lady?

FISCHER: No. I admit my Bible knowledge is not up to par. I'm a scientist. I have no qualms about that fact.

MAXWELL: I may not be as eloquent a speaker as you with all your college diplomas and whatnot. But God speaks to me and that's all the knowledge I need.

RICK: Okay. We're getting too far off topic. This isn't an evolution versus creation discussion. Okay my producers are begging me to take this call. Hello caller you're on the air. Do you have a question for Doctor Fischer or Reverend Maxwell?

CALLER: Hello?

RICK: Hello.

CALLER: Yes. I want to tell the Reverend there that he's a [expletive].

FISCHER: Clever bloke. I love you Colonialists.

RICK: Goodbye caller. Thank you for bringing such overwhelming information to our discussion. I think my head's going to burst.

MAXWELL: The message is quite clear. This calamity was brought upon us because of the queers and the false religions and the false gods. The queers sodomizing. The towel heads bowing to Allah. The Catholics still praying to Mary and the archangel Michael even though the good book says thou shalt put no other gods before me. And by not praying directly to God...

RICK: I've heard enough, Reverend.

MAXWELL: Then hear this: The Apostolic League is closing our doors.

RICK: I'm sorry sir. Did I accidentally cut your mic? So sorry. Doctor Fischer do you have anything else to add?

FISCHER: Just that I came here to spread facts and ended up arguing with this loony ponce. I have to return to Rock Forge not having accomplished a bloody thing.

RICK: It's two minutes to the noon hour and that means the morning show is coming to a close. Thank you for coming Reverend. And thank you Doctor Fischer. That's it for me. I've received word that the Federal Emergency Management Agency will be broadcasting from this station starting at noon. I'm Face-For-Radio Rick. Speaking for my absent colleague Easy-Going Earl Boy and all of us at WKTT FM 104.7 we wish you good day and good luck. Stay safe.

END OF TRANSCRIPT

WHEN THERE WERE SEVEN...

OF ALL THE mumbling and obscenities Delmas was spewing under his breath, all Leon could make out was: "*Never again in the winter. Fuck the Procurement Committee.*"

And while Leon certainly felt the same, he knew that joining Delmas' rant would only make things worse. He knew the best thing to do was keep his mouth shut.

Delmas was having enough trouble already. He had almost had the chain around the wheel on several occasions, yet each time the chain would find a way of slipping off and he would have to start over. His beret and visor lay discarded in the snow next to him and his face was red, partly from the cold, partly from anger. Though he had managed to get chains on three other tires with few complications, this wheel in particular was doing its best to be troublesome.

Delmas yanked on the chains to pull them taut, but they came loose and he stumbled backwards and fell in the snow, arms flailing. He was a stocky guy, perhaps with more fat than actual muscle, so something about it was rather comical. In situations like this Leon would normally blurt something like, '*Hey, that was almost the truffle shuffle!*' or at least point and laugh at his clumsy ass, (as the rules of their budding friendship dictated,) but he simply wasn't in the mood. Even after Delmas picked himself up off the ground —

leaving a large snow angel imprint —Leon stayed quiet.

He wasn't in the mood to joke around. Without chains around the tires, the twenty-six foot U-Haul Super Mover was going to remain stuck, quite thoroughly.

Delmas cussed again, gritting his teeth to avoid screaming at the top of his lungs and gathering unwanted attention. He threw the chain around the wheel once more, determined to win the tug of war.

Leon continued to stay out of his way.

Nearly a foot of snow had fallen in the span of just three hours, and it blanketed the entire market square. It was big, wet, sloppy snow, with flakes almost an inch wide, and looked more like torn tuffs of tissue paper than anything else. They didn't flutter back and forth as they fell either. Instead they fell straight down from the sky in big chunks almost as fast as hail. What lay on the ground now would have been perfect for forming snowballs if Leon was at all in any kind of recreational mood, but snow just wasn't fun anymore.

It was everywhere. The polished brick walkways of the marketplace, (where the well-to-do folks of the former world did their shopping,) were no longer visible beneath the white blanket. Abandoned cars were buried as well, their husks appearing as nothing more than small hills in an otherwise flat land. So much snow had fallen, in fact, that to walk through it meant lifting your leg high in the air with each step in order to unbury it. This had become a tiresome and tedious process and Leon was sick of it. He had carried more than his fair share of boxes already, so he figured he deserved this standing rest.

The sky had been clear that morning at Eastpointe and the previous day had seen seasonably warm sixty-plus degree temperatures, so the Black Berets agreed to go ahead and undertake the Procurement Committee's request. They really hadn't given it a second thought. Previous outings had proven thankfully uneventful and everyone assumed that this one would prove uneventful as well.

Alas —as Leon had learned from growing up in central Maine — *snow happens.* Even though it was the middle of March, everyone should have known better than to press their luck. Now the day had only a couple of hours of light left and just a few yards of visibility.

And to think: A few degrees warmer and it would have been

raining instead of snowing. It would have been one hell of a rainstorm, sure, but rain would cause little more than a creek overflowing its banks here and there. But no, it had to be snow.

—*Big, wet, sloppy snow. A blizzard*, in fact.

It had hit like a sucker punch and still gave no signs of letting up. Snowflakes kept landing on Leon's visor and melting into a big splash of water. Over and over he had to take the time to wipe it off with his forearm. He was tired and hungry, his last peanut butter and jelly sandwich gobbled up more than four hours ago.

His frustration continued growing, accelerated by Delmas' prolonged rantings.

Leon could stand it no longer.

All at once he ripped his visor and beret from his head, which was a mixed blessing. With the visor on he had been breathing recycled air and it had kept his lungs and throat warm.

He took a moment to swipe away some snowflakes that had gathered on his shoulders. The cold had penetrated his trylar wetsuit long ago, but he tolerated it because he thought Delmas would have gotten the U-Haul moving long before now.

Noticeably shivering and rattling his teeth, he stepped away from Delmas long enough to grab a wool cloak from the back of the adjacent humvee. He pulled it over his shoulders, but didn't wear the attached hood. He didn't want to obstruct his peripheral vision any more than it already was. The veritable whiteout made seeing more than a few yards away very difficult —let alone trying to see beyond the buildings in the market square, which was downright impossible.

But this is it, he thought. *This is what's going to kill me.*

He knew he could be asking for trouble wearing the cloak. It was a fundamental lesson any Black Beret was taught: never give a skin-eater something to grab hold of. However, with the cloak on he felt immediate warmth and he wasn't about to take it off anytime soon, advice be damned. He would take his chances.

Still, he wondered if this was the mistake that was going to cost him.

He clipped his visor and beret to his belt, then knelt down beside Delmas. They were alone up here on the other side of the square, just them, the stuck U-Haul, and the humvee.

And still they could not get their jobs done.

"I want to be in my warm house in my warm bed," Delmas gritted, still struggling with the chain. "I want to be sipping hot chocolate. Right now. Right this minute."

"I never would have guessed that, Captain Obvious," Leon replied. He reached around the tire in an attempt to show Delmas he was offering assistance, though he honestly didn't know what he was doing. He had never fit chains on a tire before. In his experience such a task was always left up to the school bus driver. After all, it wasn't that long ago that the world was normal and he was riding the bus to school every day. And from what Leon understood, Delmas had been a farmhand in one of the sunnier states far, far south of Rhode Island, so it left him wondering whether or not Delmas knew what he was doing either.

On his knees, the snow piled on the ground was reaching nearly to Leon's hips. He jumped up, feeling his scrotum shriveling up into his groin. It wasn't pleasant.

He swiped the snow from his legs and declared, "This is miserable."

Delmas nodded, gritted his teeth, and continued yanking on the chain.

Leon looked away again and peered into the whiteness of the market square.

Until now the stores here had been left abandoned and untouched in the aftermath of the apocalypse. There was a medical supply warehouse with an attached pharmacy on the east side, which had been the first building the Black Berets emptied. They filled an entire U-Haul with nothing but medicines and antiseptics and antibiotics of all kinds. (Toothpaste was in high demand this time as well; lots and lots of toothpaste.) Then came the industrial supply store to the north. All of the toiletries and light bulbs there were relocated into a second U-Haul. Then came the icing —the boutiques that gave up their designer clothing and high-end electronics. Unfortunately only the smaller ten-foot U-Haul was left, but it was being filled to capacity.

The market was indeed a good location, all things considered. It was in the outskirts of East Greenwich, roughly halfway between Eastpointe and Providence. It sat at the end of its own road and nothing else was around except for forests and small ponds. The market was probably meant to be the epicenter of a growing district that never got the chance to develop.

This was also the furthest north anyone dared to go. To venture any further meant going dangerously close to Providence, which had been a high population center in the world before.

—And a high population center *then* meant a high undead population center *now*.

Leon shivered against the cold and pulled tightly on his cloak.

He could see that roughly forty yards away the others in his group were carrying boxes out of the boutiques and loading them into the smaller ten-foot U-Haul. The Berets had brought a couple hundred folded cardboard boxes, then hastily filled them with items from the Procurement Committee's list by going up and down store isles and sweeping merchandise off the shelves.

Despite the speed of their methods, errands such as these were still day-long jobs.

But Leon could see that the smallest U-Haul was almost full now, which meant the job was just about over. Everyone was going to be wondering about the status of the stuck U-Haul.

He looked back to Delmas and asked, "You think Mike's put chains on before?"

Delmas took a moment to consider this, then glanced up and replied, "Well, he *was* a mechanic."

"Then hell with this," Leon snapped. "Let Mike do it."

"Why involve a bunch of people? This is going to turn into '*how many Berets does it take to screw in a light bulb?*'"

"Get over it." Leon pulled his walkie-talkie from his belt, held down the talk button, and said, "Mike, do us a favor. Come put these chains on."

After a few seconds a voice replied, "*Be right there.*"

Leon put away his walkie-talkie.

He knew he had learned a lesson here today: never move a U-Haul *after* snow falls. All it does is cause the snow beneath the tires to compact into a surface a lot like ice. But at the time it didn't seem like there was any other choice. The U-Haul had originally been parked under an old maple tree and the branches hovering above were getting weighted down from the snow. The biggest one was already starting to splinter. So he moved the U-Haul. It seemed like a wise move at the time, because not five minutes later that tree branch broke and came crashing to the ground. It would have busted the windshield for sure.

Now, however, since the U-Haul had already been loaded to capacity with supplies from the medical warehouse, pushing the heavy bastard with any other vehicle was out of the question. Yet somehow it still wasn't heavy enough to grind up the ice beneath the tires and find traction on the asphalt below. Unlike the other two U-Hauls and their brand new winter tires, the tires on this U-Haul were absolutely bare. The treads had worn off long ago.

An available solution? Chains.

But Leon knew he was going to catch hell from *somebody*, probably Vaughn. Or —*more than likely* —he was going to get a tongue-lashing from that opinionated Courtney Colvin, (the only female in their group,) even though she didn't know anything about snow, being the Florida girl that she was. Yet she always had something to say about *everything*, regardless of whether she knew what she was talking about or not.

"Guess this means no badminton tomorrow, huh?" Delmas asked as he stood and retrieved his visor and beret. "I thought with the weather we've been having, we could have a spot of badminton."

"Yeah, it's not looking good for the home team, is it?" Leon replied.

Delmas chuckled. It was forced somewhat, but still genuine. He said, "I like you, Leon. If we don't die first, maybe someday we can hang out again."

Leon smirked.

From the whiteness that surrounded them, Leon heard a voice call out, "Someone say badminton?"

He turned to look. Through the curtain of falling snow he saw a figure approach.

It was Mike Newcome.

"I like badminton," he solemnly declared.

Being as one-word phrases was usually the most Leon ever heard the quiet guy utter, he couldn't help but grin that Mike had made an effort to be sociable.

"Get us out of this mess and you're invited to play," Leon replied, motioning with his outstretched hand to the tire, then to the chain that lay buried under the snow beside it.

Mike joked, "*Shit rolls downhill,*" then knelt down and retrieved the chain. He twisted it around in his hands for a moment, inspecting it. He looked to the tire, then to the chain, then to the tire again. Then he spoke the revelation: "You have to adjust the chain. You've got it set too small. See these hooks?" He looked back at the U-Haul, then at Delmas. He added, "I don't even think you've got the others on right."

Delmas grunted. He lowered his head and asked, "We have to do them all over again?"

"It's not a problem," came the reply. "But someone should take my place on the loading line."

Leon and Delmas glanced at each other, but neither said anything. Leon certainly didn't want to carry any more boxes today and by the look of it, Delmas didn't either.

The work was simply getting too difficult. Raids had been easier when there were four more people on the team —and therefore more hands in which to carry stuff —but those people had met their end one way or another during previous outings.

Now there was just the seven.

Finally Leon said in a huff, "Well, hell... *I'll do it.*"

* * * * *

He trudged across the market square, cutting through the playground in the middle. The seats on the swingsets were covered in snow and the sliding board was on its side, beaten down naturally from two years of neglect. And, of course, there was a sandbox buried beneath the snow that Leon promptly found with his feet and stumbled over. He was barely able to keep his balance. It wouldn't have mattered if he had fallen anyway, as his cloak was already soaked and not much good anymore at defending him against the cold.

When he reached the other U-Hauls he saw that the rear doors of both the big one and the small one were shut. Nicholas was in front of the two vehicles, feverishly shoveling snow. It looked like he was doing a decent job of it. There was a clear path of exposed asphalt that stretched for roughly fifteen yards in front of both U-Hauls. Since they had been parked here since before the storm began, there was no compacted snow beneath the tires to worry about. Besides, the tires had plenty of tread to get them moving when the time came. The path that Nicholas made would give the vehicles a running start. Leon figured that once the vehicles were moving at a steady clip, there shouldn't be any problem with them getting stuck.

Sliding was all the drivers would have to worry about.

Nicholas was a dark-skinned fellow, barely inching above Courtney, the shortest of their group, and skinnier than Vaughn Winters, the tallest. He had a typical American way of speaking, but due to his permanent tan, somewhere along the way he got the nickname '*Arabian Nick*.' He had brought this nickname with him, so its origins must not have been derogatory in any way. After all, most people left mental baggage like that behind them.

Leon understood. Nicknames were something even the end of the world couldn't take from you.

Nicholas set down his snow shovel and leaned on it, breathing hard. He motioned to the U-Haul in the distance and asked, "Got the chains on yet?"

Leon shook his head no.

"Vaughn's gonna be pissed."

"Don't really care," Leon replied. "Vaughn's not the boss." He took a moment to glance around, wondering where the rest of his group was. There were still three unaccounted for. He asked, "Where's the rest of our merry band?"

"Ah, Chris is watching for skin-eaters on the road," said Nicholas. "And I think Courtney and Vaughn are in there." He pointed to the nearby pharmacy.

Leon opened the driver-side door of the smallest U-Haul and tossed his soaked cloak inside. It wouldn't be helpful again until it dried anyway, and there was a certain amount of relief that washed over him now that he didn't have any loose clothing to worry about.

A clear path had been created by repeated trips in and out of the pharmacy; the snow there trampled down and compacted. But the path was quickly being filled back in again by the snow that continued to fall.

Now more than ever, Leon wanted this day to be over with. He knew it was going to be a long drive back to Eastpointe.

He nodded *adieu* to Nicholas, then hustled into the nearby

pharmacy.

It had been ransacked —effectively looted by the Berets. The several isles of shelves that previously carried the over-the-counter cough syrups, aspirins and bandages were all bare, and all the prescription medication behind the counter was gone as well.

Yet he immediately discovered that Courtney Colvin was in here, apparently having found something that piqued her interest.

She was standing by the book rack near the entrance and thumbing through the paperbacks. Her nose was in one of them. Her visor and beret dangled from her belt, her hair matted in places but still flowing. She was a cute, petite chick the same age as Leon, but Leon had never gotten accustomed to seeing her carry a gun, especially in situations like this. She just didn't look the type. Right now she looked like a typical shopper in a pre-zombie world —like at any moment she might take her paperback of choice to the front counter and actually try to pay for it.

The innocent way she swung her hips as she shifted her feet, combined with the tight fit of the trylar wetsuit, caused sensual little wrinkles to appear on her posterior. They would materialize, branch off and then vanish, reform and race like streaks of lightning transversely across her butt.

Being male, Leon checked her out. But Courtney Colvin was a known shrew, all sass and no class. He figured most of his teammates saw her as just another asexual figure in a uniform. Yet it didn't change the fact that she was a sharp-looking girl, and her nonchalant attitude about it somehow made her more desirable.

The cover of the paperback she was perusing depicted a shirtless, long-haired blonde man with exaggerated muscles hovering over an equally scantily-clad woman. The wind was at their backs and they appeared ready to kiss.

The entire scene surprised Leon, since he had kind of assumed that Courtney didn't read at all, and instead spent all her time plotting more ways in which to hate everybody.

As he entered the pharmacy he disturbed the light that shone through the doorway, which was the same light Courtney was using to see her selections.

Upon seeing a shadow move across the bookshelf, she turned her head, paperback still in her hands. She saw Leon, but gave no indication that he was of any consequence, or even relief that he wasn't a skin-eater. She turned back to the bookshelf.

Instead of simply asking if she knew Vaughn's whereabouts so they could all leave, (as he later decided he should have,) something made him want to be sociable instead.

He asked, very casually, "What are you doing?"

Her eyes didn't wander from the text in the book and her posture didn't give any hint that she wanted idle banter. Moving her lips as little as possible, she just as casually replied, "I'm painting the ceiling. What does it *look* like I'm doing?"

All the same, he walked over and stood next to her. He picked up one of the paperbacks, flipped through it, then put it back without regard.

"You like the romance, do you?" he asked.

"Sometimes," she replied.

It was then she turned her head and stared at him, as if she had realized that she wasn't supposed to speak sociably with him, or — *perhaps* —that she had spoken out of character. She quickly compensated by cracking, "Are you *lost*? GAP is across the street. Or did you just notice that the credit card machines are offline?"

Leon grinned. It wasn't because her insult was particularly clever or anything, it was because her face looked kind of mousey when she was being snide. If she had been an ugly sort, it would have been easy to just tell her off. But Courtney rarely got loud and wasn't necessarily obnoxious. She was just sassy. And the best way to deal with her, he had learned, was to return the attitude. He wasn't about to be stepped on by *her*.

"Ain't lost," he said. "You just look so out of place here, is all. We're a long way from any *Hot Topic*."

She scoffed, "Do I *look* goth to you?"

"Possibly," Leon replied. "Maybe you could marry Vaughn, being peas in a pod and all that."

She let out a disgusted sigh. She glared back at him, giving him a good looking over, and sported a brazen grin as she returned, "You're one to talk. Look at you. The '*metro*' fashion died out with the rest of the world. Didn't you get the memo?"

Leon chuckled, but couldn't come up with anything better than: "Quite the sassy little minx, aren't you?"

246

"What did you call me?"

"Minx." He inched closer. "Would you rather I call you *doll*?" He lifted his hand and brushed his thumb across her cheek, then gently tucked several locks of hair behind her left ear, exposing more of her face. Strangely enough, it almost seemed like she was enjoying the attention. Leon went on, "Porcelain skin, angelic face. *Doll* suits you well."

Her face tightened up and she took a sudden step back. "Oh my god," she uttered, "You've got the nerve to *hit* on me? Do you really think you impress me with these bullshit come-ons? Do girls actually *fall* for this crap?"

Leon was taken aback for a moment. It was just the way he talked, to *any* girl, not just her. Most of them understood his mannerisms. But still, he had forgotten that this was the first time he had spoken to her as if she weren't a male. He stuttered, "Are you going to start flipping out?"

"Did you say *stat* flipping out?"

"I said *start* flipping out."

"No, you said *stat*. Lose the accent. You sound like an idiot."

Much in the manner of public speakers picturing their audiences naked, in this situation Leon tried to imagine her orgasm face. He couldn't quite picture it though. Did she scrunch up her eyes? Did her mouth hang open? Was she a moaner or a screamer? Did the shrew even *have* orgasms?

If she didn't, she sure needed one.

But Leon realized he had already reverted to a defensive mode —a desperate tactic a lot like burying his head in the sand. He didn't know what to say next.

Courtney shone him a grin that seemed to say *'better luck next time,'* then tucked her book under her arm and strutted out the door.

As he stood there trying to shrug it off, the sound of footsteps coming from the darkness further inside the pharmacy caused him to turn on his heels. He put his palm on the handle of his .45 Socom, but kept enough wits about him to not pull the gun from its holster.

A shadow approached. The accompanying voice said, *"That's funny.* I haven't seen her this mad since that house fell on her sister."

Leon recognized the voice as belonging to Vaughn Winters and immediately relaxed his grip on his gun.

Vaughn stepped from the shadows in all his gothic glory, long stringy black hair oozing onto his shoulders. Though he was somewhat lanky, he was still imposing. There was definite muscle to be seen bulging through the sleeves of his trylar wetsuit.

He leaned casually against the front counter opposite Leon, taking gulps from a bottle of purified water he must have swiped from the back of the store.

Leon turned around again to gaze at the snowbound world through the open pharmacy doors and declared, "I'll never be able to have an intelligible conversation with that girl."

"Too bad. You have *so* much in common," Vaughn returned, taking a drink of water and smacking his lips, refreshed. He then added, "*WASPs* need to look out for each other."

"Wasps?"

"*White Anglo-Saxon Protestants*," said Vaughn, matter-of-factly. "I thought you people bred like bunnies. Too bad you put *ipecac* in her water glass..."

"It was *vinegar*."

"Doesn't matter. Had the same effect. You really missed the ball on that one, champ. Think about it: if you hadn't done that, right now you could be savagely penetrating her baby factory."

Leon grunted at Vaughn's vulgarity.

Vaughn took the last drink of his water and tossed the empty bottle over his shoulder. It landed somewhere behind the counter. Unfazed —perhaps even *inspired* —he continued, "Why bother with a female that has such a snobbish upper lip anyway? I just can't quite picture her ever lowering herself to give you a blowjob, no matter how much you look like a member of her favorite boy-band. It would be blasphemy. But don't fret, man. If the world had stayed normal, she'd be addicted to prozac right about now."

Leon was speechless. He wasn't sure just who Vaughn had been insulting. Words danced in his head but couldn't be vocalized.

Vaughn stepped towards the magazine rack next to the bookshelf and scoured it from top to bottom. After a moment he reached in and grabbed one of them. He opened it in his hands and started flipping through the plastic pages, obviously searching for one in particular.

Without turning his gaze from the magazine, he asked, "Leon, you're —what —not even twenty years old yet?"

Leon turned to face him and answered, "Nineteen."

"It shows."

"What did you do in the world before, Vaughn?" Leon stammered. "Just go around spreading evil?"

"Is this a *getting-to-know-you* chat?"

"Pretend it is."

"Well, actually, I was *famous*," said Vaughn. "A *lord*, really. I sat in my throne room all day long while half-naked women laid around me like housecats, trained to break open Cadbury Eggs and pour the filling straight down my gullet."

This statement was followed by a smartass grin.

Leon rolled his eyes.

Vaughn chuckled heartily, then handed Leon the magazine he had been looking at, opened to page forty-seven. As he walked out of the pharmacy, he said, "In the world before, I was just like you, man. I was on the verge of *what could have been*."

Leon watched him until he stepped out of sight, then glanced down at the open magazine in his hands. His eyes glanced over the page, but it was too dark inside the old pharmacy and the text in the magazine was terribly small and cluttered by lots of unnecessary clipart. He didn't have enough time to comprehend what he was reading.

—Or perhaps he didn't care enough to bother trying.

A voice coming over the walkie-talkie squawked, "*I see deadfucks.*"

Leon dropped the magazine and dashed outside. He joined with Vaughn and Courtney as they ran to the road.

* * * * *

Christopher Gooden was a militant-looking fellow. He had sunken cheekbones and a shaved head, though his hair was beginning to peek through his scalp again. Surprisingly, however, he wasn't in the military before the apocalypse. Like most of them, he hadn't even held a gun until after the first corpse decided to rise.

He had been a gymnast, so far as Leon knew from listening to him talk, yet his affinity for fighting and firearms was quickly realized. He was stoic, had eyes like a hawk, and was definitely the group's sharpest shooter.

For these reasons, everyone felt safe when Gooden was on the lookout.

As they gathered on the road that exited the marketplace, there was a bluish fog rising from the ground. Snow was still cascading from the sky, but there was only a half-light now —a ghostly glow reflected upon the blizzard.

Twilight was upon them.

Leon said, "I don't see anything."

"About fifty yards down," Chris told him, handing him a pair of binoculars. "The locals don't like our shopping spree."

Leon put the binoculars to his eyes and brought them into focus. At first he saw nothing but close-up snowflakes given profound clarity and detail —a whirlwind of intricate patterns and designs.

Then, seen vaguely amidst the whiteness, Leon made out several stumbling shapes coming down the road. They were human figures, yet they had an awkward gait and dragged their feet through the snow. Their heads and shoulders were covered with it, but it didn't seem to be slowing them down.

The longer Leon watched, the more of them that came into his view. He counted at least fifty before giving up.

He lowered the binoculars and mouthed, "*Damn.*"

"Let me see," Courtney told him.

He handed her the binoculars and she put them to her eyes.

"So what do you think?" Christopher asked. "Do we abandon the U-Haul? Take what we got and run down the deadfucks on our way out of here?"

Courtney passed the binoculars to Vaughn. She added, "We should definitely quit while we're ahead."

Leon lifted his walkie-talkie and said, "Delmas? Mike? How are the chains coming along?"

After a moment, Delmas squawked from the other end, "*Mike's on his third wheel right now.*"

"He might not have time to finish," Leon told him.

"*Why? How many skin-eaters are coming?*"

Vaughn lifted his own walkie-talkie and pressed the talk button, effectively cutting off Leon. He told Delmas, "Just stay cool. Tell Mike to get it done."

Leon gritted his teeth, but stayed calm. He asked, "And just what are we going to do?"

Vaughn stood tall. He declared, "We're going to cancel all these motherfuckers, *that's* what we're going to do." He lifted his walkie-talkie again, pressed the talk button, and barked more orders. This time it was, "Nick, bring us some Hornets."

Leon looked down the road again. He recalled when they had driven up this road that morning, before all the snowfall. It was mostly straight and completely clear, though now there wasn't even really any hint of a road underneath all the snow. But there was no abandoned cars, no toppled trees —nothing to stop the advance of the dead people.

He squinted his eyes. Though the zombies were still just a dark blur in the distance, he could now see them without the binoculars.

That meant they were getting closer.

Courtney must have seen them too. She commented, "*There's too many.*"

Her frequent bitchiness aside, Leon admired Courtney's rationale. She always played things safe —acted only when the odds were in her favor. It was probably why she was still alive.

"I'm not leaving the U-Haul," Vaughn told her, quite firmly. He turned to face Leon and Chris, and stated, "This is a cushy fucking job. Don't you realize that? We work maybe a couple of days a month. You guys want a day job? You want to be planting potatoes? Cutting up cows in the slaughterhouse? Mowing grass? Shoveling shit on the farm?"

Nobody said anything.

Vaughn went on, "Fuck that. I don't shovel shit. *This* is my job. We're not leaving anything behind. The more we take home means the less times we have to go out. So the U-Haul goes with us." He paused a moment, taking the time to stare directly into Leon's eyes, then Chris', then Courtney's. He added, "The dimwits back in Eastpointe call us a Strike Team, so why don't we fucking *strike* for once?"

Nicholas came running up then, his arms bogged down with three .22 Hornet rifles and another strapped on his back. On top of the pile of rifles was a green lockbox containing more ammunition.

Leon took the lockbox and one of the rifles. He cocked the rifle to make certain it was already fully loaded. Vaughn grabbed one, followed by Courtney. Chris, being the prime example of a Black Beret, already had his rifle. He had been lugging it around with him all day, even while loading the U-Hauls.

"So what's the situation?" Nicholas asked.

"Go back and warm up the U-Hauls," Vaughn told him. "Get them started and ready to go."

"Hell with that," said Nicholas, retrieving the rifle from his back and holding it at ready. "If there's shooting to be done—"

"—Do what I tell you," Vaughn interrupted.

Nicholas scoffed. He looked to Leon for support, but Leon rolled his eyes and turned away. Courtney and Chris weren't much help either.

Finally Nicholas turned back to Vaughn and declared in a huff, "You're not the boss."

Leon moaned. He knew why Nicholas said it —because *he* had said it earlier —but it was never meant to be something one would proclaim directly to Vaughn's face.

Vaughn turned to Nicholas.

His arm sprang out.

Before Leon could even discern what happened or what exact motions had been made, in the next instant Vaughn was holding Nicholas' rifle, and Nicholas was holding nothing. It was even stranger that they were both still standing and in pretty much the same positions they were in before. *Something* had happened, but the actual movements were a blur.

All Leon knew was that Vaughn had somehow snatched Nick's rifle while Nick stood there looking dumbfounded.

Krav Maga, Leon remembered. *Vaughn's instructor taught him that.*

Nicholas stared at his rifle now in Vaughn's hands, a pouting frown forming on his lips.

Without raising his voice, yet still carrying the slow, methodical firmness of speech he was known for, Vaughn told Nicholas: "Now you ain't shooting shit, Aladdin. Go start the truck."

Nicholas stepped back. He then quietly turned and headed back to the vehicles.

Everyone else was quiet. Leon glanced over at Courtney and

noticed that her knees were trembling ever so slightly. Maybe it was the cold. Or maybe Vaughn made *her* nervous as well.

"Let's get to work," said Vaughn. He removed his visor from his belt and fit it over his face, then situated the beret on top.

Leon, Courtney, and Chris followed suit.

They formed a straight line crossways in the street outside the marketplace. Vaughn took the left. Leon took the spot beside him, Courtney was third, and Chris took the spot furthest on the right. They nestled two arms-lengths apart. The Black Beret training manuals had called this formation *Frontline*. They opened the ammo box and situated it between them for easy access. It sunk deep into the snow, barely peeking above the surface.

Leon raised his .22 Hornet and peered through the scope.

The first zombie that came into view looked like it had been something of a redneck in its previous life. Its jeans were torn at the knees and a black and red checkered flannel adorned its upper half. It was ripped all over. The left side of the zombie's face was peeled away and stained in black, likely caused by blood that had once flowed and then coagulated over time, gathering all kinds of muck in the process. Its skin was a cold blue color. Snow hung like a carpet across its head and shoulders.

They don't change, Leon thought. *Why don't they fucking rot?!*

He was freezing, shaking so much that the zombie's image bounced and wobbled through his scope. He tried to keep his shakiness from being noticeable by any of the others.

He reminded himself that he had done all this before.

He forced himself to stay calm. To focus.

—To be an *adult*.

The zombie ambled closer, filling up more of Leon's view through the high-powered scope. He tried to focus the crosshairs on the dead man's forehead.

"Why don't they decay?" Courtney whispered, speaking to no one in particular as she, too, peered through the scope of her rifle. "How can they keep moving?"

"Ask God when you meet him," Vaughn replied, keeping his focus on the throng of dead people walking up the road. He instructed, "Keep steady. Choose your shots."

Leon slowed his breathing. Any long-winded exhales were

causing the inside of his visor to fog up. He tried to avoid doing it.

He centered the crosshairs on the redneck zombie's forehead, steadied himself, then pulled back the trigger. The gun discharged with a healthy-sounding *crack*. Up ahead, the left eyeball of the targeted zombie suddenly exploded in a mist of white gunk and the back of its head let loose a maelstrom of brain and skull fragments. It fell face-first in the snow and didn't move again.

However, there were plenty of walking corpses behind it to take its place. Soon they were stumbling over their fallen companion with nary a downward glance.

They lurched closer.

Vaughn's gun discharged, followed by Chris' and Courtney's. Up ahead, three more zombies collapsed in the snow.

Leon cocked his gun and took aim again.

The zombie he focused on next had been a short fat lady. Strangely enough, her purse still dangled from a strap over her head and down past the opposite shoulder. Her midsection was torn away and a chunk of pale intestine was peeking out like a hibernating snake. Her eyes were glazed over with a milky-white haze.

Everything was given so much clarity through the high-powered scope of the .22 Hornet that Leon could see a maggot slithering on the fat lady's face. It had crawled halfway up her left nostril and the exposed tail was waving back and forth across her upper lip as if trying to hail a cab.

Leon swallowed hard, resisting the urge to gag. He centered the crosshairs on the fat lady's forehead and pulled the trigger. She collapsed in the snow. The other zombies stepped over her.

Vaughn fired. Courtney fired. Chris fired.

Three more zombies dropped in the snow.

Leon cocked his rifle and took aim again.

There was a zombie in the vanguard that was pushing ahead of the others, probably sensing food was closer than ever. It was walking in full strides now, its feet plowing through the snow, its arms outstretched, its head tilted back and its mouth wide open.

Leon made an example of it by putting it out of its misery.

The mob had gained roughly ten yards, and were now easily visible with the naked eye.

"Be shooting a little faster if you don't mind," said Vaughn.

The other rifles discharged and three more zombies fell.

Leon lifted his rifle again.

Aiming was easier now that the mob was closer. Leon quickly situated the crosshairs on a random forehead and shot a zombie down. He cocked his rifle, aimed, and did it again.

The other Berets in the line were doing the same, quickening their pace to match the approaching speed of the undead mob.

Leon reached down and grabbed more ammunition from the open lockbox. He shoved five bullets in the chamber of the Hornet, cocked it, then lifted it towards the zombies. He could hear them making all kinds of noises now, gaspless moans and raspy snarls. Those at the front were going into a frenzy and it was spreading through the horde like a plague within a plague. They were pushing through the snow even faster, nearly trampling over each other like crazed fans chasing a tour bus. The four Berets kept putting them down, one after another. Still they shuffled closer, unfazed by the loss of their brethren.

Leon continued reloading, aiming, and shooting. Every shot fired by the Berets brought down one of the targets. This went on for a while, until the lockbox and the ammunition belts were all empty. By this point the zombies had shuffled to within twenty yards of the firing line.

The Berets dropped their rifles and pulled their .45 Socoms from their holsters. They flicked off the safeties and switched on the targeting lasers.

The attached silencers muffled the gunshots, but the approaching mass of zombies was dropping one by one. The fallen were replaced by more, marching over the motionless bodies like a squad of army ants.

Vaughn emptied his clip and reloaded. He calmly instructed everyone, "Remember the formation. If one of us steps back, the others follow. Don't obstruct the firing line."

Leon focused his eyes over the barrel of his Socom. He went in short bursts from left to right, highlighting undead foreheads with the targeting laser and putting bullets in them in rapid succession. When all fifteen rounds were spent, he dropped the empty clip from his gun and loaded another.

The zombies continued to advance. Though they had no plan,

no grand strategy, and nor were they capable of making one, their fearless persistence was the greatest threat. The group was inadvertently widening and enveloping the Berets.

The Berets started picking off the wings of the ranks to prevent themselves from getting surrounded. They needed the battle to remain straight on.

All the zombies were frenzied now and moving in fast strides. One of them got within five feet of the firing line. The Berets began taking small steps backwards, but continued shooting.

Zombies continued dropping.

Others continued stepping over them.

"Need another clip!" Christopher Gooden shouted.

"We're out!" Vaughn shouted back. "Switch!"

The last of the .45 ammunition depleted, the Berets hurriedly holstered their Socoms on the right side of their belts. An audible scraping sound was made as all four Berets, in unison, drew their wakizashis from their sheaths. That noise was followed by a satisfying wisping sound as the blades cut through the bitter air and into a defensive position.

"Keep it simple," Vaughn told them. "One-two."

Even through all the commotion Leon was getting sick of the condescending drivel. He was tired of Vaughn treating him and the rest like children —like they didn't know how to handle themselves —like they hadn't been drilled on these techniques umpteen-million times just like he had.

A hideously ugly dead person approached, eyeballs bulging, mouth open and ready to bite. Its arms were outstretched, raggedy sleeves dangling.

Leon cut off one of its hands at the wrist with one swing of the blade, then made a clean slice through its forehead with a second, gelatinous brain matter leaking from the cut. The zombie dropped at his feet.

Another approached. Leon went through the same process; off with the hand, followed by a slash through the brain.

All down the line the other Berets were mimicking this method.

One-two.

One-two.

One-two.

The zombies continued advancing, continued falling, and the Berets kept taking subtle steps backwards to maintain distance.

Now, however, a possible end to the battle could be seen. There were no more heads lingering behind the mob of walking corpses. That meant no more reinforcements —No more to deal with after this last rush of roughly twenty to twenty-five.

Leon was aware of his exhaustion. It was evident in the way he swung his wakizashi. His muscles were hot despite the chill of the air around him. His arms were feeling swollen and cumbersome.

But he kept swinging.

And then he fell.

There had been something on the road, buried beneath the snow. By the feel of it, he guessed it to be a bicycle wheel. He had stepped on it with his heel and it pivoted up like a seesaw, slapping against his calf. He stumbled and fell backward. Though there was a large cushion of snow to land on, it still hurt. He was learning that extreme cold served only to enhance the effects of pain.

Suddenly he could see nothing but the deadfuck falling on him —a Rambo-looking survivalist freak, snarling, old bite wounds all up and down its arms.

Leon remembered his Jiu-Jitsu training and kicked away at the creature from his back, hoping to stall it long enough so he could stand up again. But it was relentless. When it finally came down, Leon trapped it in his legs. He put the blade of his wakizashi to the monster's throat, then put his free arm around its head. He pulled his two arms together, forcing the blade through the zombie's neck and cutting cleanly through the spine. Gooey blood poured from the severed trachea like day-old gravy.

The decapitated head slid from the neck and ricocheted off Leon's visor, leaving a black smudge in the shape of open lips.

However, as Leon went to shove the headless corpse off of him, he was mauled by another.

A salesman-looking type came down on him, pinning Leon's hand and sword against his chest. Then another zombie approached from the left, this one resembling the nanny he had in his younger years.

Leon's vision was blinded as a glob of snow that had piled up on the corpse's head slid off and caked on his visor.

He didn't have a hand available to wipe it away.

The zombie opened its mouth and sunk its teeth around Leon's forearm. It chomped down, hard. The pain was worse than one of his old pointless, boredom-induced experiments in high school shop class, when he had fit a C-clamp on his skin and twisted the screw until he could stand it no longer.

The corpse continued biting and clawing, turning Leon's forearm in its palms as if it were kneading dough.

Leon screamed, "Fuck!"

He then felt the same painful sensation again, this time on his left leg, directly on his calf. He could feel his skin being tugged on. When he tried to kick the zombie away with his other leg it only made it worse. His skin —through the trylar wetsuit —was firmly between the teeth of the creature and it gave no hint that it was going to ease off.

Leon was gritting his teeth and breathing hard, panicking now, still blinded by the glob of snow on his visor.

Then he felt the zombie biting at his leg let go, shortly followed by the one chomping away at his arm.

Finally free, he swiped his forearm across his visor to clear away the snow. He saw that the two zombies that had been attacking him now had sword slices through their skulls.

He felt a hand grab him by the collar of his trylar wetsuit. He was then dragged through the snow several feet before the hand released him.

Looking up, Leon saw a tall, lanky figure that could only be Vaughn Winters.

Vaughn saves me? Leon mused.

He brought himself to his feet. He was numb from the overwhelming coldness of laying in the snow. He was tired. Weary. Breathing hard.

He hoped he wouldn't have to fight anymore.

Thankfully, with the last snicker-snack of someone else's wakizashi, the final zombie fell flat on its face.

The battle was over.

Leon ripped away his visor and beret and let them fall to the ground, unconcerned with where they landed.

Vaughn, Courtney, and Chris gathered around him.

Shaking, Leon brought his aching forearm close to his face and inspected it. He looked closely for any sign that the zombie's teeth had penetrated the trylar and sunk into his skin. He saw nothing — only little pointy indentations where the incisors had been. He then hurriedly knelt down and checked his leg. The trylar was wrinkled there, perhaps even stretched. But it wasn't broken.

—*Thank God it wasn't broken.*

His eyes were watering. He wasn't sure if these tears were there because he was crying, or if it was simply nature's way of preventing his eyeballs from freezing over.

It didn't matter. He felt downright *exhilarated.*

He glanced up and saw that only one of his teammates was still watching him. It was definitely Courtney, her feminine form unmistakable. She was standing just a few feet away. However, he couldn't see her face through her coppertone visor, and therefore couldn't determine what emotion she was conveying.

Was she relieved that he was going to live? After all, losing a Black Beret would only succeed in making the survivors all the more aware of their own mortality.

Or was she dismayed? Was she hoping that she would outlive him so that it could be her that put a bullet in his brain? Was she really that morbid?

He panted, "Got something to say, doll?"

"No," she replied in a hush.

She walked away and started picking up the Socom clips that had been discarded in the snow.

Leon forced himself fully upright and stared down the road. He was still breathing hard —smiling a little, even —rejoicing in the fact that he would survive this day.

The road was lined with a long trail of bodies —maybe a hundred and fifty, maybe more, some lying face down, some lying face up, some stacked up to three high in little piles. Snow was still falling on them, attempting to cover the evidence. Yet there was no denying that a battle had taken place here.

Their enemies had probably once been townsfolk from East Greenwich. Most were plainly dressed, others had on suits and ties. Fathers and mothers. Sons and daughters.

Now they were all dead a second time.

* * * * *

The scene that waited for them when they arrived back at the U-Hauls was entirely unexpected. Leon figured that everyone was still working off of their adrenaline and exhilaration —as he was —so it was quite sobering indeed.

A slap in the face.

It wasn't fair. It wasn't as if they all really needed to be reminded of their ever-present reality. Leon felt as though some invisible entity had kicked him square in the balls. He wondered how the others felt.

They gazed down at the ground.

—At the bodies.

One had been a zombie. It had a clean-cut hairdo and wore a fancy white shirt with a blue tie. A pair of khakis covered its legs. A nametag pinned to its pocket protector read, '*Regal Pharmacy – My name is DAN. How may I help you?*'

This zombie was not going to move again. The blade of a wakizashi was shoved up through its mandible and out the top of its head. Its tongue was hanging halfway out its mouth. Its glazed-over eyes remained open as well, staring up at the sky. In its clutches was a visor and a beret.

In the snow next to the nonfunctioning zombie was Nicholas, on his back in a supine position. Blood stained the white snow beneath his head, but it had stopped flowing some time ago, the wound frozen and clotted over. In one of his outstretched arms, an empty pillbox lay in his open hand.

He had swallowed his barbiturates.

Arabian Nick was dead.

A mental evaluation of the scene led Leon to one conclusion: The walking corpse had blindsided Nicholas, yanked away his visor and beret, and chewed a chunk of skin from the back of his head. There were dragged footprints originating from the side of the pharmacy and came all the way up to the rear of the U-Haul where Nicholas had probably been standing. No one —including Leon — suspected that a skin-eater had been stuck behind the dumpsters near the service entrance, and had spent the last several hours quietly pulling itself free.

It had stumbled upon a lone Black Beret, and it had got the better of him.

The engines of both vehicles were running, exhaust spewing from the tailpipes in a great gray cloud, intermingling with the wintry air and the pure white snow. Because of the noise, Nicholas must not have been able to hear the approaching zombie.

He had been surprised. He had been bitten. He had spun around and shoved his sword up the zombie's head.

And then they both fell to the ground.

Nicholas hadn't radioed for help. He had known, as Leon did, that a bite from a zombie was lethal. He knew he was going to die and become one of them.

So he did what any Black Beret would do —He swallowed his barbiturates.

Had Nicholas been too embarrassed? Leon wondered, *Too ashamed to radio for someone to join him so he wouldn't have to die alone? Or had he been brave? So brave he wasn't afraid of dying alone?*

After an eternity of silence, Vaughn lifted his walkie-talkie and said into it: "Are the chains on?"

A moment later, a reply came: "*In a second... Yep. There, they're on.*"

"Then get over here," said Vaughn. He put away his walkie-talkie, neglecting to tell Mike and Delmas on the other end what had happened.

However, they found out soon enough. They brought the humvee and the previously immovable U-Haul to the center of the market and parked them next to the others. They got out of the vehicles, leaving the engines running, and joined the other Berets next to the bodies.

Mike didn't say anything.

Delmas asked, "How much time do we have before he comes back?"

After nobody spoke up, Courtney told him, "Maybe twenty minutes."

"Then let's take him inside," said Vaughn.

* * * * *

With the approaching night came added cold. The wind picked up and the snow wasn't as big and chunky anymore. Now it was sweeping sideways through the marketplace at the urging of any stiff breeze, a lot like the powdery snow Leon was accustomed to growing up in Maine.

The inside of the pharmacy was somewhat warmer, thankfully, simply because its air was old and stale.

It was as good a place as any to draw straws.

Vaughn took a *Get-Well-Soon* card from the Hallmark rack, disregarding whatever limerick may have been printed inside. He ripped up the card lengthwise into six strips. He then took one of those strips and ripped it in half.

Now five of the six strips were of equal length and one was not.

He shuffled them around in his hand, then extended them in his fist towards the other Black Berets. Obscured by Vaughn's fingers, it was impossible to tell which of the six strips was the short one.

Vaughn stated, "Let's get this over with. I want to go home."

Courtney took a step back. She said, "I'm not in this."

Delmas grabbed her by the arm to stop her, gently, yet with a firmness. He softly told her, "You can't keep avoiding these things, Courtney. Every time this comes up you avoid it. Take your chances like the rest of us."

She shrugged him loose and stammered, "Fine!"

She stomped over to Vaughn and yanked away one of the strips he was holding. She didn't pause. She didn't hesitate. She simply picked one at random.

She held up the strip she had singled out, displaying it for all to see.

It was long —definitely not the cursed one.

Leon saw her eyes close and a long exhale escape through her slightly parted lips.

He mused, *Add 'extremely lucky' to her personality traits.*

After a moment she opened her eyes again and traded glances with everyone. She snarled, "Happy now?"

She hurriedly stepped out the door, rubbing her eyes with her forearm. They heard her mumble, "*Goddammit,*" and then she was gone from sight.

Vaughn declared, "Next."

Christopher Gooden stepped up, looked over the strips growing out of Vaughn's fist like a cartoonish porcupine, then selected one.

He slowly pulled it free.

It was a long one.

He stepped away. He put his head down and quietly slipped past the others and made his way outside, into the cold.

Delmas was next.

He, too, drew a long one.

And he, too, quietly withdrew from the huddle and walked out the door.

Mike pulled next and his was long as well.

He joined the other winners outside.

Only Leon and Vaughn remained. Nicholas' body still lay on the cold tile floor of the pharmacy, still not moving.

—*Yet.*

Leon stared at the remaining two strips sticking out of Vaughn's fist. He didn't figure that it would ever come to him. People had died in their group before, and two of those bodies had been recovered. On the first occasion, Christopher had been the trigger man. The second time it was Delmas.

But Leon never really thought it would happen again, nor did he think it could possibly come down to him to be executioner.

Eenie-meenie-miny-moe...

Fuck it.

He pulled the strip on the left. He wrapped his fingers around it, concealing its length from both Vaughn and himself. He looked down at Nicholas' body, then looked back up at Vaughn.

They quietly stared at each other.

Leon whispered, "You wanna be the boss? Then you should do it."

Vaughn smirked and let out a soft chuckle. He whispered back, "Is that what you think? That I want to be in charge?"

Leon nodded.

"Well, it's not like that at all," Vaughn told him. "I abhor any kind of responsibility. Haven't you figured that out by now? Truth be told, I'm not a leader and I'm no follower either. I'm just not a *joiner* —I'm a *survivor*, nothing more, nothing less."

Leon rolled his eyes and commented, "Whatever. That stunt you pulled? Making us fight when we could have just left? You're the laziest bastard I've ever seen, but you act like you should be in charge."

Vaughn very sarcastically retorted, "My pa always said, *work smarter, not harder.*"

"I don't think so," Leon snapped back. "I'm tired of your dickhead attitude."

"I just saved your ass out there," Vaughn scoffed.

"And one day I'm sure the favor will be duly repaid," Leon fired back. "But let's talk about what's happening *now.*"

"Fine. Let's talk about it. I think it's *you* that wants to be in charge."

"Oh really?"

"Yeah, that's what I think. You don't like being undermined. I guess I don't either. But you were probably captain of the locker room. You take it personally."

Leon was tempted to cuss him at this point, but decided against it. He didn't want a fistfight.

Vaughn went on, "I'm telling you this right now, regardless of whether I hold the short straw or not: *I'll shoot Nicholas.* I would have shot him outside, but I didn't. You know why? Because all of you would have thought I was a totally heartless bastard. Someone needs to shoot Nicholas. We both know it. But we gather in a circle-jerk and draw straws like it's the most reprehensible thing in the world. Your mindsets are outdated."

There was silence. Leon didn't know what to say.

Vaughn continued, "But, you see, it won't do any good for me to shoot him, because we both know I'm capable of doing it. The question is, are *you*? Can you be a man? Can you grow the fuck up? Can you prove to me —*to all of us*—that we should listen when you tell us what to do? Or are you really just a pretty boy afraid of getting his hands dirty?"

Leon swallowed hard and let his eyes wander away from Vaughn's. They eventually focused on the fallen Black Beret, who still lay on the floor, abandoned. His eyes were still closed. He was still dead.

A shout came from outside.

It was Delmas asking if it was over yet.

Leon returned his gaze to meet Vaughn's peculiar, indifferent stare.

He was a gothic motherfucker indeed, with a long face and shadows under his eyes. He had big eyebrows and a lengthy nose flowing to a point just above his upper lip. A day's worth of unshaven scruffiness was appearing on his cheeks.

Vaughn then whispered, "It isn't about wanting to be in charge. It's about doing what needs to be done. It's time you grew up, man. Whether you want to be in charge or not, a lot of dimwits depend on you. Prove you can get us out of this deep shit we're in." He paused a moment, then stated with finality, "Prove you're worth a damn."

Leon drew his Socom. He stated, "You think I can't shoot him?"

"This isn't a pissing contest," Vaughn replied. "Do it because you *have* to."

Under Vaughn's watchful gaze, Leon loaded a healthy clip, then switched on the targeting laser. He allowed his arm to drift off to the side. He followed it with his head, watching the red dot swim across the floor, bouncing over fallen books and magazines, until the red dot appeared above Nicholas' dead eyes.

He then situated the red dot on the wrinkles of his forehead.

Leon held his aim for a long time, making certain it was steady. He didn't want to have to shoot more than once. It would be uncalled for. It would somehow be disrespectful.

Finally he pulled the trigger.

There was a muffled blast as the shot found its mark, straight and true, the red dot replaced by a bleeding bullet hole.

Nicholas' head jolted as the bullet penetrated his skull and buried itself deep in the brain. And then he was still again.

Leon holstered his Socom.

Vaughn, expressionless, patted him on the shoulder before walking out the door to join the others.

Alone, Leon uncurled his fingers on his left hand and allowed the straw he had been holding to flutter out of his sweaty grip. It swayed this way and that, side to side for the longest time before coming to rest on the cover of a Harlequin Romance.

Whether the straw had been long or short, Leon didn't know.

He didn't bother looking.

*   *   *   *   *

They wrapped Nick's body in the cloak Leon had been wearing earlier, able to cover everything but his leather-booted feet. They loaded him in the back of the humvee so he could be returned to Eastpointe and given a proper burial in the ever-growing cemetery.

Leon chose to drive the humvee and take point in the convoy, with Delmas riding shotgun next to him. The other Berets followed; Courtney driving the ten-foot U-Haul Mini-Mover, then Mike and Chris in the first twenty-six foot U-Haul Super Mover, and Vaughn driving the last. The vehicles didn't have too much trouble getting along, other than sliding every now and then.

But it was all under control.

At one point a family of white-tailed deer sprinted in front of the headlights, their majestic, grayish coats untainted by the distorted world in which they freely roamed.

Here, in a moment of clarity, many things came to light in Leon's mind.

Firstly, he couldn't help but be saddened by the realization that never again would he see Nicholas shoot a zombie, followed by the words, *"That's five more experience points. Only a thousand more and I'm level twenty."*

He suddenly wished that he had gotten to know the guy a little better, but this thought was overshadowed by something deeper.

Events of the day replayed in Leon's mind. He remembered when they had first pulled into the marketplace that morning, and loading the U-Hauls before the blizzard hit.

He remembered Vaughn disappeared from the group for roughly ten minutes. Such characteristics weren't entirely unheard of — Vaughn was known to occasionally find a corner somewhere and take a quick nap.

But when Vaughn returned to the group he was carrying a two-by-two cardboard box with an X hastily scribbled on the side. He had loaded the box into a U-Haul with no fanfare, and then went back to the task of assisting the other Black Berets. At the time, Leon had thought nothing of it, and during the commotion of the day he didn't have time to think *about* it.

Yet that very box, he remembered, had been loaded into the same U-Haul that got stuck.

He looked into the side-view mirror of his humvee, past the two U-Hauls behind him, and stared at the last vehicle in line.

—The U-Haul Vaughn was driving.

It was the same one the box was in.

The same one that had to have chains installed on the tires.

The same one that just seemingly couldn't —under any circumstances —be left behind, even when an army of the undead was approaching, even when any other time Vaughn just would have agreed, "Leave it, let's get out of here."

Leon snapped his head forward just in time to steer his humvee back into the center of the road. He had almost gone into a ditch.

"What the hell was that about?" Delmas asked.

"Just zoned out," Leon told him. "Don't worry. I'm cool."

He couldn't stop thinking about it. There was no proof, of course, just a nagging suspicion. He wondered if all that macho bullshit from Vaughn was just a clever way of pulling his strings like a goddamn puppeteer.

If the contents of the box were just something Vaughn wanted to claim for himself, then surely it wasn't so important that it necessitated a gun battle with a horde of zombies to defend it. After all, Vaughn wanted for nothing. Leon had once heard him say, '*I love life now. Everyone who ever wronged me is dead. What more can you ask for?*'

But...

Leon then recalled all the times Vaughn would come directly out of the Superintendent's office before an outing. And now Leon wondered if Vaughn's meetings were really just so some bigwig could wish him luck.

—And if Vaughn *was* in a loop that Leon wasn't, just what was he being offered in return, if he wanted for nothing?

Leon was young, but he wasn't necessarily stupid. Eastpointe's Black Berets were a patchwork team, nearly all the members having come from different trainers and factions, but Leon was slowly learning their personalities. He had been trained by an instructor who focused immensely on the Judo and finesse aspects of the art. He knew he stood out from the rest. But he also knew he was still just another mask —another visor above a black and turquoise uniform.

And perhaps today he had been manipulated as such.

"Son of a bitch..."

Delmas jerked his head toward Leon with a *did-you-say-something* look on his face.

Leon glanced over at him, then settled his eyes back on the snow-covered road ahead.

He neglected to elaborate. He didn't want suspicions to outweigh the somberness that Nicholas' death deserved. He told himself that thoughts of conspiracies were just crazy. He told himself that his mind was simply muddled, what with the death of a fellow Beret and all.

Regardless, Leon grew up a lot that day. He knew he was too charismatic to be a *follower.* From then on he would be a leader — or, if nothing else —present such a confidence that he could not be ignored.

For the time being, however, he would lead the convoy home in silence.

He saw only one skin-eater on the way back to Eastpointe. It was a child, perhaps five or six when it had died. Several inches of snow were piled on its shoulders. It was pulling a red Radio Flyer wagon along behind it, (also loaded with snow,) as it meandered through the blizzard, going nowhere.

one two when
ril showers and
? I didn't know
nothing else for
to m. Will any
s. I'm seriously
an intermis-
ately wasting
ver rampage.
the more likely
text. I laughed
here's a differ-
e hair." That
ks does it take
hen the article
omb was only
tomb is des-
re's no end in
ass off when
ce between a
Corey is a riot.
e to get to the
vas originally
ve years old.
d beyond and
There's no one
led majesty of
dance, both
ght, each dark
ncontrollable.
in a game with
dguns involved
ything about
over there. Be
r deep feelings

can moviegoers expect when she wears a tight black leather cat-suit and taunts us? I wasn't much of a fan of Christina Beck before this film, but she's really winning me over. Highly recommended. A+

—*Loki Agarri*

TM

The dark musician known as Xafan (the "F" in his logo resembling an athame jabbed thru the letters; kudos to the marketing department,) will definitely be more than just a flash in the pan. We at *Musick Nocturne* were fortunate to receive a sampler of his premier album *Gazing Into The Abyss*. Let us tell you, this tenor-turned bass-turned poet really has us on edge. You'll never hear a better dark metal cover of Billy Joel's *Pressure*, but a clear highlight is Xafan's haunting love ballad, *Forbidden Rendezvous*, within which his voice goes from shrill to soothing and all shades in between. (The song itself is creepily plausible.) We can't get over the ethereal elegance of his vocals. This new signing could be just what Leviathan Records™ needs, since three of their last six artists have forfeited their contracts. We'll have more info closer to the official release date.

—*Devon Pickman*

NEXT:

AFTER TWILIGHT

Walking with the Dead

Printed in the United Kingdom
by Lightning Source UK Ltd.
123791UK00001B/80/A